“There is
Not anyw

Jake’s voice was ragged.

Ramona could do nothing but reach for him.

“There is peace, Jake,” she whispered. “Right here. Right now…let go of the pain, Jake.”

He moaned. “I want you, Ramona.”

It was her turn to close her eyes. To resist. His soul was bleeding, as was his heart, and he needed her. She ached to give him what he thought he wanted, but her instincts told her it would be wrong. “No, Jake. Not like this…”

Dear Reader,

I hope you've got a few days to yourself for this month's wonderful books. We start off with Terese Ramin's *An Unexpected Addition*. The "extra" in this Intimate Moments Extra title is the cast of characters—lots and *lots* of kids—and the heroine's point of view once she finds herself pregnant by the irresistible hero. The ending, as always, is a happy one—but the ride takes some unexpected twists and turns I think you'll enjoy.

Paula Detmer Riggs brings her MATERNITY ROW miniseries over from Desire in *Mommy By Surprise*. This reunion romance—featuring a pregnant heroine, of course—is going to warm your heart and leave you with a smile. Cathryn Clare is back with *A Marriage To Remember*. Hero and ex-cop Nick Ryder has amnesia and has forgotten everything—though how he could have forgotten his gorgeous wife is only part of the mystery he has to solve. In *Reckless*, Ruth Wind's THE LAST ROUNDUP trilogy continues. (Book one was a Special Edition.) Trust me, Colorado and the Forrest brothers will beckon you to return for book three. In *The Twelve-Month Marriage*, Kathryn Jensen puts her own emotional spin on that reader favorite, the marriage-of-convenience plot. And finally, welcome new author Bonnie Gardner with *Stranger in Her Bed*. Picture coming home to find out that everyone thinks you're dead—and a gorgeous *male* stranger is living in your house!

Enjoy them all, and don't forget to come back next month for more of the most exciting romantic reading around, right here in Silhouette Intimate Moments.

Yours,

Leslie Wainger
Senior Editor and Editorial Coordinator

RECKLESS

RUTH WIND

Published by Silhouette Books
America's Publisher of Contemporary Romance

For Chuck Walker, who is fondly remembered and often missed.

ISBN 0-373-07796-3

RECKLESS

This edition published by arrangement with Harlequin Books S.A.

Printed in U.S.A.

Books by Ruth Wind

Silhouette Intimate Moments

Breaking the Rules #587
**Reckless* #796

Silhouette Special Edition

Strangers on a Train #555
Summer's Freedom #588
Light of Day #635
A Minute To Smile #742
Jezebel's Blues #785
Walk In Beauty #881
The Last Chance Ranch #977
Rainsinger #1031
**Marriage Material* #1108

*The Last Roundup

RUTH WIND

is the award-winning author of both contemporary and historical romance novels. She lives in the mountains of the Southwest with her husband, two growing sons and many animals in a hundred-year-old house the town blacksmith built. The only hobby she has since she started writing is tending the ancient garden of irises, lilies and lavender beyond her office window, and she says she can think of no more satisfying way to spend a life than growing children, books and flowers.

Excerpt from the diary of Louise Forrest...

Jake is at it again! He's lived in these mountains all his life, and he knows better than to go climbing on rotten rock, especially half-drunk. That's a tourist stunt. And it isn't the first time lately he's done something like that.

It's as if he's asking for trouble all the time: driving too fast, drinking and partying too much with a different woman every night. Just being reckless. He isn't sleeping or eating, either. And he hasn't cut his hair in months. Could be I'm making too much out of it, but a mother has her instincts. When he was younger, the army—the honor and the discipline—was his entire life, and I don't think he took much time to sow his wild oats. So, if he was enjoying himself...well, maybe I could understand. But he hates it! You can see it in his eyes.

Something's gone deeply wrong in my oldest son's life. Wrong enough to make him give up the military and bury himself in that sterile apartment of his. Maybe I'll have Ramona Hardy talk to him. She's a doctor, and she's done a lot of work with veterans. Besides, there's something so peaceful about her....

She may be the last chance I have to find my son again.

Chapter 1

Jake Forrest had not slept well last night. In fact, he hadn't slept at all. He'd lain in bed and stared at the ceiling, thinking that if he could only rest, he might not look so haggard for his brother's wedding. Twice, he'd nearly gotten up for a belt of whiskey—that usually put him out—but he'd been afraid he might just stay up drinking till dawn. It had happened before, when the demons were on him.

And the demons were on him now. They had been for more than a week, climbing from the trunk where he managed to periodically wrestle them and tormenting him with haunting memories and visions burned forever into his mind.

Now, standing beside the altar as his brother took his vows, Jake swayed in exhaustion. He held himself rigidly erect, focusing on Lance and on the joy that shone in his eyes as he kissed his brand-new bride. In spite of himself, Jake smiled. Wasn't that something? Lance married. Jake had honestly believed his brother would never settle down.

But then nothing was turning out the way Jake thought it would.

Tyler, supposedly the happy family man, had walled himself off up on his mountain, shunning women as if they were rats carrying plague. Lance, the footloose ladies' man, was married with a child. And Jake was supposed to be the soldier. Likely a lieutenant colonel by now if he hadn't bailed out four years before he could have retired in style.

No, things were not turning out the way he had imagined.

The wedding party started their march down the aisle. Jake automatically held out his arm for the woman he was paired with—a small brown wren with a bosom that could hardly be contained in the unfortunate choice of bridesmaid's dress. The rest of the bridesmaids looked like confections in the simple yellow satin. This woman was a little too round for it, a little too pale to be wearing that sunny shade.

She smiled at him, and he felt ashamed of his critical thoughts. In return, he managed to muster something like a smile. She squeezed his elbow as if offering support. "Are you all right?" she whispered.

Jake scowled. What had she seen? Did he look as haggard as he felt? He'd forgotten to get his hair cut, and it was too long, and he'd nicked himself shaving, but he thought the black tux made him look a bit like his old self. Maybe not.

"Just tired," he said. The words came out on a gruff note he hadn't intended, making him sound worse than he felt.

The woman—what was her name?—nodded. There was something empathetic in her eyes, something that made him feel annoyed and hungry all at once. How dare she look at him as if she knew his thoughts? As if she knew it wasn't a hangover that made him feel miserable, but days and days without a single restful minute of sleep. He swallowed the fury it roused in him.

"We're almost finished here," she said. "Then we eat."

Judging by her rounded shape, she probably looked forward to that, he thought darkly. Again, his meanness shocked him. In repentance, he tried to find something he liked about her as they stood on the church steps waiting for the limos that would take them to the reception.

For one thing, she wasn't really overweight. She was, as his mother would say, buxom. With generous hips and breasts, and arms that were a little fuller than the current emaciated standard. He didn't like buxomness particularly, but looking at her, he had the sudden feeling she would be very soft. Warm and soft and easy to hold close in the darkness of a sleepless night.

Her name suddenly popped into his mind: Ramona. Ramona Hardy. She was one of Tamara's friends, but he didn't know much more than that.

"Lance has done this up right, hasn't he?" she asked with a grin. "And Tamara looks like Cinderella."

Jake looked at his new sister-in-law. She wore an elaborate white gown, covered with beads and lace and pearls. Her dark hair was swept into a knot on top of her head. As he watched, Lance put his hands on his bride's face and kissed her, pulling away with an expression of stunned wonder on his face. Tamara glowed.

And just like that, Jake wasn't standing on the church steps on a bright, late-spring day in Colorado. He was in a Kuwait village still smoking from the missiles that had tumbled buildings to rubble. Somewhere, a child screamed, and Jake couldn't find it. Couldn't find it until he ducked into the half-standing ruin of a house and saw the boy pinned—

He shuddered violently at the flashback, slamming back to the happy noise of the wedding party. He blinked hard to clear the dry graininess of his eyes and tried to hold himself upright. To hide the trembling of his hands, he shoved them into his pockets.

Ramona looked at him, steadily, clearly. Her eyes were big and brown, as big as a doe's, and once again he thought she saw more than she should. She didn't say anything, just kept her small hand on his elbow. He was absurdly grateful.

"He's spent a damn fortune on this wedding," Jake managed to say aloud.

"From what I understand, he can well afford it. What good is money if you can't spend it on something like this once in a while?"

Jake shrugged. "They look like Barbie and Ken."

Ramona smiled gently. "I think that's the whole idea."

"Yeah," he said. "Barbie and Ken and picket fences and the whole happily-ever-after game." Jake stared at the bride and groom with a fierce, hollow ache in his chest. "I don't believe in happily ever after."

"Not for anyone?"

"I've never seen one." Jake looked at her. "You make plans and have big dreams, and everybody tells you hard work makes things happen. And there you are one day, thinking you built something solid, something concrete you could put your hands on, and what happens? Life has a way of turning concrete dreams into a house of cards." He spoke out of his despair, unaware he was giving voice to his thoughts. "No," he repeated, "I don't believe in happily ever after." His words held a harsh rasp born of his weariness.

Her small, strong hand tightened on his upper arm, and those wide, sympathetic—no, *empathetic*—eyes saw far more than he wanted them to see. Appalled that he'd been so brutally honest at a moment when he should have been taking pleasure in the joyful wedding of his brother, Jake looked away.

And to his amazement, Ramona said nothing at all. Nothing placating or soothing or nullifying. As if she knew how he felt.

The roiling disturbance in his chest increased in intensity. How dare she think she knew anything? He stiffened, pulling himself away from her, but that small hand stayed firmly wrapped around his arm, almost stubbornly giving him comfort and a measure of strength he didn't want to accept.

The limos arrived, sleek and black, hired out of Denver at an outrageous price. "See," Ramona said mildly. "That wasn't so terrible, was it?"

"Better hurry up," Jake said, moving forward. "Before they turn back into pumpkins."

At the reception, Ramona watched Jake Forrest carefully. Her instincts screamed that he was in trouble. Big trouble, judging by the hollows under his eyes. Gauntness had whittled away the handsome boyishness she remembered from high school, turning his face into something coyote-hungry.

Ramona cornered Louise Forrest as the older woman left the dance floor, flushed from waltzing with an amiable-looking Latin man Ramona didn't know. Smiling at the color in Louise's cheeks, Ramona teased, "New boyfriend?"

"Oh, heavens, no!" Louise protested. The ruddiness in her cheeks deepened. "I'm well past the age of boyfriends. He's just a wonderful dancer."

"I saw that." Ramona glanced over her shoulder. The man, short and spare, with a thick black mustache, watched Louise depart with a twinkle in his dark eyes. "Who is he? I haven't met him."

Louise snagged a paper napkin from the buffet table and blotted her lips. "Alonzo Chacon. Lance hired him a couple of months ago. He does authentic adobe bricks, the old way."

"I'll have to go see how he does it," Ramona said, and meant it. She admired craftsmen.

"You should." Louise looked straight at her. "What's on your mind, honey? That boy of mine got you worried?"

"Yes." Ramona wasn't surprised at Louise's perception. She halfway suspected it was no accident she and Jake had been paired in the wedding party. "You're worried, too, aren't you?"

"You bet your life I am. For one thing, I don't think he ever sleeps, not unless he's flat-out drunk."

"That's pretty evident." Ramona glanced at Jake. He stood at the bar, a glass of something amber in his hand, giving his trademark grin to a slim, leggy blonde. "I thought he might pass out on the church steps."

Louise scowled at her son. "He hasn't got a lick of sense about women lately, either. They're all a bunch of loose, fast girls with only one thing on their minds."

Ramona smiled. Leaning negligently against the bar, tall and well formed, with his carelessly long, dark hair and vivid eyes, Jake looked like a movie star. "Well, you have to admit he's a very attractive man."

"Who's going to get himself killed if he doesn't make peace with himself." Louise thumped her empty glass on the table. "I saw the same thing happen to my father, when he came home from World War II. They called it combat fatigue back then. He was among those troops who went into Dachau, and he had nightmares that made him wake up screaming night after night. He didn't eat. He couldn't work. It was a terrible thing."

"Did he get well?"

Louise pursed her lips in an ironic expression. "I'll never know. He went off to look for work one morning and never came back."

Ramona put her hand on Louise's arm. "I'm sorry."

"Ancient history," Louise said with a shrug. "But I don't aim to lose my son the way I lost my daddy, you understand?"

"Of course." She inclined her head. "I have the feeling you think I might be able to help him, and I don't think you understand that I'm a G.P., not a psychologist or psychiatrist. I treat bodies, not minds."

Louise made a scoffing noise. "I know that. I'm not that dumb."

"Do you want a referral for a good counselor? I know the man who leads the support groups at the VA home."

"Nope," Louise said firmly. "He won't go to one. I want you to help."

Ramona grinned. Few women could be as steadfastly stubborn as Louise Forrest once she'd made up her mind to something. Patiently, Ramona said, "I'm not qualified to treat him."

"So why do you spend all that time out there with those old coots at the VA home, huh?"

"Some of those old coots are in pretty bad shape physically. They need medical doctors."

"Mmm-hmm. You think I don't remember *your* daddy?"

Ramona looked away. "I don't."

"I know you don't, honey. You were pretty little when he went off to war. And it's a terrible thing that you lost him to it, but look what good things have come out of it."

Ramona felt a small clutch of emotion in her throat. The reasons for her devotion to the vets at the home were a lot more complicated, but Louise would not know all that. Lightly, Ramona said, "There are no mysteries about my psyche, are there? I'm a doctor because I wish I could go back and save him."

"That's what I mean, sugar. God can turn anything into a positive."

"Maybe." Ramona wasn't entirely sure about that, but a wedding reception hardly seemed the place to hold a philosophical debate.

"Listen." Earnestly, Louise took her hand. "I'm not asking you to perform miracles, but Jake's out there at the VA home a lot. He goes in the evenings. Maybe once in a while, you could just...be there."

Ramona waited.

"You having a calming way about you, Ramona. It might be real nice for him just to have a woman *friend*—" she shot a dark glance toward the bar "—he could talk to."

Louise would not give up until she extracted a promise, and Ramona gave her a resigned smile. "All right. I'll see what I can do, okay? No promises. If Jake is suffering posttraumatic stress disorder from his combat duty, he'll need more than a friendly shoulder to cry on."

Louise winked and patted her hand. "Good girl. I knew I could count on you."

"Louise, don't expect too much. It's a serious condition."

"I understand."

"Are you taking your blood pressure medicine properly?"

"Like clockwork."

The man Louise had been dancing with joined them. "I must steal this woman," he said to Ramona. "She is the only one here who can dance. Okay? You done?"

Ramona was charmed to her toes by the lilting accent and twinkling eyes. "I'm done."

"This is the doctor, Alonzo. Ramona Hardy. She said she'd like to see your work sometime."

"A lady doctor? You must be very smart." He inclined

his head. "Sure, sure you can come. Anytime. I am always working."

"Thank you."

Louise pushed none too gently at Ramona's arm. "Go get something to eat," she said, and sent a meaningful glance behind Ramona. Jake had filled a plate and now sat at his place at the table. Ramona's bouquet was on the chair next to him. As she watched, Jake took a long breath as if preparing himself for some painful task, then picked up his fork.

For one moment, Ramona was transported backward over the years. She was sixteen and very studious, a shy girl who hid behind thick glasses and tried her best to camouflage her overdeveloped bosom under baggy clothes. Her shyness was only increased by the comments the boys constantly made about her chest, as if it belonged to them. As if it had something to do with who she was.

And across the years, she remembered standing in the doorway of the cafeteria, mortified by a knot of boys who had trapped her as she went in to buy her lunch. They made crude remarks in quiet, snickering voices and shoved each other until one "accidentally" put his hand right there.

Jake Forrest had come to her rescue. Big and strong, and as clean-cut then as he now was ragged, he had grabbed the boy manhandling her and twisted his arm behind his back. With a quick jerk of his head, he indicated Ramona should go, and she had. When she tried to thank him the next day, he'd just shrugged. "No big deal."

He didn't remember her, Ramona thought now—and maybe that was for the best. He wouldn't remember what a terrible, nerdy little wallflower she had been. How many times had she wished there had been someone like Jake Forrest to rescue her a year later from another group of boys?

She shoved the thoughts away. She was over the trauma

of that awful day. More, she'd won. The boys had gone to jail.

And because she had survived that brutal day when she was seventeen, because she had built a solid, warm life in spite of the evils in the world, she knew she could help Jake Forrest.

If he would let her.

At the very least, she could offer kindness to repay him in some small way for that long-ago act in her defense. Catching up the skirt of her ridiculous bridesmaid's dress, she headed across the room.

Jake felt better after he allowed himself a solid belt of single malt Scotch on the rocks. Scotch was good medicine—and not only for sleeping. It blunted the edges of his rage and sorrow and lostness. Enough of it could even make him forget everything entirely for an hour or two. Some days, the idea of simply crawling into that tall green bottle and never coming out was very appealing.

Trouble was, a drunk couldn't afford imported Scotch, and Jake really didn't care for anything else.

The food was very good—catered by an upscale establishment that had grown used to satisfying celebrities and the simply wealthy who kept second homes in Red Creek to be close to the best skiing to be had this side of the Atlantic. He ate wafer-thin slices of smoked salmon and strawberries and whole-grain bread with real butter, and the knot in his gut eased. By the time he spotted Ramona returning to the table, he felt much mellower and not nearly as defensive about her all-too-knowing eyes.

Pretty eyes, he could think now, without danger. Big, soft, get-lost-in-them brown. As she made her way across the room, he noticed that people stopped her often—and bent down to hear her gentle voice. They smiled after her, and even the restlessness of children confined by patent-leather shoes and unfamiliar dress clothes seemed to settle a little as she moved among them, stopping to touch this one's shoulder, murmur a joke in that one's ear, scold another who was teasing his sister.

Peace and calm followed after her like the glow of a good wine.

He grimaced. Fine and well if you were looking for a mother, or maybe even a mother for your children. She was the type of woman who wanted to domesticate the world—probably had herbs hanging from her kitchen rafters and rows of home-canned tomatoes and beans on her shelves.

Not his style.

Restlessly, he scanned the room, feeling his disturbance rumble in his loins. Sometimes sex helped almost as much as liquor, and there were several possibilities in the room. Somehow, he couldn't seem to rouse himself enough to get out of the chair.

When Ramona sat down beside him, Jake briefly imagined her in his arms, all warmth and softness. A little of the tight anxiety eased out of his neck. "I bet you put up your own jelly, don't you?" he said before he could help himself.

To his surprise, she laughed. The sound was much huskier and richer than he expected. It made him think of thick woolen blankets on a cold, cold night. "You make it sound like something criminal. Don't you like jelly?"

"I don't think about it." He picked up a roll and suddenly did think about the rows of ruby soldiers his mother had made every year. "Do you ever make chokecherry?"

That laugh again. A little fuller this time. "I made a lot this year. There were so many chokecherries last fall I gave thought to starting a new hunger drive—chokecherries for the world." Her dark eyes danced. "What do you think?"

He smiled, almost against his will. "So do you have any left?"

"Well, I don't know. If putting up jelly is a criminal activity, maybe you ought to be careful about becoming an accomplice." She speared an artichoke heart on her fork. "Did you taste these? The sauce is wonderful."

"Slimy green vegetables aren't my thing."

"Shame on you." She popped it into her mouth and made a noise of pleasure. "Wonderful!" Spearing another, she held it out to him. "Try one. Really. You'll be glad."

He looked at her for a long moment. Maybe she wasn't as plain as he first thought. Her coloring was nice—the hair that was swept up into some elaborate system of braids was not just brown, but brown and blond all mixed together, and very healthy. He wondered how long it was and what it would look like spread over her shoulders.

A faint, almost unnoticeable ripple moved down his thighs. Impulsively, he leaned forward and snagged the triangle off her fork, knowing she had meant him to take it with his fingers.

The taste exploded on his tongue. He widened his eyes to show his approval. "That's good."

She grinned, and he decided her mouth was very nice. A nice mouth was one of his requirements in a woman. How had he missed it earlier?

"You might be surprised how many wonderful, slimy green vegetables there are," she said.

He picked up his fork. "May I have another one?"

"Of course." She leaned back to give him access, and Jake speared another from her plate. He smelled something nice coming from her skin, very light, a perfume or something.

"You smell good," he said.

"Thanks. So do you."

He met her gaze and felt a flame arc between them—that undeniable frisson that passed between a man and a woman, a frisson that had nothing to do with anything except perfect chemical alignment. Chemicals didn't care if her figure was the kind he usually admired, or whether she had home-canned peas on her shelf. He let his gaze sweep over her face, light on her mouth, travel downward to the plump breasts too tightly confined in the ridiculous dress. For a minute, he was a little dizzy—his exhaustion rising to the fore—and had to close his eyes. With an effort, he opened them again and made a stab at flirting. "You like my cologne, huh?"

Maybe he'd expected her to be flustered. She was not. She met his gaze steadily, a tiny smile hovering at the corner of her mouth. "Yes."

Something about that expression teased his memory, and he frowned for a minute, trying to place her. The snippet jelled and he saw her laughing with an old soldier as she checked his blood pressure. "You work at the VA home, don't you?"

"That's one of my stops, yes."

"Are you a nurse or something?"

She raised her eyebrows. "These days, women aren't only nurses."

"A doctor?" He couldn't keep the slight surprise from his voice. Not because she was a woman, but because he associated women who achieved such grueling positions with a much more aggressive personality. "You're a doctor?"

"Amazing as it may seem, I am."

"I didn't mean it like that." He shrugged and took another artichoke heart from her plate. "Most women with big-time careers are kind of..." He stopped, noticing the tightness of her mouth. "Ah, never mind."

"No, please," she said in a silky tone, "I love to hear sexist comments from the lips of macho soldier boys."

He laughed. It just came out of him all at once, sounding

rusty and unused because it was. "Touché," he said. "I'm sorry."

"Accepted." Tiny flames of humor danced in her eyes. "I mean, you can't really expect a soldier to be politically correct, now can you?"

"Ex-soldier," he said automatically.

"Ah, that's right. You're retired, aren't you?"

"No," he said without the usual pang. Amazing how far a little Scotch, a little food, and a woman to flirt with went toward silencing his demons. "You have to complete your commission to retire. I resigned."

"I see." She picked out a perfectly shaped, bright red strawberry and admired it on her fork. "That's beautiful, isn't it?"

"I guess."

"You guess? Look at it again. This is the queen of all strawberries, and by some fine accident, she ended up on my plate. And my mouth." She bit into the flesh, and Jake found himself admiring the movements of her pretty lips. A bawdy comment bloomed in his mind as he watched her savor it, eyes closed, all concentration focused on the task. Another prickling wave of desire washed down his thighs. A little more insistent this time.

"Are you flirting with me, Doctor?"

She smiled. "Maybe a little. Isn't that what one does at these things?"

She made it sound so harmless and innocent and simple. He'd forgotten innocent pleasures even existed and he was suddenly quite glad to realize they still did. "I guess it is." Impulsively, maybe because she made him laugh, he held out his hand. "In that spirit, I think you should dance with me and let me flirt back."

She frowned. "I'm not much of a dancer."

"It's easy." He stood up, still patiently holding out his hand. "Just follow me."

She hesitated for a moment, just long enough to make Jake want to reconsider. He wasn't kidding himself for a second. He wanted to get laid, and this was the woman his body wanted, no matter how inappropriate it was. Or impossible. He couldn't go around sleeping with the local doctor.

Plus, in his current mood, it was dangerous to give in to any whim. Once he had her softness close to him, he wouldn't be thinking about appropriate or inappropriate. He'd be thinking about how to seduce her.

Bad idea. Even Jake had some honor. He stuck to the fast, brittle women his mother despised, simply because they didn't want anything more than he did—a quick, impersonal roll in the hay. Ramona, with her soft eyes and plush warmth, was not the same kind of woman at all.

But before he could sit back down, she took his hand and rose gracefully. "I hope you don't fall down from exhaustion," she said.

"You can hold me up," he replied, and led her onto the floor.

Chapter 2

Ramona followed Jake out to the small square cleared for dancing, all too aware of the eyes that followed their progress. She'd seen the measuring examination of the women here, many of them the kind of woman Jake was known to enjoy.

When he stopped in front of her, waiting for her to catch up, she felt a strange, quick swoop of dizziness. She wished she were wearing something besides the unflattering bridesmaid's dress. She wished she were tall and lean and elegant, with a swath of butter-colored hair. She wished she had spent her youth making small talk instead of buried in her studies, so now she would know what to say to catch this big, beautiful man's attention for more than a moment.

But because she had no illusions, she simply smiled up at him and moved into the circle of his arms.

She tipped her head back to look at him. "I hope I don't trip you."

He simply shook his head, not even a faint pretend smile

breaking the graveness of his dark face. Against black lashes, his eyes were almost painfully blue, that bright, rare shade that defied naming. Only the mountain sky on a hot summer day in the mountains ever came close to that color.

"Dancing is just two bodies moving," he said. "Relax and let yourself feel me."

Feel me. An image of her putting her hands on his skin rose up with vivid and erotic insistence—a vision all the more surprising because she simply didn't get those kinds of thoughts very often. Her introduction to sex had been violent, and it had been a long time afterward before she'd even allowed a man to hold her hand. Once in a while, she saw a movie that made her wonder what it would be like to feel passion, or she dreamed of a man whose face never came clear, a man of vast tenderness who disrobed and worshiped her as if she were an angel.

But Jake was real and male, and smelled not only of his cologne, but of a distinctly earthy note that she thought must be that skin she thought of touching. Beneath the fabric of his coat, she felt the muscles of his arm moving easily, and she wondered what color his skin was there. Tanned a golden shade? Or white from the long winter?

With a frown, she realized she was making too big a thing out of it. He had only asked her to dance, for heaven's sake. Not a particularly revolutionary act at a wedding reception.

Taking a deep breath, Ramona exhaled slowly and tried to release the tension in her shoulders, tried to let her hands rest lightly upon him instead of gripping so tightly.

"There you go," he said. "Relax and listen to the music. Let it move inside of you." As if to make it easier for her, he stepped a little closer.

Her breasts brushed his chest, and his knee rubbed the side of her thigh. Trying to ignore those details, Ramona concentrated on the music. It was a song from high school, and she knew it well enough that she didn't have to stumble. When she finally relaxed a little, she caught a glimmering of what he meant by letting herself feel his body. A dozen nearly imperceptible movements signaled her to move this way or that—the faint pull of his hand, the nudge of his knee, the sway of his hips.

But then her awareness of his body led to an increased awareness of her own, and she tripped on his feet. "Oops," she said with a grin. "I don't think that's what you meant."

"You're still thinking too much." Now there was a little humor in his eyes. "Have you ever ridden a motorcycle with someone?" he asked.

"Sure."

Jake put one of her hands on his waist and settled his free hand on her shoulder. His palm was cool against the bare flesh above her gown. "You know how you have to lean into turns and both of you have to lean together?"

Ramona nodded. He slipped his arms closer around her, and their bodies touched at chest and thighs. She swallowed against the sudden jolt of desire that passed through her, fast and hot.

"Close your eyes," he instructed.

"If I close mine, you have to do it, too," she countered. "I don't want anyone thinking I'm swooning over you."

A grin cracked the somberness of his face. "It's a deal."

So she did. Closed her eyes and leaned into him lightly, then let him lead her in a dance. He smelled of coffee and Scotch and the heady after-shave she liked so much. His jacket brushed her arms. And dancing, which had always eluded her, seemed an effortless thing.

"You're a very good dancer," she said quietly.

"Mmm."

The song changed, sliding into something else from the same era. "'American Pie,'" Jake said, his voice coming to her both through his chest and from above. "They played it at the homecoming dance when I was a senior."

Ramona smiled. "I remember it, too. I bought the 45."

"Forty-fives. Do you still have them?"

"Probably some."

"I'd love to see what you have sometime."

"No problem."

At his urging, she gave in to the impulse to rest her cheek against his shoulder, to relax completely against his body, moving sinuously against her. Their thighs slipped and slid, and their hips swayed in perfect harmony.

Distantly, she was aware of his hands moving almost absently against her back, up and down. Was it normal to dance like this with a stranger? Ramona didn't really know—nor, oddly, did she care. It felt as if it were the right thing to do, and that was all that mattered. Maybe it would give Jake a little peace.

"Am I leaning on you too much?" he asked.

"Not at all."

A silent sigh moved his chest, and Ramona felt the tension ease out of him as if someone had pulled a plug.

The song ended, and the band suddenly switched gears, moving into a rowdy reel. Jake straightened abruptly, blinking. Ramona thought he looked as if he'd been suddenly awakened from a nap—and that probably wasn't far from the truth.

She smiled. "Thank you for the lesson."

A puzzled look crossed his face. "My pleasure." He glanced over his shoulder. "I think I'll go have a drink with my brother. Maybe we can dance again later."

"Sure."

The reception lasted a long, long time. It was well past dark, and Jake was amazed to find himself still upright. He didn't dare drink much for fear of keeling over where he stood, but in his current state, it didn't take much Scotch to give him a little buzz. He danced when asked and drank a toast to his brother, but mostly, he stationed himself at the bar and drank water, watching the room with the same sense of distance with which he'd viewed everything for longer than he cared to admit.

Nothing ever seemed real. He had a sense of being on the outside, as if he were watching a movie—even when he had sex with a beautiful woman, or ate a good meal, or pretended he was having a conversation with one of his brothers. He could manage to participate for about five minutes in any one thing, then some switch in his brain kicked in and he was no longer a part of the moment, but instead observing it from some faraway place, with the sound turned low.

He was fairly sure he was losing his mind. But even that roused no emotion in him. He didn't much care.

There were only a couple places he felt his old self—at the VA home and when he cooked. Six months ago, he'd purchased a long-established restaurant at the edge of town. He'd done it on a whim, wanting something to do. He'd always enjoyed food and cooking, and the business was handled by a manager. In the short time he'd been running the place, the profits had slowly increased. But it was in the big, old cluttered kitchen that Jake found peace. If only he could retreat there now and spend the rest of the night making up dishes, Jake thought he could weather this bout of—whatever the hell it was. But much as he half-wished to retreat to the restaurant now and spend the rest of the night making up new dishes, sometimes a man had to turn up for certain occasions, and his brother's wedding was one of those times.

So he watched the movie playing on the dance floor, complete with soundtrack from the band. Colors seemed a little overbright, as if it were an old Technicolor film. The blondes were brassy, the lipsticks too red or too pink, the dresses just a little too flagrantly pastel.

A hand fell on his arm, and Jake smelled Ramona's perfume. "How you doing, soldier?" she said, and half hopped up to the seat of a stool beside him.

He couldn't rouse a lie. "I'm dead on my feet, Doc."

"I thought so." Her hand rested lightly on his sleeve, and it didn't annoy him as he might have expected. It was soothing. "Why don't you let me drive you home?"

A picture of his sterile condo flashed through his mind, and Jake found himself gritting his teeth. "No, thanks. I might run over to the Wild Moose after and cook up something interesting."

"I'd forgotten you bought the place. How's it doing?"

"Great. All it needed was a little modernization—some low-fat salad dressings and upscale presentation. I've tried to keep the old feeling, too, somehow make it okay for the town, as well as bring in that fit crowd from the mountains."

"I'll have to stop by."

"Do. I'll hustle up something special just for you." He found his face stretching into that weird, sincere smile. "No artichoke hearts, but I'll have to see about getting them on the menu."

Ramona laughed. "Don't bother. There's so much fat in the dressing, no one in the ski crowd will touch it, and I suspect most of the townspeople would avoid artichokes on general principles."

"I'll bet I can come up with a sauce that tastes exactly like that one, and cut ninety percent of the fat."

"You make it and I'll eat it."

Her smile was warm as morning, and he liked the gentleness in her eyes. Against the Technicolor surrealism in the rest of the room, she was as real and as tangible as the earth itself. There were no artificial harsh highlights in her hair, no lipstick blurring her pink mouth. Her bare toes peeked out from beneath the awful dress and her feet seemed the most real thing of all. "Where are your slippers, Cinderella?"

"I hate high heels." She looked at her toes. "And anyway, Tamara is Cinderella, remember? I'm the mouse turned into a coachman for the day."

"Not a mouse," he said, and inclined his head. "A deer, maybe. You have eyes like a doe, all big and brown and shiny."

"A deer?" She grinned. "You mean those tall, leggy creatures that leap gracefully through the forest?"

He chuckled and cast an appreciative eye over her lush curves. "Well, doe eyes anyway." He lifted an eyebrow. "The rest is more like—" he narrowed his eyes teasingly "—a hen."

"Oh, thank you very much!" she exclaimed without rancor. "Now I know exactly how awful this dress is."

Jake *had* thought she looked like a hen at first and hadn't thought it kindly. But now, as she sat next to him, all real and earthy and shapely, he thought of how she'd felt against him when they danced: giving and soft. He raised his eyes. "I was thinking more like a succulent, freshly roasted hen—juicy and rich and delicious."

Ramona blushed. The color rose instantly, burning in her cheeks and faintly along the rise of her breasts. "Oh," she murmured.

He leaned forward. "Are you really blushing?" he teased, and touched her cheek. "I haven't seen a woman blush like that in a long, long time."

She wouldn't look at him. "You embarrassed me."

It pained him a little. "I didn't mean to, Ramona. I was trying to give you a compliment."

A reluctant smile curved that pretty mouth. "Well, then, I suppose I should thank you."

"I think so." Distantly, he realized he shouldn't be flirting with her, not this good, kind, honorable woman, who was unsophisticated enough to blush at a bawdy compliment, but he was too damned tired to think it through. He ought to take his randiness to one of the brittle women he'd danced with and be done with it. But he didn't want one of them. Not tonight. It was more pleasant to simply sit here with Ramona.

The band shifted to a new song, and Jake felt the notes pluck something inside him. It was a good rendition of Van Morrison's "Listen to the Lion." Impulsively, he took her hand. "Dance with me again, will you?"

She lifted her dress to show him her bare feet. "Not this time. Without my shoes, I'll be way too short."

Jake stood and took her hand. "No, you won't. You can stand on my feet, like a little kid."

"No way!" She laughed and tried to pull her hand out of his grip.

He didn't let go. "I won't take no for an answer. You might as well just give in."

She gave him a wry, disbelieving look. "Or what?"

"Or—" he let her hand go and reached for her waist "—I'll carry you out there."

"Now that would be typical macho behavior."

Jake chuckled. "We've already established I don't have to be politically correct." With a quick movement, he picked her up and threw her over his shoulder.

"Jake!" she cried. "Put me down before I have to scream."

She wasn't exactly light, and he did set her on her feet. "Let's go, then."

"Fine. But I'm not going to stand on your feet like a four-year-old."

"That's up to you." In spite of the little scene at the bar, no one paid them much attention. Jake slid into a spot on the darkened floor and pulled Ramona close, bending over a little to do so. "You are short, Miss Hen."

She slapped his arm. "I tried to warn you."

"That's all right. This will work."

It worked just fine. Her breasts pushed softly into his ribs, plush and comfortable. He slid his hands down her back and put his hands on the upper edge of her hips, liking the flare of solid flesh under his palms.

But she was a little stiff again, and he rubbed the hollow of her back for a moment. "Just relax, Ramona. Remember?"

He felt her breasts push into him as she took a breath. Under his hands, the stiffness in her back eased. Jake closed his eyes. Gently, he used one hand to push her head into the hollow of his shoulder. Her hair felt as healthy as it looked, and he allowed himself one moment to savor the sensation. Cool, thick, clean hair.

"There," he said. "Isn't that better?"

Her answer was low and faintly muffled. "I guess."

Jake took a deep breath and let himself fall into the simple movements of a slow dance. Holding Ramona was as comforting as hugging a favorite stuffed animal. All thought, all worry, all despair simply flowed out of him, leaving his mind to drift on the quiet eddies of a romantic song.

He didn't know how long they danced like that. By now, the band was playing all slow songs for the romances developing at the reception. The lights were low, and the crowd had thinned enough so that there were no real distractions.

And he didn't know exactly when the feeling of Ramona's body changed against him, either. When she stopped being simply a comforting teddy bear and became a warm, lush woman. The awareness drifted in slowly. The change came in snippets: the smell of her citrusy shampoo, the slight sway of her breasts against him, the giving warmth of her body against his faint arousal, the swishing sound of her satin skirts. The sensation of slippery satin over warm flesh proved an alluring combination, and he couldn't seem to keep his hands still. Up and down her back they moved, over the curves and into the channel of her spine, down again to the dip of flesh over her bottom, then along the swell of her hips and over her dress up to the bare skin of her shoulders. The sudden encounter with pliant flesh after the slick satin gave him a pleasant jolt each time.

What would it be like to make love to so small and lush a woman as this? How would they fit together, and how would she sound when she made love? The questions flitted through his mind, undemanding and unalarming. He didn't open his eyes or resist, only allowed a vision of their lovemaking to drift through his mind. It was surprisingly erotic to imagine her nude and aroused beneath him, surprisingly inviting.

And because he was so tired, because he had no will to think or consider, he acted on impulse, guiding her into a darkened hallway that led to the back rooms of the hall.

Ramona didn't notice until the darkness around them was absolute. She lifted her head and, with a half-dazed look around, said, "Jake, what—"

Her uptilted face was white in the darkness, her eyes dark and limpid and deep. He curled his hand around her neck and bent his head close.

And kissed her.

She made a faint, surprised sound as their lips touched, and one of her hands flew up to his chest. But she did not push him away, only tilted her head to fit her mouth to his more perfectly. Her lips were as warm as the rest of her, and he liked the plumpness that molded to the shape of his own mouth. He liked the taste of lemon and caramel that lingered there, and the sudden catch of her breath.

Deepening the kiss, he pulled her tightly to him, pressing all of her against all of him. Her body and his seemed to meld, and Jake felt himself respond, felt her notice that response, and he told himself he should stop, that he was taking greater liberties than he ought.

But just then, she opened her lips to his tongue and invited him in, and Jake gave a groan of pleasure. Women liked kissing. He had perfected his technique for that reason, learning how to coax a soft response or a furious one, learning to kindle the flames that he needed for his own satisfaction.

Now as he kissed Ramona, he remembered those techniques, the slide of a tongue, a grazing nibble, the suckling of a lip.

Somehow, he did not use them. He meant to, but he kept getting lost in the feeling of her tongue against his, parrying and darting and tangling. He lost himself in the tenderness of her inner lip and the feeling of her body against his. She smelled right and felt right, and in the darkness, with music playing softly in the distance, it was a uniquely sensual experience. It had never seemed so easy to simply drift along on a kiss, to take such pleasure in the soft heat of her breath coming in a little rush.

He wasn't ready for the flare of heat that exploded inside him, sending a message of urgent need into his belly. Reacting to this overwhelming desire, he shifted to press her close against the wall, thrusting his hips against her in an instinctive and earthy movement that was totally unlike him. She did not protest or make a sound of disgust, only arched against him with the same instinctive need as his own. The kiss grew wilder, more demanding. He plunged and retreated and finally grasped her face in his hands so he could kiss her as deeply as he wished.

He yearned to slide his hands over her breasts, to lift that ugly skirt and touch her thighs, but he didn't. He only kissed her and kissed her and kissed her, as if they were really at a high school dance, where they had to be careful and they both had parents waiting up to ask questions when they got home.

It was this feeling that made him finally reel himself under control and slow their kiss, letting its fierceness ebb into a low, soft burn.

At last, he lifted his head.... And only then, seeing the stunned expression on her face, the look of vulnerability in her eyes, did he realize what he had done. A thud of regret erased all his pleasure. What had he been thinking? She wasn't the kind of woman who would take such a kiss casually.

Gently, he brushed a wisp of hair from her cheek. A dozen possible responses rose to his lips, but in the end, he only murmured, "That was nice." His voice sounded raw.

Ramona managed even less. She simply nodded, her doe eyes round and stricken in her face.

He didn't move, even though he knew he should. "I shouldn't have done that. I'm really not your kind of guy, am I?"

"No," she said, "you aren't."

A thread of dismay wound through him, but he forced himself to straighten, move away from her and plaster an ironic and well-practiced grin on his face. "Well, you can't blame a guy for trying."

"No," she said again. She, too, smiled, and he was relieved to see it wasn't a cowed or uncertain smile at all, but wise and teasing. "And as kisses go, I've had worse."

His smile turned real. "Me, too, Ramona."

A sudden commotion from beyond the dark hallway drew their attention. Both looked toward the reception room without moving, then listened to the announcement that Tamara and Lance were off to their honeymoon.

"Well, I guess we're free to go at last," Jake said, and reached for his bow tie. "Thank God."

"Amen," Ramona returned. "I can't wait to get out of this dress."

His erotic vision of her nude and pliant body beneath him rushed back, bringing with it a certain heat and hunger that surprised him. "I'd be glad to help," he said with a raised eyebrow.

She only smiled and held out her hand. "I'll see you around, I'm sure."

Jake shook her hand, faintly aware of the absurdity of such a formal gesture after the kiss they had just shared. "I'm sure."

"Go get some rest. Doctor's orders."

Then she was gone, disappearing out into the bright room, leaving Jake to stare after her with the oddest sensation in the area of his chest. Finally, he blinked, put the whole strange thing down to exhaustion and decided to follow the doctor's orders.

He'd go home and get some sleep.

Chapter 3

But still Jake didn't sleep. Not that night, or the next, or the next. Not real sleep anyway. Sometimes exhaustion simply kicked in and he fell into a state of virtually comatose oblivion for an hour, or if he was very lucky, two. If the cards were in his favor, he might catch a couple of those short naps in a twenty-four-hour period.

In the four years since he'd quit the army, these insomniac episodes had occurred on a regular basis, but they'd been worse since his father died last year and Jake had come home to Red Creek for the first time in almost twenty years. If he'd had the energy, he would have worried about it.

Instead, he relied on a steady intake of sugar and caffeine to keep him going. His thoughts grew brittle, easy to shatter. He found it hard to concentrate. His face looked whittled away to pure bone. He had trouble holding conversations. The persistent sense of the world as being a movie he could only watch from a distance increased.

Since he'd be a danger in a kitchen, he stayed clear of the restaurant and left it in the capable hands of the manager.

He was fortunate his father had left him investments and the profits of the restaurant could support him. Work of any kind was impossible when he had one of these episodes.

That left only one place for him to feel comfortable—at the VA home, in the company of a World War II vet named Harry, a Medal of Honor winner, though he never discussed it. As a youth who revered all things military, Jake had mowed lawns for the old man and had hung on his every word. When it came time for Jake to apply to West Point, Harry's letter of recommendation had been key to his acceptance.

So now, every other day, Jake smuggled in a bottle of Guinness and a pack of Winstons to his old friend.

The Friday after the wedding, he showed up in the morning and nodded to the nurse on duty. She grinned at him and shook her head. "He's in the sun-room."

They all knew Jake and Harry's small duplicity and looked the other way. Harry had been pronounced terminal four years before and no one had the faintest idea why he was still alive. Jake—and he suspected many of the nurses along with him—figured Harry had earned the right to indulge these last small pleasures.

"Hey, old man," Jake said as he entered the euphemistically labeled sun-room. It had a wall of windows, but the planning committee had neglected to realize that the windows faced north. North and mountains pretty well assured it would be the coldest, dimmest room in the hospital, but it was set up with checkers and a television, and the view was spectacular. Harry especially liked the view of Mount Gordon since he'd spent his life gauging the weather by the way the light fell on the peak.

Harry turned at the sound of Jake's voice. Wizened and

frail, he nonetheless dressed in a clean white shirt every morning and wet combed his thinning hair back neatly. "Jake!" he said, his voice reflecting the same surprise it always did. He frowned and peered over his round, wire-framed glasses. "You look like hell. You aren't a young man anymore, you know."

"Don't I know it. You ready to take a little spin in the garden, you old codger?"

"Hell, yes, I am. They found my last pack in my shoe and took it away last night." He scowled. "Treat us like a bunch of children."

"I got you covered." Jake pushed the wheelchair outside and down a bricked pathway to a sunny spot next to a grove of scrubby trees, twisted and anemic from the long, icy winters. From beneath his jean jacket, worn for the express purpose of hiding the dark brew, Jake pulled out the bottle of Guinness, a keyhole opener and a red pack of Winstons. He glanced over his shoulder, checking the area for an orderly or a nurse who might feel obligated to reprimand them. "All clear," he said, and popped the lid off the ale.

Harry drank gustily and lit a cigarette with hands as steady as a twenty-year-old's. With a contented sigh, he exhaled. "At my age, that's a hell of a lot better than sex," he declared. "Though I wouldn't object to that, either. Got a woman in that coat of yours?"

"Well, Harry, the trouble is, I keep trying to bring one, but they're plumb worn out by the time I get done with them."

"Huh. Selfish little upstart."

Jake chuckled and leaned back against a tree. He closed his eyes against the warm sunlight and let it seep into him. "Nice day," he commented idly.

"Be better with a woman."

"Nah, women talk too much."

"True enough." Harry lifted his cigarette and inhaled

with satisfaction. "That was what I always liked about my Jean. Never much of a talker, that girl."

Harry's wife, Jean, had died, while Jake was away. From his days mowing Harry's lawn, Jake remembered her as a small, birdlike woman with curly hair that never stayed brushed. She was always busy with some household task, washing windows or mending clothes or digging in her pretty garden. "I remember," he said.

Harry settled into some place a long way from the veterans' home. Maybe he was thinking about Jean. Though she had died some ten years before, Harry still spoke of her daily.

Letting the sun soak into his bones, Jake lazily wondered what it would be like to have loved a woman so long and so well. To have shared a life with another person day in and day out, so by the time you were old and sitting in a garden on a sunny summer morning, the fabric of your life would be so interwoven with that of your spouse that the whole color of your existence would have changed. In his lazy, musing state, the metaphor pleased him, and he imagined that Harry was red and Jean blue, and their lives had woven together to make a warm, rich purple.

Nice, but it didn't always work out that way. His own parents had been ill-matched and their life together had been an uneven and blotchy weave. No blend. Just clumps of one color or the other, jarring the eye no matter how many times you expected you'd get used to it.

He might have drifted in the color metaphor for a long time, but Harry said, "You gotta get some sleep sometime, boy."

Jake jolted and leaned on his knees. "Yeah. Tell me about it."

"I had a nightmare about Bataan last night," Harry said, picking a bit of tobacco from his tongue before lifting the cigarette to his lips again. "Always the same one, for more than fifty years now." He cracked a grin. "Sometimes I think heaven would just be never having that dream again."

"I understand."

"Yeah, I reckon you do." He drank a little more Guinness. "You oughta join one of the support groups. Good bunch of fellows. Nobody else is ever gonna know what you're feeling."

Jake rubbed his face. "Yeah, maybe." He was reluctant to turn down Harry's advice straight out, but the idea of wandering into that group of World War II and Korean and Vietnam vets shamed him.

"It don't get better on its own, boy."

Jake nodded. That much was obvious. It had been more than five years now, and he only seemed to be getting worse, not better. "Sometimes," he said quietly, "I really think I'm going insane."

Harry merely nodded and went back to smoking, his pale blue eyes fixed on something far, far away. Feeling safe and protected with Harry only a few feet away, Jake leaned back against the tree and slept with the sunlight against his lids, burning away any image that might sneak in.

Ramona pressed her stethoscope against her pregnant patient's belly, and listened quietly. "Sounds good. Fast heartbeat still—probably a boy."

The young woman smiled. "My husband is dying for a boy."

The nurse popped her head in the door. "Dr. Hardy, do you have time to see Louise Forrest before lunch? Her son just brought her in with a sprained ankle."

"Of course," Ramona said. "Which son brought her?"

"The oldest boy. Jack? Jake?"

Ramona smiled. Now why wasn't she surprised that Louise would have a little accident just before the end of office hours on a Friday and just happen to call her eldest son to take her to the doctor's office?

"No problem," she said to her nurse. "Put her in three, and I'll be in there in a few minutes."

"Okay. I'm going on, then, if you don't mind. I need to leave early for the school party."

"That's fine. See you Monday."

Ramona finished with her expectant mother, then headed down to exam three, half-smiling at Louise's predictability. She would bet a large sum of money there would be nothing at all wrong with the ankle—Louise wasn't above subterfuge to get what she wanted.

"Good morning, Mrs. Forrest," Ramona said cheerfully as she came in. Louise sat on the table, an ice pack on her bare ankle. Jake sprawled on the chair in the corner, his face turned away, and Ramona frowned. He looked haggard as hell. "How are you, Jake?"

It seemed to take him a long time to turn his head, and when he did, Ramona found that his eyes were just exactly as blue as she remembered. The color called Persian blue, the color of columbines. "Fine, thank you," he replied politely.

A lie. His jaw was shaded with the dark bristles of an unshaved beard, and his eyes were sunk into purple hollows. She thought that in the short week since she'd last seen him he'd lost weight. The wonder was that he was able to sit upright at all.

But she let the lie slide for the moment and turned to Louise. "What did you do?"

"Oh, it was the silliest thing. I slipped on the steps going to take out the trash."

"Hmm." Ramona lifted the ice bag to examine an ankle as trim and neat as a girl's. She poked at the unswollen, unbruised, untraumatized flesh with two fingers. "Does that hurt?"

Louise frowned. "A little."

"We'll fix you up."

"Jake," Louise said, "why don't you wait outside and let me talk to the doctor about my medication while I'm here."

He shrugged and stood. Ramona resisted the temptation to gawk at his long, lanky form, but it was impossible to avoid sneaking a peek from the corner of her eye. She had not forgotten the way he'd felt against her, nor the wonder of the kiss they had shared.

Not to mention the sheer size of him. In the small examining room, he seemed to take up most of the available space. "I'll be in the waiting room," he said, and ducked out.

As soon as the door was closed, Ramona put a hand on her hip. "There's nothing wrong with this ankle. You want to tell me what's going on?"

"I know, I know. I'll pay your regular fee, just like a patient who really has something wrong."

"Louise, you know it isn't the money."

The older woman raised a hand and waved all that away. "I had to get him in here somehow. He's bad, Ramona. I don't think he's had any real sleep since before the wedding. For a bit there, right after he bought the restaurant, he seemed to be getting better, but he's gotten worse again. You can see it for yourself. I'm scared to death he's going to kill himself."

Ramona frowned. "You think he might be suicidal?"

"Not strictly." She pursed her lips. "Not as in taking a rope and hanging himself or anything like that, but he could very well kill himself another way—wreck his car, drink too much one night, fall, something. You know what I mean."

"Yes."

"I just want you to talk to him, Dr. Hardy. Maybe he'd take sleeping pills."

Ramona sighed. "He needs more than I can give him, Louise. I'm only a medical doctor, and he needs counseling. He can get it through the veterans' office."

"He won't do it." Louise grabbed her hand. "Honey, I feel certain you can help him a little, maybe just get him going in the right direction. Everybody knows those old soldiers love you like you're some kind of queen. Please?"

Ramona narrowed her eyes. Much of what Louise said was true. She had survived her own case of PTSD and she'd been able to use that knowledge with some success. She was also predisposed to take combat veterans under her wing. "The thing you have to understand is that I can't help him until he's ready. It's like trying to get an alcoholic to stop drinking. You can beg and plead all you like, but the decision to accept help comes from within or it isn't successful."

"So you'll talk to him?"

Ramona laughed. "I knew we should have barred you stubborn Texans from this state a long time ago."

Louise jumped nimbly off the table. "Right, you go, then. I'll just wait until you call him into your office."

"Okay." Her hands in her lab-coat pockets, Ramona paused by the door and felt compelled to offer another warning. "Don't expect miracles, Louise."

The stubborn Texan winked. "Oh, I'm always looking for miracles, sugar."

Ramona left Louise and walked down a short hall to the waiting room.

Jake sat in one of the chairs, his head flung back against the wall. His eyes were closed. With his hands folded on his stomach and his long legs stretched out in front of him, crossed at the ankles, he looked very peaceful. Ramona hated to disturb him.

It seemed impossible that he should still be so gorgeous, even with the torture that lay on him like a banshee, eating him from within, but he was. He looked like exactly what he was: dangerous and haunted and unbelievably sexy.

Ramona was well-educated and had basic good sense. But she was a woman, too. A woman who had never had much time for relationships until she reached her thirties, and she'd liked it that way.

But she had the normal hormones, and they worked as predictably as any other woman's. For a long time after the rape, she had felt no interest in men at all, but eventually she'd made peace with the difference between acts of violence and acts of sex. There had been a sweet, gentle boy in college who had eased her through the worst of her fears, and in matters concerning sex, Ramona believed she was no different from any other woman. She'd been too busy to date a lot, but on the rare occasions that she actually met a man whose company she enjoyed, she had no mental block about a physical relationship.

Jake somehow aroused an altogether different reaction in her than the usual pleasant attraction. When she did date, she tended to choose calm, intelligent, nurturing men. Jake was not like them. He was volatile. He was intense. He was hard and wary.

And the visions he roused in her imagination were also different. She didn't imagine a life spent going for walks or fixing him supper. She imagined panting, tangled, sweaty bodies. She imagined that beautiful mouth kissing hers again and again and imagined how he might sound when he made love.

Pretty earthy stuff. Admiring him in her waiting room, she had to smile. In a way, it was rather comforting because she knew her daydreams would never amount to anything. They might become friends, and she might be able to help him with his problems, but Jake was not her kind of man—

and she wasn't his kind of woman. They were mature enough to realize that.

She walked over to him and spoke his name quietly. "Jake, can I talk to you for a minute?" No response. "Jake?" A little louder this time. She bent over and touched his knee. "Jake."

In an instant, he was upright, his hand curled around her wrist in a fierce and painful grip, his other hand raised as if to strike her. A feral, brutal expression burned in his eyes, and Ramona couldn't help the protective gesture she made.

"It's me," she said, holding up a hand to guard her face.

Several long moments passed before his grip eased, before he seemed to realize where he was and what was happening. Abruptly, he let her go. "Don't ever touch me when I'm sleeping."

It wasn't an uncommon trait among ex-soldiers. Sometimes even very old men still reacted to a sudden awakening this way—but few of them retained Jake's powerful strength. "I'm sorry," she said. "I won't do it again."

"What do you want?" he asked gruffly.

"Can you come into my office for a minute? I'd like to talk to you."

He blinked. "What's wrong?"

She only responded, "Why don't we go to my office? We can talk there." Before he could protest, she moved away, knowing he would follow.

Blinking tiredly, Jake followed Ramona into her small office in the back of the clinic. She looked different today, efficient and brisk, her hair in a knot up on the back of her head, her lab coat hiding her figure. As he sat down in a chair upholstered in a floral print, his heart thudded uncomfortably. What could be so wrong with his mother that they had to have a private conference about it?

It seemed to take Ramona forever to round the desk and

sit down. "Spit it out, Ramona," he growled. "What's wrong with her? Cancer? Her heart?"

She smiled. "It isn't your mother, Jake. She's as healthy as a horse, and I expect she'll be around to meddle in the lives of her great-grandchildren."

Relief flooded through him, followed quickly by perplexity. His sleep-deprived mind couldn't seem to make the jump from there to—whatever it was he was here for.

His expression must have reflected his confusion, for Ramona sobered and inclined her head. He'd forgotten how velvety those big brown eyes were, how much they invited him to just relax, let her take over. Resisting her spell, he sat up very straight in his chair.

"She doesn't even have a sprained ankle, actually. It was ploy to get you in here."

"Damn."

"She's worried about you, Jake, and probably with good reason."

"I'm fine. She's just projecting. Her father lost it after combat, so she thinks anybody who's spent a little time in the field is going to go crazy."

"Are you fine?"

He forced himself to look at her. "How long is your hair?"

She chuckled. "Nice try. Answer the question."

"I already did. I'm fine." Restlessly, he stood and wandered toward the window that looked out toward a view of the town, tumbling down the slopes of the mountain like a storybook village. "It just takes a while, you know."

"To do what?"

He shrugged a shoulder, peering out at the sunlight. "Adjust to civilian life, I guess."

"Well, that's true. You were in the military a long time."

"Sixteen years."

"Didn't you go to West Point?"

A thick, panicky feeling rose in his throat. "Yeah."

She said nothing for a minute, and Jake employed his favorite tactic. Stay quiet, and the rest of the world will do the talking for you.

But Ramona's silence stretched way longer than usual, and he was finally curious enough to turn around to look at her. She calmly sat behind her desk, her hands folded on the blotter in front of her. When he met her gaze, she asked quietly, "How long has it been since you slept, Jake?"

He didn't know why he answered her, but he did. "Forever."

"I thought so. I can give you a prescription that would help, but I think you need to consider counseling to go along with it."

"I don't need any—" he halted the foul word rising to his lips "—damned counseling."

"My hair is to my waist," she said, picking up a pair of wire-framed glasses.

"What?"

"My hair," she said patiently, pulling over a prescription pad. "It's long. To my waist."

Jake couldn't quite summon a smile. "Touché," he said, and sat back down in the chair. "Is that prescription for me?"

"Yes, if you'll take it." She finished writing and ripped the note off the pad. She held it out to him.

The glasses radically changed her appearance, hiding the softness of her eyes, obscuring the nice, clean line of her cheekbones. They made her look serious and purposeful and a lot more like a woman who had the drive and ambition to become a doctor. Jake felt a sudden wash of memory. "I remember you," he said. "You were in some of my classes, weren't you?"

Ramona grinned. "Yep."

"How could I have forgotten your name?" He narrowed his eyes. "In the eighth grade, you took the regional spelling bee. I wanted to kill you."

"I also seem to recall a science fair that annoyed you a tiny bit."

This time, Jake did manage a smile, which was followed by a small, miraculous chuckle. "Don't remind me. I still remember your project, too—the heart/lung demonstration. The minute I saw it, I knew I was cooked. It made me furious to be beaten by a girl."

Ramona laughed. "Oh, I loved beating you at any academic contest. You took it so seriously."

Jake fell quiet, reminiscing. He had taken it seriously, and he'd loved the rush of competition, the fierce pleasure of pitting his brain against others. "I did." He met her patient gaze. "Nothing feels like that anymore. Did I just get old?"

"No." She paused, then removed her glasses. "No, that's not the problem. I think you're suffering from a pretty serious case of posttraumatic stress disorder, Jake."

"Yeah, right." He rolled his eyes. "You know, Desert Storm wasn't like Vietnam or World War II or Korea. We didn't lose thousands and thousands of our men. It didn't drag on for years. We kicked the enemy's butt, got out fast and came home heroes." He felt his jaw tense, his throat tighten. "No big deal." She inclined her head again and nodded, and it suddenly made Jake furious. "Don't play counselor with me, damn it. Don't start thinking I'm some pity case just because I can't sleep."

"Jake, did you like being a soldier?"

"Is this some trick question?"

"No." Her voice somehow managed to soothe the anxiety her questions and probing raised. A gift, that calming voice, part of her healer's bag of tricks. "I've never approved of the army, actually. I don't believe in war."

"How nice for you."

"Hear me out." She leaned forward. "I don't disapprove of the choice someone makes for his or her life. We have to make our way in the world, and we do that as well as we can, but there's such a gap between a healer's mind and a soldier's mind that I've never been able to understand why someone would choose that life. Didn't you always want to be a soldier? I'd like to understand that."

Her words spun into him, stinging like hornets in a hundred raw places, buzzing and burning against his open wounds. Memories rushed in. He saw himself raking Harry's leaves when he was twelve, listening in rapt fascination to Harry's battle stories. The noise, the action, the bonding of men. He saw himself chortling when the letter from West Point came and his dream was so close. When he'd actually entered those hallowed halls, his heart had swollen so large in his chest he'd almost passed out.

And though he tried to stop the rest—the tormenting visions—they all came in a tumble, too. The dun-colored sand and the smell of burning flesh and the noise that meant children had died, and the tanks and—

"Damn." He clamped his hands over his eyes. "I don't want to talk about this," he said in a raw voice. "Leave me alone."

He bolted for the door then, but Ramona stopped him, grabbing his arm before he got through the door. "Take the prescription," she said. "At least you can get some sleep."

Without thought, conscious only of his urgent need to flee, Jake grabbed the slip of paper from her hand and escaped.

Chapter 4

Louise took one look at her son's face and abandoned all attempt at faking a sprained ankle. His expression reminded her of when he was twelve and furious with himself for falling short on some standard he'd set—generally way too high—for himself.

When he came out of Ramona's office, he shot his mother a single, blazing look and growled, "Let's go."

Louise glanced over her shoulder at Ramona, who only shook her head. A sword pierced Louise's chest, but she wisely said nothing as she followed Jake out to his low-slung red Miata. She said nothing as he unlocked the door or as she buckled her seat belt. Nor did he.

Maybe this time she had overstepped her boundaries. Jake was not easily directed. He listened only to some voice inside of him, a voice she suspected echoed the authoritarian bark of her late husband, Olan. No matter what Jake had achieved as a child, Olan had only pushed him harder—and Jake had learned to do the same for himself.

In his own estimation, he was never strong enough, smart enough, good enough.

All that, in spite of his astonishing record. In school, he had always scored highest on tests, and graduated valedictorian. If he played sports—and naturally a boy like him had to play—he had to be captain of the team. He'd set his sights on West Point and gotten it. He'd determined to attain the rank of major by the age of thirty and had achieved that, too.

He was the most driven man she had ever known. All of his life, Louise had worried about it. Experience had taught her no man could keep up that hard pace without eventually collapsing.

Oh, she'd tried to counteract it. When he'd achieved a goal, Louise encouraged him to revel in it, to take pride in the new achievement, but Jake was always heading for the next pinnacle. Always striving, always looking ahead to the next challenge.

She didn't see anything wrong with ambition. Ambition and drive were good things, but like everything else, they were only good in moderation. Jake never seemed to get any joy out of his accomplishments.

Four years ago, he'd abruptly resigned his commission with only a handful of years to go to retirement. Upon hearing the news, Louise had immediately suspected all was not well with him, but she hadn't been able to see for herself until he came home last fall. Once the neatest of her three children, he hadn't had a haircut in months, and it was plain he hadn't shaved in at least a few days. Looking at him now, she noted with concern the blue shadows under his eyes, the grimness of an expression held in check to hide everything going on inside.

She pressed her palm to the sick place at the top of her stomach. "Jake, I'm sorry for buttin' into your life, but you can't expect me to sit back and watch you waste away into nothing.''

His hands tightened around the steering wheel, but he stared straight ahead. ''I'm fine, Mama.''

''Fine, my foot! When was the last time you ate a real meal? When was the last time you slept all night? Can you even *remember* the last time you enjoyed yourself at anything?''

''As a matter of fact, I had a great meal at Lance's reception, and I really enjoyed myself, too. Does that make you feel better?''

''That was almost a week ago!'' she protested, thinking of the food.

Jake gave her a half smile. ''Mama, this may come as a great surprise to you, but a good many single men and women don't eat full-course meals three times a day.''

''Just because they don't, doesn't mean it's healthy.''

He gave an exasperated sigh. ''What do you want, Mama? You want me to be back in the army? You want me married and goo-goo-eyed like Lance? You want me to cut my hair and wear clean shirts like old Harry? What? Just tell me.''

''I just want my Jake back,'' she said quietly. ''I want to see that spark in your eye again. I want to see you really living instead of just drifting like this.''

He pulled up in front of her house and put the car in Neutral, but didn't turn off the ignition. He stared at the house with a singular lack of expression. ''The old Jake is gone, Mama. I'm sorry, but he's not coming back.''

Louise opened her mouth to protest, then thought of Ramona's warning. Jake had to be ready. ''All right, son. I'll try to accept that.'' She opened the car door. ''You're welcome to come eat anytime. You know I can't stop cooking.''

He caught her arm. ''Ramona gave me a prescription for

sleeping pills. I'll try them, all right?'' He kissed her cheek quickly. ''Just mind your own your business, will ya?''

''I'll try.'' She patted his cheek and winked. ''I'll try real hard.''

And in fact, it was nearly miraculous what those pills did for him. Jake didn't know if he was simply just too exhausted to think or even ache anymore, but the pills put him to sleep in minutes. For the next few weeks, he didn't exactly sleep blissfully through the night and wake up refreshed—his nightmares were a little too energetic for that kind of rest—but he at least got enough rest that he could function again. He went back to work and started experimenting with a low-fat sauce for artichoke hearts. When his cook broke both legs and a wrist in a climbing accident, Jake cheerfully took his place, playing rock and roll on the radio as he juggled orders.

Because of his pinch-hitting, he was late going to see Harry one Saturday evening. He'd called to leave a message, but it still bothered him—Harry counted on Jake. It was almost dark when he got to the hospital, but Jake found Harry in his usual place, looking out the windows toward Mount Gordon.

''Hey, Harry,'' Jake said, ''sorry I'm late. Did you get my message?''

Harry nodded. ''I did. You know you don't have to wait on me, son. I got by without you before you came home. I'd get by without you again. You got something to do, you go on and do it. Don't put anything on hold for me, you hear?''

Jake chuckled and grabbed the handles of the wheelchair. ''You want a sweater or anything? It's cool tonight.''

''I guess I do. There's a jacket in my room if you want to go and fetch it for me.''

''Will do. Don't go anywhere.''

Harry didn't smile. He didn't answer. Just sat facing the windows. Jake saw the purpling mountainsides reflected in Harry's round glasses and noticed the yellowish look of the old man's skin and the deeply etched lines in his face.

"Are you all right, man?"

"I'm old," he said, and coughed heartily. "Nothing a good Winston won't cure."

"All right. I'll be right back."

Jake wasn't in the home much this time of day, and it was different. He waved at old soldiers in their beds, thinking it seemed lonely here tonight, with the sounds of canned television laughter unable to completely drown the mechanical whooshes and beeps of health support equipment. Fluorescent tube lights gave everything a cold greenish cast. Jake thought absently that the rooms should be painted more cheerful colors. Maybe some warm blues and greens, or stripes in bright primaries.

He ducked into Harry's room and quietly opened the narrow closet, careful not to awaken Harry's roommate, who slept with his mouth open, snoring robustly. He found the light cotton jacket Harry favored and crept back out to the hall, closing the door behind him.

A woman's laughter spilled into the hallway. It was a warm, life-giving sound in the quiet of the home, sexy and utterly female. Jake smiled, thinking of all the men who would turn to that sound and grin to themselves, or maybe yearn to hear it in response to one of their jokes.

A man's voice murmured just a couple of rooms down, and the woman laughed again. Low and husky, somehow very rich. Nice. He thought it belonged to a young woman, and his dulled libido perked up. He'd been too tired even to do much automatic flirting the past few weeks. Maybe he'd peek in to see who it was. A lot of these guys had children and grandchildren in the area.

Just as he neared the door, however, the woman came

out, looking over her shoulder to offer a slightly ribald joke to the old man in the bed.

Ramona. Jake stopped, clutching the jacket in his hands. For one brief moment, he wanted to duck into one of the rooms along the route so he could avoid her. He didn't like the astuteness of those clear, steady eyes.

But for once, her hair was down, and she had on something that actually flattered her coloring and figure. It was a pretty, springlike dress made of some floral fabric, very light and airy—and kind of transparent, like those old dresses from the forties.

Beneath the red-and-blue fabric, she had on some kind of dark slip. He saw the straps on her shoulders and followed the line of the slip over her breasts.

She didn't see him until she nearly ran right into him, swinging out of the room with her dress fluttering around her legs and her hair tumbling down her back. He caught her arm to keep her from bumping into him.

"You really do have long hair," he commented.

Her eyes showed a flare of pure womanly pleasure before she managed to don her professional manner. "Jake! It's good to see you."

"Yeah?"

She gave him a smile that crinkled the corners of her eyes. "Yes. You look a lot better. Did the sleeping pills help?"

Annoyance rose in him. He didn't want to be her patient. He wanted to slide his hands over that slippery dress and feel the way her flesh gave against his palms. He let his gaze wander over her body, and his sex gave a small, approving shout. "Nice dress," he said.

"Thank you," she replied as if she hadn't noticed his perusal. "It's one of my favorites."

There was a long, long row of tiny buttons from the

demure neckline to the hem. "Must be hard to get on and off. You'd about have to use tweezers on those buttons."

She took a step away from him and crossed her arms. One breast swelled prettily against a red fabric petal. "Cool it, Jake," she said.

"Cool what?"

"The seductive act. You don't have to flirt with me." She smiled. "I'll be nice to you anyway."

"Sorry," he said, and realized he meant it. "Habit."

"I know. But it isn't necessary with me." She inclined her head. "How are the pills working?"

"Actually, they help a lot. Thank you."

"Good. Maybe in a few weeks, you can think seriously about contacting one of the counselors, huh?"

"Maybe." He wouldn't, and she probably knew that. It was her job to suggest it and he didn't blame her.

"Are you here to visit Harry?"

Jake lifted the jacket. "Yes."

She nodded, and her smile was very sweet. "He really looks forward to seeing you, you know. His children only come once a month."

"I know." The children all lived in Denver. "It's a long drive, I guess." He looked at the khaki jacket folded over his arm and knew Harry would be anxious to get outside for his cigarette, but Jake was somehow reluctant to move.

But he also couldn't think of anything to say. He raised his head and met her wide brown eyes, and his breath caught in his chest. "I guess you have a lot going on, huh? Things to do when you finish here?"

"Not really." Her voice blew like a warm breeze over his nerves. "This is my last stop."

Still no words came to mind. He wasn't sure exactly what he wanted to tell her. He only knew that he wanted to spend a little more time with her, maybe just listening to that peaceful voice and letting himself drift in the softness of her eyes. "Can I buy you some supper or something?"

She hesitated, and Jake felt an unfamiliar embarrassment wash over him. Women didn't turn him down as a rule. In fact, he really couldn't remember the last time.

She took a breath. "This is hard for me to say, so don't laugh, okay?"

He gave her a puzzled frown. "Okay."

"I know I'm not your type, and you aren't really mine, but there does seem to be an...a..." She paused, sighed quickly and met his eyes. "There's something pretty physical between us."

He grinned as wickedly as he was able. "I was afraid you hadn't noticed."

"I noticed. But my point is, I think it would be a very bad idea for us to be involved sexually." Only a tiny hint of color betrayed her discomfort. "But I wouldn't mind being friends."

It was rare that anyone, man or woman, could so frankly confront such a subject, and although Jake felt a slight urge to reciprocate and turn the tables on her for her rejection—however well-meant—he wouldn't demean her honesty by pretending he wasn't attracted to her.

"Okay." He grinned again and let his eyes sweep over her luscious curves. "But I can't promise not to speculate about what I might do if you'd let me."

"I mean it, Jake. I would enjoy matching wits with you again, but I don't want any complications. We're just too different."

He sobered. "I mean it, too, Ramona. It would be nice to have a friend." To his amazement, he was sincere. "I'd better get back to Harry. Think about where you want to eat."

"Okay. Take your time with Harry. I've got rounds to

finish, and I'll wait for you in my office. Ask one of the nurses where it is."

Ramona couldn't help a shiver of anticipation as she walked out into the cool night with Jake Forrest at her side. She had meant what she said about a sexual relationship. It would be disastrous. Aside from the very real problem of his PTSD, Jake brought an intensity and a kind of wildness with him, and she didn't have the time or the inclination to deal with that personality.

As he opened the car door for her, however, she couldn't halt the rush of awareness he aroused. Standing there bathed in the weak white light of a gibbous moon, his hair shone fiercely, and his face was an alluring arrangement of planes and shadows. One high, arched cheekbone and the bridge of his elegant nose caught edges of moonlight.

She paused, remembering a moment when she was sixteen. She'd been late for class and had rushed to her locker for a forgotten notebook, then rounded a corner at a run. There, in a secluded hallway, had been Jake and his girlfriend, making out. Jake's hand had covered the sweatered breast of the girl, and she had a nearly delirious expression on her face as he kissed her neck. Petrified and shocked and aroused all at once, Ramona had stared at them for a long minute, mesmerized by those long fingers stroking and teasing and moving over the girl's flesh.

Finally, ashamed, she had hurried away, her face burning.

The memory had lost little of its power over the years, and Ramona felt a familiar heat flood through her.

As if he noticed nothing amiss, Jake said now, "How about the Moon Café? I hear they have a pretty good Celtic trio. You seem as if you'd be the sort to like Celtic music."

She smiled. "I do, but it doesn't strike me as your kind of thing."

"Oh, really?" He raised a brow. "What would be my kind of thing?"

Ramona shrugged. "I haven't thought about it. Something loud."

He gave her a pained look and closed the door, then climbed into the driver's side. "That makes me sound so uncivilized."

The car was small and Jake seemed to fill every inch of it. Ramona smelled the same cologne he had used at the reception and inhaled appreciatively. "You do smell good."

"Thanks." His smile flashed in the darkness, and Ramona reminded herself that he was quite practiced with women. The car, the cologne, the easy, knowing smile. His confidence showed even in the way he drove—too fast, but very much in control—as if the machine were only an extension of his body.

"So what kind of music do you like?" she asked.

"I think you should guess. No more stereotypes."

"Stereotypes?"

"You assumed I'd like something loud."

Ramona shook her head. "I wasn't stereotyping any more than you were when you said I seemed the type to like Celtic music."

"Ah, but you do like it, don't you?"

"Yes."

"So I wasn't stereotyping. I was making a judgment call about you and what I know of you." He negotiated a steep, tight curve, then shot an amused glance her way. "You, on the other hand, were making a sweeping generalization."

"Touché. I was thinking of soldiers and what I used to hear on their car stereos when they went blazing down the street." She narrowed her eyes. "Let me see, then. Country or bluegrass, maybe?"

"Not my thing, though I don't mind it."

"Hmm. Blues? Jazz?"

"Closer."

Ramona frowned. "I don't know...you might get excited about some classical, but I have to put my money on fancy guitar." His face went blank and Ramona knew she'd scored. "Let's see...you're a year older than I am...so what? Led Zepplin, ZZ Top, maybe a little old Aerosmith?"

Jake pulled smoothly into the downtown lot behind the café, then turned off the engine before he spoke. He looked at Ramona and gave her a singularly gorgeous grin. It lit his eyes and warmed his face and kindled a tiny fire in the nether regions of her body.

"Pretty good, Doc." He pulled out a hand-lettered cassette tape, and gave it to her.

Ramona read the handwriting: *La Grange.* She laughed. "ZZ Top!"

"Pretty adolescent, huh?"

"Not at all. I used to love this. I haven't heard it in a long time, though. My friends and I used to play it while we got dressed for parties, just to get us in the mood."

"I don't remember seeing you at parties."

"We didn't exactly travel with the same crowd."

"True." He slipped the cassette back into the tape deck. "I'll play it on the way back. Let's go eat. I'm starving."

The Moon Café was as up to the moment as any place in Red Creek, a coffee shop that would have been at home in any downtown string of upscale shops in any city in the U.S. It had been established by a San Francisco couple who'd fled the coast after the last earthquake. Ramona often stopped in for lunch and the owner waved to her as she took a seat.

The late-evening crowd was mostly young and at least pseudointellectual, local kids who listened to Enya and dreamed of wider horizons, and summer-idle ski bums.

They sat in the dimly lit room and listened to the Celtic trio and talked of world hunger and white witchcraft and fantasy novels. Ramona liked them.

"I guess you've been here before, huh?" Jake remarked.

"Sure." She flashed him a grin. "In spite of being stereotypically my kind of place, it really is my kind of place."

Jake smiled appreciatively. "Too bad there were no coffee shops like this when you were in high school. Then you wouldn't have had to suffer through parties."

"I found the coffee shops in college just fine, thank you."

"And I bet you dated really earnest guys with round glasses and long hair."

She couldn't help the chuckle that rose in her throat. Mark, her college sweetheart, had looked as gentle as he was—blond, thin and bespectacled. "My main squeeze was a music major. He played in all the clubs."

"I'll bet he didn't play electric guitar."

"No. Fiddle."

His eyes twinkled. "Bingo."

The waiter stopped by and they ordered the coffee of the day, something dark and rich and African. When hers came, Ramona sprinkled nutmeg over the top and stirred in sugar. Jake, not surprisingly, drank his straight.

They ate exotic sandwiches made of sprouts and tomatoes and guacamole on thick slices of multigrain bread. Ramona had to fight to keep her weight even in the moderately plump range and usually watched every gram she put in her mouth, but she felt beautiful tonight, and free, and for once she allowed herself to eat until she was really full.

The trio, a harper, a flutist and a wistfully beautiful singer who looked about thirteen, was very good. A waiter brought a backgammon board over at Jake's request, and as they set it up, Ramona asked, "How do you like the music?"

"Not bad. It would be nice if they sang in English."

"Some groups do."

"Didn't you have a girlfriend at one time who was Irish? An exchange student or something?"

"Bridget."

"Yeah. The little red-haired girl. She was scared of her own shadow."

"She's a writer now. Big, glitzy potboilers about the English upper classes. She's done quite well."

"Really? That's amazing. You'll have to point her books out to me sometime."

"I have all of them. If you're serious, I'll send them to you."

"I'd love to borrow them. It's interesting to find out something like that about some kid you knew way back when. Seems to me most of my friends from high school didn't ever..." He shrugged.

"Didn't what?" She rolled the dice and got a natural, five and six, and moved automatically.

"I don't know. They just didn't do anything. Or at least not what they thought they'd do."

"Like what?"

He moved his pieces, then lifted his head. "Like my friend, Jed, who wanted to be an astronaut. He really wanted to go up into space. I mean, his room was covered with model rockets and star maps and all kinds of things. He was good at math and science and all that—but he's selling insurance."

Ramona's healing instincts prickled, and although she hated herself for it, she found she could not resist drawing him out on the subject. Perhaps he would reveal some key to his own troubles. "Okay. I set out to be a doctor, and I am one. You were a soldier."

"'Were' being the operative word in my case." There was only a hint of rancor in his voice. "I don't know what I mean, really. It just seems at times that nobody ever really gets what they want." He gestured toward a table nearby, filled with a crowd of young people. "I mean, look at those kids. I bet there are aspiring writers and singers and world leaders among them, and how many will really do what they want to do?"

Ramona didn't speak for a moment, mulling over the right words. He looked at her, and for a fleeting heartbeat, she saw raw, screaming pain in the depths of his eyes.

Then it was gone and he nudged the dice toward her. "Your turn."

She rolled and moved. "Your friend, Jed, leads the local astronomy society."

"Oh, that's very exciting."

"No, now that's not fair. He loves the stars, and he gets to share that love with others. Maybe he isn't going to walk on the moon, but that doesn't change his love of it or the passion he feels toward space, does it?"

"It isn't the same, Ramona, and you know it." His eyes narrowed. "Leading the astronomy society is not the same as being in space."

"You're right," she said slowly. "But I know Jed. He's one of the happiest men I know." She smiled gently. "He has six children, did you know that? Two are foster children he adopted. His wife worships the ground he walks on and she's one of the kindest, most loving people you'd find anywhere. Jed didn't become an astronaut because she got pregnant when they were first married, and he chose to come back to Red Creek so his child would have the same childhood he did."

"Don't you think he ever wishes things turned out differently?"

"I have no idea. Maybe. We can't ever know what's way

down deep in someone's heart, but my guess would be no. I don't think he minds. Maybe sometimes when he's gazing up at the Pleiades, he wonders what it would have been like to build a space station, but I bet it's just a moment's twinge. I doubt he would trade the life he has for the life he wanted.'' She looked at the table of earnest young people. ''The aspiring writer in that group might end up doing technical writing, and the singer might only end up with one of the biggest CD collections in the state, but both of them will be the richer for having dreamed, for having striven to reach something beyond themselves.''

He nodded, but Ramona could tell he didn't agree with her. Not for one second.

''You don't buy it,'' she said. ''Why not?''

''It's not that. Look, I'm sure Jed is happy. He always liked kids,'' he said slowly. A thoughtful frown creased his brow, and he looked consideringly over his shoulder at the crowd. ''Maybe it's like that old expression, 'Be careful what you ask for.' My mom always told us to be careful, because what you end up getting may prove to be a disaster.''

Ramona only murmured assent quietly, afraid to disturb the flow of his words.

''She wanted a rich man—or thought she did.'' Jake gave Ramona a wry smile. ''Hard to believe she really thought that was what she wanted, isn't it?''

She nodded. ''She's a very down-to-earth woman.''

''She is. But her dad ran off after the war, and her mother had to take in sewing and clean houses and work as a waitress to make ends meet. They didn't have anything, and my mother hated it, so she made up her mind to find a rich man.''

''Was your father rich? I had the impression he was a self-made man.''

''He wasn't rich when they met, but she said she could

tell he was going to be. And he was.'' Jake suddenly seemed to realize where he was and rolled the dice, then moved his pieces. ''He was also one of the most selfish, hard-nosed men I've ever met.''

It was hard to find words of praise for Olan Forrest, that was sure. But Ramona was more interested in Jake at the moment. ''So what do you think your mother should have wished for?''

The question surprised him. ''I don't know. A good life, maybe. A good man.''

''And you, Jake? What would you wish for, knowing what you know?''

The vivid blue eyes flickered, and in the space of a second, all the honest thoughtfulness was safely hidden beneath a smooth, untroubled expression. ''Are you counseling me, Doc?''

''Sorry.''

They dropped the conversation after that and concentrated on the game, reminiscing idly about the various people in their past. Ramona had been on the alumni committee for several years and knew at least a little about most of the kids they had graduated with. Not many had stayed in Red Creek.

Learning that, Jake shook his head. ''Seems odd, doesn't it, that all the natives are fleeing and so many outsiders are coming in?''

''You never appreciate your own backyard.''

''That's true, I guess.'' He pursed his lips. ''There's always been a lot of tourist traffic, but it wasn't like it is now. Some mornings this past winter, I walked where I wanted to go. It was faster than driving.'' A short, comfortable pause fell between them. Jake asked after a while, ''Do you ski?''

A cold fist struck her heart, then was gone—the last, and

probably permanent reminder of her own trauma. "I used to cross-country, but I don't anymore."

"I like cross-country, too. Why'd you give it up? Get too old to hack it?" He grinned.

Ramona swallowed and forced herself to meet his friendly, guileless gaze. "I guess so."

"Maybe I can drag you out there this winter. I've missed it."

"Maybe." She glanced at her watch. "I'm going to have to call it a night. I have to work tomorrow."

"No problem." He reached for the check and called the waiter.

He drove her back to the hospital to pick up her car. It was a very quiet drive, but not awkward. She liked the fact that she didn't feel obligated to fill the silence. Nor did he.

By the time he had come to a full stop next to her car, Ramona had her hand on the door handle. "Thanks, Jake," she said.

He caught her arm. "Do I have bad breath or something?"

Ramona blinked. "What do you mean?"

"It's like you can't wait to get out of the car."

He held her arm loosely, and their faces were only inches apart. Ramona stared for one longing moment at his beautiful mouth, then eased away. "I'm just avoiding temptation," she said, and her voice was a lot throatier than usual.

His fingers moved on the bare underside of her arm, and Ramona felt the shivery reaction all the way down her spine. "Fair enough."

He straightened, and Ramona was aware of a tinge of regret. Firmly, she reminded herself it had been she who had set the parameters of this relationship. "Good night, Jake. I had a nice time. We'll have to do it again."

"Yeah." When she was about to close the door, he suddenly leaned over to look at her. "Hey!"

Moonlight silvered the planes of his face and glittered in the uncommon and beautiful eyes. "What?"

"Would you bring me some of that chokecherry jelly?"

Ramona chuckled. "Sure. I'll leave it with Harry the next time I come over here."

"Thanks."

He waited until she had safely climbed into her car and started it, then he drove away much too fast. Ramona watched the retreating lights musingly, then put her own car in gear and headed home.

Chapter 5

There was an odd little lump of sorrow and regret in her chest, vague and unfocused, as she drove home through the moonlit forest toward her mountainside house. Part of it was the lingering trace of that long-ago day, a trace that would never entirely disappear, but that wasn't all of it. She felt uneasy about Jake. He had seemed much better tonight, but she couldn't forget the sudden, raw pain she had glimpsed in his eyes.

At the gate to her long drive, she got out, unfastened it and drove through, then latched it again behind her. It wasn't so much a security measure—though she did value her privacy and had fenced the entire twelve-acre spread some years ago to keep out the tourists—but rather a means of protecting her dogs.

They gathered around as she stepped out of the car, and Ramona greeted each one by name. Her three dogs barked or whined according to their temperaments, and she rubbed each head in turn, murmuring greetings. Some of the knot in her chest dissolved. "What would I do without you guys, huh?"

They happily trailed her inside. The cats, eager not to be overlooked, jumped on the back of the couch and on the table near the door, and she greeted both of them, too.

All five animals padded behind her into the kitchen. Ramona dutifully filled food dishes and checked water levels, then sat at her kitchen table to take off her shoes and give each creature a little one-on-one attention.

She had never intended to be responsible for so many animals, but each was a rescue of one kind or another. Venus, a delicate little white female cat, had been huddled under a car, shivering in the November cold. Her consort, Pandora, a mixed Siamese with enormous blue eyes and a skittish nature, had shown up on the clinic steps as a starving and wary kitten.

The dogs had similar stories. Manuelito, a lean, rangy husky with wolf blood, had been abandoned in the woods nearby before finding his way to her house to beg for food. Guinevere, a homely terrier-shepherd mix, had belonged to a hospital patient. Arthur, a black Lab with more jubilance than good sense, had followed her home from the grocery store, and none of her repeated ads, signs or posters had led his owner to her.

She loved them all, especially tonight when they blunted her sorrow and loneliness. Rubbing the head of Manuelito, while Venus curled up in her lap, Ramona also had to admit she was helplessly softhearted, unable to resist helping those in distress.

And that was what made Jake so dangerous. He brought to the fore every Mother Earth instinct she possessed. She wanted to cradle his head on her breast and stroke his glossy hair and chase his demons away.

Wearily, she sighed, stretching the stiffness from her neck. The fantasy went deeper than that, actually. Jake was the ultimate warrior. He had all those old-fashioned attitudes about honor and integrity and noble quests. He would fight to the death to protect the small and weak and vulnerable.

Those were the qualities that made him suffer now. She would put money on it. For all that the sleeping pills had given him respite, she knew he was a long way from being healed. His demons, whatever they were, had not been scared away, only buried.

The healer in her recognized he needed to release those demons before they destroyed him. The woman in her knew more—that the real fantasy was not the actual soothing of his wounds, but a wish to have him trust her enough so he'd be willing to dismantle his protective walls and let her in. As a woman, she ached to win that trust.

Which led to a very real, very dangerous conflict. Since she was a doctor, it would be wrong for her to allow an attraction to her patient to grow. She would lose her objectivity. It was also unethical. To treat him effectively, she would have to maintain some kind of emotional distance.

It wouldn't be easy. She was very, very attracted to Jake Forrest. He had an air of almost magnetic virility about him. She liked his hair and his eyes and his long body and his laughter. She had really liked his kiss....

She breathed out a sigh of frustration. "Enough of this," she said aloud. "I'm going to bed."

The dream was always the same. She glided along in the stillness of a clear mountain morning, the sky overhead a vivid turquoise in contrast to the blinding white of the snow. She skied well and often made a five-mile circle up the mountain and back to her house on weekend afternoons. She liked the way her blood pumped harder in her veins, and how the sunlight caressed her face, and the easy, graceful movements of the skis and poles. It made her feel strong.

The dream ended the same way every time, too—with Ramona hiking out of the forest at dark, minus skis, her body bruised and almost preternaturally sensitized. She tasted the cold night air in her lungs and breathed thanks. She trudged down the hill on trembling legs that threatened to collapse beneath her and wept in relief. Without gloves, her fingers were almost surely frostbitten, but Ramona only put them against her belly and prayed she would not lose any of them.

And then, like always, she awakened in her big bed with the animals arrayed around her and moonlight spilling in the lace-curtained windows. The familiar hollow feeling was back in her stomach. She reached over the side of the bed to touch Manuelito. He groaned and stretched, then settled back into sleep.

It had been a long time since she'd had the dream, but it wasn't surprising after the casual question from Jake. She had never skied again and now and then she wondered if that were healthy. She'd managed to keep the incident from ruining her life. She had pursued her goals and moved onward, but the truth was, if she tried to put on skis, she felt sick to her stomach.

Thankfully, she only dreamed the beginning and end of that day, not the part in between. At least she wasn't tormented by that.

She had been seventeen, three months from her high school graduation. That day, there had been three boys skiing, too, which in itself was not unusual. She waved companionably, and they waved back.

But near the top of the mountain, she had come across them again, swilling something out of a wineskin. People never realized how fast alcohol went to your head at high altitudes, and the boys were very drunk.

She recognized their state in an instant and tried to turn around, but they were on her before she could escape.

They had raped her. It was that simple and that brutal. When at last they passed out, Ramona had gathered her clothes and hiked down the mountainside. She had seriously considered letting them freeze to death, but had instead gone to the police, allowed the humiliating tests that would confirm the crime and told the forest service where to find them.

They had been hospitalized for exposure, under guard. Three Eastern college boys who had come to Colorado to ski during spring break. The local paper did not run a story, and the few officials who knew what had happened did not wish to add to Ramona's troubles by making the story public. The prosecutor in the case asked for a change of venue for the trial in order to protect Ramona's reputation, and it had been granted.

Within a year, all three were behind bars, with sentences as severe as the law would allow....

Beyond her moonlit window, a blackbird began to sing, and Ramona lifted her eyes to the sky. It was almost morning.

She knew she had been very lucky. Because the crime had been so brutal—three against one—and because Ramona was a small, studious girl with a good reputation, the jury had thrown the book at them. One boy had eventually written Ramona a letter of apology. She read it, then in a choking fit of violence, tore it to tiny pieces, which she then burned.

Most of the time now, she didn't think about it. But back then, she had suffered her own case of PTSD. For months afterward, she had been fearful and easily shaken. Her belief that the world was a benevolent, supportive place had been totally shattered, and Ramona was afraid to do anything or go anywhere alone. That included the grocery store or even out in the backyard. It wasn't so much that she expected to be raped again, but she'd come to believe there were dangers everywhere. No place was safe. Only long-standing study habits had saved her grades, and she had almost delayed going to college—a move her mother had fought.

Over that long summer, Ramona had become angry. She had raged against the unfairness of the rape, against the shattering of her innocence, against the theft of her safe, calm world. In spite of her mother's efforts to help her, Ramona became bitter and unable to trust anyone.

But when fall came, she went off to college, teeth gritted. She even managed to function, after a fashion, by pouring her rage and alienation into her studies.

And then there had been a rape, on the campus. But the circumstances of this attack were quite different from Ramona's. It happened to a girl who, unfortunately, had a less than pristine reputation. She'd been partying late at night with two boys from a neighboring dorm when it happened. The crime was reported in all the local papers, and the entire dorm seemed alive with the news.

Ramona knew the girl only marginally from a couple of her classes. But for a week, she watched her trying to continue with her life and ached for her. The need to love and heal would not let her leave the girl alone, and finally, Ramona had gone to the girl's room. There she had spilled her own story, and the two of them had cried bitterly together. All the seething poisons that had been destroying Ramona's life were flushed away. In offering support to another victim, she herself had been healed.

The other girl had not fared as well. By the end of the term, she'd left school. Ramona never heard from her again, although she thought of her often.

One of the cats crept up Ramona's leg and settled on her hip to purr. Smiling softly, Ramona reached out a hand to stroke Pandora's silky head and took comfort in the warmth. The animals always seemed to know when she was upset.

Even after the initial healing, it was a long time before Ramona was able to get interested in men again. She didn't dislike them or avoid them, she just felt nothing. Nothing.

This lack of response had frightened her. Before the rape, she enjoyed a healthy fantasy life, if not the real thing. Like most girls her age, she spent endless hours daydreaming about kissing various boys who caught her attention. Jake Forrest had starred in more than a few of those daydreams, if Ramona was honest with herself. After the incident in the hallway, she had a hard time avoiding the occasional, forbidden fantasy about his hand on *her* breast.

In other words, her developing teenage libido was quite healthy and normal.

After the rape, she couldn't summon any interest in boys, and it scared her. She'd been afraid she would never be able to have a normal relationship, that her enjoyment of sex would be forever destroyed by her brutal introduction to it.

A music student at the college had shown her that was not true. She met Mark at a student-union meeting. He was gentle almost to a fault, a sweet, soft-spoken man whose greatest trait was his sensitivity. For more than a year, they had been only friends, but Ramona found herself trusting him enough to let him kiss her. Then touch her. Then finally introduce her to the pleasurable side of physical union.

Their relationship had been comfortable and satisfying, bounded by mutual respect, but when the inevitable decisions had to be made at graduation, they mutually agreed to pursue their own dreams—his to be a musician, hers to continue with her education.

The parting had been a friendly one. Ramona still heard from him on the odd occasion. He had married and had children and worked as a studio musician. She was quite fond of him. Because of Mark's gentle, loving touch, she had been able to heal all her old wounds. With him, she had learned to love making love, to make the distinction between sex and violence.

In the end, she had triumphed.

The memory gave her a smile, and she yawned. Her last thought before she drifted off was that she needed to find the key to help Jake unlock his demons, too.

A woman's hand roved over his back, warm and small and ever so enticing. A tumble of hair fell over his stomach. Jake, not even a quarter of the way to actual awakening, felt himself go hard and shifted in the bed, pulling the warm female into the cradle of his arms. A plump breast pressed into his ribs. Jake sleepily reached for the comfortable weight, feeling deeply aroused, but in no hurry. He skimmed his fingers over the round flesh and slid lower, to a belly as soft and round as her breast.

Her hands moved on his body, spreading heat and arousal through his every nerve, teasing closer and closer to his ever more fiercely aroused sex. He awoke, ready to reach for her, a pleased growl in his throat.

He was alone. Sunlight streamed in through the high windows of the loft in his condo and lay on his body in warm bands. Disoriented, he blinked twice and then swore.

His body took a few minutes longer to catch on to the fact that he'd only been dreaming. There was no plush, warm body in his bed, no small hands edging close to his engorged organ.

With a curse, he rolled over on his belly and pulled a pillow over his head and tried to call the dream of Ramona back.

Instead, he only noticed that his mouth tasted like ashes,

and there was a thick, thudding headache in the back of his skull. Sure signs of too much Scotch.

Scotch? But he hadn't been drinking, not with the pills. He knew better. He rubbed his tongue over his teeth and frowned. Definitely Scotch.

The night rushed back, unreeling like a badly lit French film. Feeling restless and caged, he'd left the apartment last night at nearly ten. He'd worked all day, but the work was mental, not physical, and he'd felt the need for activity. He drove out to the VA home, hoping to find Ramona somewhere about, but she'd already left.

Instead, he'd gone to a trendy little bar nearby, where long-legged, good-looking, coldhearted women were known to hang out. He'd drunk quite a lot of whiskey, danced with a blurry parade of partners, and sometime after closing, he'd let someone drive him home. She came in with him, too.

Then what? He couldn't really remember, and it made him faintly sick. He couldn't recall the woman's name, or call up her face.

He pulled the pillow more tightly over his head, the guilt from his hangover crashing into him. What kind of man did these things?

And suddenly, he remembered resisting the woman's overtures, her passionate, skillful kiss and his gentle refusal. She had only smiled. "Your loss," she said as she left.

Relief, vast and clear as a plunge into a mountain lake, washed through him. Thank God. He hadn't driven drunk and he hadn't had anonymous sex with some faceless woman.

He felt so much better, he jumped up and showered, ignoring his headache. In the same restless mood as the night before, he rushed through shaving and left the apartment with his hair still damp.

Surely Ramona would be home on a Sunday morning.

Chapter 6

At the entrance to her property, Jake parked his car and walked up to the gate. "Hello!" he called. "Anyone home?"

The lot was thick with spruce and pine and aspen, and Jake couldn't tell how far back the house might sit. When there was no answer to his call, he went back to the car, grabbed the bag with his goodies and opened the gate.

It was beautiful up here. From some hidden place, he could hear a creek gurgling, and bird song filled the air. The trees looked healthy and Jake thought he saw the flash of a deer's tail, but when he turned to check, the only sign was a bobbing branch. He ambled up the walk, breathing deeply of the spicy mountain air.

"Hello!" he called again. Still nothing. Jake frowned. It was awfully isolated up here. If she didn't have any kind of alarm system in place, he didn't like to think how dangerous it was for a woman alone.

The house came into view, just a slice of bright blue

through the trees, and he called again, "Hello! Ramona, are you home?"

A beast exploded out of the trees, rushing Jake, who immediately froze. He had an impression of bared teeth and a savage bark and enormous size before the animal halted a few feet away, growling a low warning for Jake to stay put.

He didn't argue. The dog was at least half his weight, and by the look of the long snout and the unmistakable eyes, it was at least half wolf. Probably more.

Ramona came behind, carrying a rifle. Cocked. When she saw Jake, she put on the safety and lowered the gun. "Manuelito," she said to her dog, touching his back in a soothing gesture. "Good dog. This is a friend." Holding on to his collar, Ramona said to Jake, "Come here and let him smell you, and see me touch you. Don't lower your hands until I tell you to."

Jake moved with slow, deliberate movements. The beast stopped growling, but there was a fierce, intelligent awareness in his eyes. "What a beautiful creature," he said quietly.

Ramona, one hand firmly grasping Manuelito's collar, put her other hand on Jake's arm. "Friend," she said. Manuelito stretched his nose out to sniff the seam of Jake's jeans and followed a line down to his feet. Apparently satisfied, the dog licked his chops and sat down. Ramona scrubbed his neck. "You're my baby, aren't you?" He licked her chin in agreement.

Ramona grinned at Jake. "Okay, you're safe. Hold out your hand and let him lick you if he will, and the next time you come sneaking up my driveway, he might not tear out your throat."

Slowly, Jake extended a hand and Manuelito nosed it curiously, then with more interest as he whiffed the sugar glaze from the doughnuts Jake had bought at a grocery store on the way over. Manuelito gave his palm a dry lick, then another, then sniffed around his wrist.

"Okay, Manuelito, that's enough," Ramona ordered.

"It's okay," Jake said. "Can I pet him now? Will he let me?"

"Sure. He's not really mean. He's just a good watchdog. If I had brought you in here, he wouldn't have blinked an eye—unless you tried to hurt me."

"Will you take this for a minute?" Jake asked, handing her the grocery bag. He knelt in the dirt at the dog's level and lifted his hands to scratch the wolf dog's ears. "Oh, you're a beauty, aren't you?" he said, smiling as Manuelito made a low, approving noise in his throat. "Smart and fierce and beautiful."

Manuelito lifted his head and gave Jake a delicate lick on the chin.

Ramona laughed. "In like Flynn, Jake Forrest. You're one of those dog charmers, aren't you?"

Jake got to his feet and brushed the dirt off the knees of his jeans. "I don't know about that. We seem to get along well enough. This one is pretty fantastic."

"He is." She turned toward the house. "Come in and I'll get some coffee. What did you bring?"

"Doughnuts."

She opened the bag and inhaled. "You evil, evil man."

"Evil?"

"Evil," she repeated. "Big, strapping soldier boys with muscles all over them can afford to eat doughnuts. Some of us—" she gestured meaningfully toward her body "—don't have that luxury."

She was wearing a pair of loose-fitting shorts and a simple gauzy blouse with a low neck. Like the rest of her, her legs were rounded, a little fuller than the current fashion dictated, but the skin was smooth and tanned, and he saw muscles shifting when she walked. Strong legs.

"You look all right to me," he said mildly.

Her grin was wry. "And your reputation precedes you, Mr. Forrest."

"What reputation is that?"

"The same reputation as all the Forrest men—you're skirt chasers."

He laughed at the old-fashioned word. "Well, my dad was, that's for sure. I think Lance was just a ladies' man until he met the right woman." He sobered, thinking of his youngest brother, Tyler. "Ty's problem is just the opposite—he's a one-woman man and she died on him."

Ramona paused one step above him on the porch. "Poor Tyler," she said in her throaty voice. The sound purred down Jake's spine, and he found himself remembering his dream. "He still hasn't come out of his recluse mode?"

"No. I'm not sure he ever will."

"His wife was my patient. I felt sick about it for weeks afterward. I warned her against pregnancy, but she was adamant."

Her eyes, up close, were not an unbroken, unwavering dark brown. At the edges of the irises, Jake saw tiny flecks of gold and light brown. Her lashes were extraordinarily long and thick, which gave her that doe-eyed look. "You really have pretty eyes," he said without thinking.

"And you," she said with a grin, "are an incorrigible flirt."

"I like skirt chaser better."

She laughed and led the way into the kitchen.

It wasn't until she had brewed the coffee and settled a napkin in front of him—a cloth napkin of all things—that he realized his imaginary picture of her kitchen could not have been more on the mark. There were herbs hanging from the ceiling in neat bundles, and rows of home-canned goods in the glass-fronted cupboards. Plants grew in a tangle on every windowsill and more hung from hooks in the ceiling or tumbled from atop ledges and cabinets. A braided rug covered the pine floor. The wallpaper border, her dish towels and her curtains all sported a pattern of unruly sunflowers.

Ramona herself, in bare feet, her tanned skin glowing and her hair shining, her good health obvious, could have been on a poster extolling the virtues of natural foods.

With almost a zooming sound, the surrealistic sense of distance Jake so loathed suddenly reappeared. One minute, he was smiling and admiring her long hair; the next he was yanked from the scene and forced to view it from a distant perspective, as if some cruel puppet master wanted to remind him that life was only a foolish drama played out on stage. Everything now seemed ridiculous. Her airy humming as she poured the coffee, the bands of rich gold sunlight in the room, the fecund plants...

Panic suffused him. His mouth went dry so fast he couldn't even swallow the bite of doughnut, and he reached blindly for his coffee. He knocked it over and the hot liquid spilled over his leg, scalding him. At the same moment, he choked on the doughnut. He jumped up, pulling at his jeans and trying to catch his breath.

He couldn't breathe and couldn't see and couldn't decide which problem to address first—the searing pain of the coffee burning his thigh or the doughnut cutting off his air. Every second seemed to last an eternity. Then he became vaguely aware of Ramona moving toward him. Her sharp blow on his back that dislodged the doughnut. She pressed a napkin into his hand and he spit the food out.

Tears streamed from his eyes and he inhaled a huge gulp of air.

"Take off your jeans," she barked. "You'll have third degree burns if you don't."

Jake didn't wait for a second invitation. He unbuttoned and unzipped and peeled off his jeans in an instant. Cool air struck his thigh and he looked down to see an angry, already-blistering burn that stretched from his knee to mid-thigh in a wide angry slash.

"Damn," Ramona said. "Sit down. I'll be right back."

She returned carrying a big plant with pointy spikes and knelt in front of him. With a steak knife, she sliced a thick branch from the plant and slit it lengthwise, then slapped the opened side onto the burn. It was cold and stung at first, but almost immediately, the heat went out of the scald. "That helps," he said, embarrassed that his voice sounded rough. Like he was some kid getting a scrape bandaged and trying not to cry.

She repeated the procedure several times until the burn was covered with the cool, moist leaves. The incident had jolted him violently back into reality, and Jake found himself watching her small, efficient hands moving on his thigh, so close to his briefs. As she leaned over him, her blouse revealed a fulsome display of cleavage, creamy smooth flesh that invited a man to open his mouth wide and taste...

No. If he started fantasizing, there wasn't much between them to hide his reaction. He focused on a pair of wrens quarreling in a tree beyond the screen door.

"There," she said. "Is that better?"

Jake raised his eyes. She was kneeling in front of him, her braid tumbling down over one breast. The blouse had slipped to one side and her shoulder was gorgeous—satin-skinned and round and smooth. She seemed completely unaware of the provocative pose or how seductive she looked. "Yeah," he said. "Thanks."

"You need to sit there for a minute and let the plant take the heat out of the burn. I'll get you another cup of coffee if you like." She stood and gave him a wicked smile. "And maybe a towel to wrap around your waist."

He looked down at his briefs. "My swimming trunks are a lot smaller than this." He grinned. "It's up to you."

A touch of color pinkened her cheeks. "I'll bring you a towel."

Jake laughed. "Whatever makes you comfortable, Doc."

Chapter 7

Ramona carried the aloe plant back to its sunny spot in the living room, then went to the bathroom for a towel.

Sex sex sex sex sex.

Jake Forrest was sex personified. It emanated from his skin like a scent, danced in his eyes, whispered through his voice. It was in the lazy, easy way he moved, in the careless toss of his head, in the way he touched things. He seemed particularly sensitive to the texture of things. Ordinary things. He'd fingered the cloth of the napkin and rubbed a thumb over the rough finish of the earthenware mug she'd given him. He'd put both hands on her dog and opened his hand as if to feel the fur on every inch of his skin.

Or was she just projecting?

She turned on the cold water and splashed her face repeatedly. She was a doctor. She had treated plenty of men—plenty of gorgeous, sexy men—and had never had a single moment of trouble separating her professional and personal responses.

But it had taken every shred of her self-control to treat Jake's burn. It had to be on his thigh. Coffee spills usually were. And he was right—he was wearing more than most bathing suits.

As if her libido cared. It didn't seem to put much trust in logic.

Ramona plunged her face in the water, gasping at the cold. It didn't help. She couldn't seem to dislodge the picture of his sex, cradled between his thighs in a harness of soft cotton. Her fingers tingled with the lingering need to weigh that flesh in her hands. She was thirty-six years old and never in her life had she felt quite such a surge of pure, questing, curious—well, *need.*

Over and over she washed her face in the ice-cold water. It finally began to help. Out of the cupboard she took the biggest bath sheet she could find—appropriately bright red for danger—and took it back into the kitchen.

At the threshold, she paused. Jake sat by the open back door, his face in his hands. Or rather, on his knuckles, which were white with the tension in his fingers. Scatters of black hair spilled over his hands, hiding his expression, but his posture screamed of both resistance and pain—and she doubted very much that it was the burn causing him that much anguish.

She had not questioned his appearance at her door this morning. He wore that vaguely ragged look of a bad night. The hollows had come back to his face, and he hadn't shaved. Although he flirted and teased and gave the impression of a friendly visit, she sensed he just needed her.

She didn't question that. It was something she had grown used to over the years—people came to her when they hurt. She trusted completely her ability to soothe them. It was something she'd always known how to do, the way some people made perfect bread or sewed wonderful clothes or, like Jake's brother, Tyler, could see the way wood should be cut or carved even before the bark came off a log.

And she had seen that Jake was in the grip of a panic attack seconds before he choked and floundered and burned himself. She'd gone instinctively to the sink to get him a glass of water.

Now she eyed the line of his shoulders, rigid and hard, and the weary set of his head, and knew the sleeping pills had not done him any good at all. If anything, they'd made matters worse by removing the urgent need to confront his demons.

Making no sound in her bare feet, she moved into the room. He did not look up. Remembering his earlier reaction to her awakening him in the office, she started humming as she approached him. He shifted, but didn't immediately look at her. She suspected he was not happy about being caught in such a vulnerable pose.

Gently, she rounded him and put the towel around his waist. "It's for me, okay?" she said lightly. Standing behind him, she put her hands on his shoulders.

He tensed. Ramona used her thumbs on the pressure points in his neck. "Relax a little, okay? I can see you had a bad night. And I'm good at this."

She had good hands, something else she trusted about herself. They were strong and they could give at least momentary peace. As she worked on the knotted places in his muscles, she hummed a little ballad.

Slowly, he began to relax. Once, she pressed a spot made sore by all the tension, and he groaned.

"Too hard?" she asked.

"No. Just right."

Golden morning light fell over his dark hair and gilded his strong-looking arms and caught in the dark hair on his legs below the towel. Ramona kneaded his shoulders and neck with expertise and breathed deeply of his exotic scent.

She mused about the nature of pheromones, the scent-calls men and women put out for one another, and wondered if Jake had an unusually powerful scent. It would account for a lot.

After a while, he reached up and caught her hand. "That helped. Thank you."

"You're welcome."

His hand engulfed hers. She started to pull away, but he didn't let her. Instead, he pulled her hand to his lips and pressed a kiss to her palm.

A bolt of arousal shot from the center of her hand to her thighs, and Ramona felt her hips melt. His mouth was warm and she could sense the heat just beyond. Against her fingertips, his prickly jaw seemed terribly fragile. Without conscious thought, she stroked the bones that formed his extraordinary face.

He raised his eyes and Ramona felt herself snared in the captivating intensity of his jewel-like blue gaze. With one hand on his shoulder, the other caught close in his against his cheek, she simply let herself fall.

He was unimaginably handsome. No man who looked like this had ever given her a second glance, but in Jake's eyes she saw a hunger mixed with that grave soberness that always seemed to haunt them.

"I dreamed about you last night," he said, and his mouth moved against her life line.

She couldn't quite remember how to breathe. "What kind of dream?"

"I thought you were in my bed when I woke up." He pressed a kiss to her inner wrist, oh so gently. "I was very disappointed when you weren't."

Against the rush of images his words evoked, Ramona closed her eyes. But it only made her other senses more acute, and she felt his mouth, lush and skillful, moving over her hand. It touched her wrist and thumb and lingered on each fleshy rise below her fingers. Tinglings of desire sped up her veins until Ramona was sure her body was glowing a rosy red.

Impossible she should feel so instantly, fiercely, ready to make love to him, right here in the kitchen, when all he had done was kiss her hand, but there it was. She opened her eyes to let in the sight of him and could not resist letting her fingers stray over his cheekbone and the fragile skin at his temple.

"I'm not your type," she said.

"I know."

But he didn't look away. Instead, his free hand lit upon her waist and restlessly skimmed up to her ribs, then back down and up again, going even higher until his thumb brushed the underside of her breast. Ramona stilled, her heart thundering in her chest, and she suddenly remembered the sight of his long, elegant, questing fingers hungrily kneading the breast of a girl in a secluded hallway many years ago. A pulse leaped to life low in her belly, and she heard a soft, longing sigh escape her throat.

His hand slid back down to her waist, and he let go the hand he held against his face. Ramona, lost in the erotic shocks of the past few moments, felt a blush rising over her chest, up her face. That sigh had given her away. How...?

Jake didn't move away. He simply stared up at her, a peculiar intensity lending his eyes an electric vividness that seemed almost unreal. There was no teasing there, no glittering amusement, only a fierce solemnity—and yes, a hunger as bewildering and powerful as her own. He shifted so he could pull her into the angle between his thighs, then put both hands on her waist, spreading his fingers as if to absorb the sensation of her body into every cell of his hands.

Waiting, Ramona felt the air in the room grow thick,

thick with unspoken needs and wishes and long-buried fantasies and dreams. With a sense of wonder, she stroked his high, intelligent forehead and the thick black line of his brows.

When his hands at last began to move over her chest, Ramona knew she ought to be alarmed. Maybe even uncomfortable. When a man touched a woman's breast for the first time, it seemed he ought to be kissing her when he did it.

But Jake didn't kiss her. He simply skimmed upward over her tummy, his hands rumpling the fabric of her blouse, then over her ribs, and finally, finally, covered her breasts. Bright with passion, his eyes embraced hers as he did it, and Ramona could not look away, even knowing that he'd see how much he affected her.

He touched her breasts the way he'd touched everything else, as if he was extraordinarily aware of each and every nuance. His fingers stroked her nipples, curled around the curves, lifted her flesh to gauge the weight and fit. Each small movement sent new waves of awareness and desire through her.

Nor was Jake unaffected. His breath came unevenly, and when he lowered his gaze to look at what his fingers touched, he made a low, soft sound that was almost a growl of yearning. She touched his cheeks, the edges of his jaw and the fan of lines around his eyes. And when her knees would no longer hold her, she swayed forward and pressed a kiss to his brow.

His mouth grazed the upper swell of her breast, and he moved his hands to pull her close against him, pressing his face into the hollow of her throat, his fingers fierce against her back. She ran her fingers through his thick, dark hair and stroked the long, corded muscles at the back of his neck.

"I dreamed you were naked." His voice was a quiet

rasp. Moving his mouth in tiny kisses along the curve of her shoulder, he murmured, "I dreamed of your breasts and belly, all soft and round next to me."

Ramona found herself kissing his silky crown and cradled his head against her breasts. A wave of something much too deep and hungry washed through her. Dangerous. Dangerous to care too much about a man who was so lost.

This was too much, too fast, and she couldn't let herself just fall into bed with him. Gently, she pulled away. "Jake…" she began.

His fingers clenched on her sides. "I know. I do know."

With an obvious effort, he straightened, and Ramona stepped back, then away, moving toward the counter to hide her face from him and give him time to compose himself. "Do you want some more coffee?"

"Ah, sure, I guess." He cleared his throat, and when he spoke again, his voice was utterly normal. "How long do I have to keep these leaves on here?"

Ramona grasped at the distraction. "You can take them off now, if you like." She poured his coffee and put it on the table, frowning as she looked at the burn. "You are not going to want to wear jeans for at least a few days."

"Which does present a quandary, doesn't it?"

She grinned. "You don't want to walk down my driveway in your underwear?"

"Not particularly. And I doubt you have anything in your closet that will fit."

"No, that's certain. What about Tyler? He lives close by—call him and ask him to bring you some sweats or shorts."

Jake nodded. "Listen, I know you probably don't trust me, and I'd understand if you didn't think I could behave myself, but I came up here intending to ask you to go sailing with me. Would you think about it?" He held up three fingers. "I swear I won't come on to you again."

Sailing. With Jake Forrest. In the sunshine and heady air of the mountains. She hesitated, aware again that he was very dangerous indeed. She had this appalling tendency to really like him, in addition to being furiously attracted. Bad combination.

He caught her hand. "Please. I don't know why, but you make me feel alive."

Ramona looked away. Of course. He needed healing, and she was the healer. Because he was a very sexual man, his visions of healing came to him in those terms. "You'd make more progress with a therapist, Jake."

"What?"

With an effort, she looked at him. He dropped her hand. "You're lost and needy and you sense that I'll be able to offer healing. But I'm not that kind of healer. You aren't broken physically, but wounded emotionally. A good therapist can help you more than I can."

"No, you don't understand. It's not like that." He seemed to struggle to find the right words. "Most of the time, I feel like I'm watching a movie, you know? Like I'm by myself out in the audience, just watching. Like I can't make contact."

Disassociation—a classic symptom. She nodded to let him know she understood.

"When I'm around you, the movie goes away, and everything seems real again." He paused. "Somehow, you're alive and no one else really is."

A sensation of pain squeezed through her chest. Humbled, she said quietly, "I'll go sailing with you." She paused. "But you have to let me ask you one question today. One question you answer honestly."

"What kind of question?"

"Any question of my choosing."

He said nothing for a moment, his mouth hard as he considered her request. "Deal."

* * *

Ramona met Tyler at the gate after he agreed to bring Jake a pair of shorts. Anyone else might have made bawdy jokes or teased lewdly, but not the serious, upright Tyler.

Of the three brothers, Tyler was the youngest and the tallest—made into a recluse by tragedy. A widower for four years, he lived with his young son in a cabin a couple of miles up the mountain not far from Ramona and looked every inch the loner. His gilt-blond hair had grown to below his shoulder blades, and was tied back with a leather thong. "How are you, Dr. Hardy?" he asked politely, the shorts over his arm.

"Just fine, Tyler." She had repeatedly asked him to call her Ramona, but he stuck to titles with everyone. "You?"

He gave her the shorts. "Very well, thank you. I got a nice commission from the Harrow House renovation—oughta keep me in peanut butter for a long time." His narrow face lightened with a smile. "Never gonna be a rich man like my brothers, but Curtis and I get along just fine."

A blond head—then a second almost like it—poked out of the truck window. "Hi, Dr. Mona!" called Curtis, Tyler's son. His cousin, Cody, one year older and not to be outdone, yelled out another greeting.

She grinned and waved. "Are you boys being good?"

"Yep!"

Cody said, "My mommy and daddy will be back tomorrow. They're bringing us presents, so we have to be good."

Ramona laughed. "I bet you'll be relieved to have Lance and Tamara back. Has Cody spent the whole time with you?"

"Pretty much—either with me or their grandma." He gave her a slanted smile. "And speaking of Grandma, I hear she faked a sprained ankle, the meddling little busybody."

"She did." It felt oddly uncomfortable to realize the subject of that doctor's visit was even now inside her house. He had not wanted to see his brother for reasons Ramona decided not to plumb. She grinned up at Tyler. "You'd best beware—now that one of her boys fell to marriage, she won't rest until she gets you all neatly wedded."

"She knows better with me." He raised one eyebrow. "Besides, two can play at that game. She keeps pretending she's too old for love and romance, but have you met Alonzo?"

"The adobe-brick maker from Mexico?"

Tyler nodded. "The very one."

"I met him at the wedding. Quite a charmer."

"Mmm-hmm."

Ramona chuckled. "Perfect match."

A loud, piercing whistle cut the air. A blue jay. Ramona looked around for it.

"That's Jake," Tyler said. "He must be getting impatient for the shorts. I'll see you." He raised a hand in parting and climbed into the truck. Ramona watched him lean over and make sure the buckles on the seat belts were firmly fastened over the boys. She waved.

The blue jay whistle rang out again. Ramona smiled and walked back up the drive, Manuelito tagging alongside. When it came a third time, Ramona lifted her chin and whistled back in the voice of a blackbird, which was the only birdcall she had mastered. He answered, and she whistled again.

As she rounded the last turn in the drive, a real jay swooped by her to land on a tree near the house and called out. Jake, sitting in the sun in his red towel, whistled, and the jay answered.

She gave him the shorts with a grin. "Not only a dog charmer, you're a bird charmer, too."

A white smile cracked the darkness of his face. "I'm just

a charming kind of guy. Turn around and let me get decent—that is, if you're sure you want me decent.''

''I'm sure.'' She did as he asked him.

''Last chance,'' he said.

She grinned to herself, but didn't move.

''Okay.''

''Are you ready to go? I have a lunch packed.''

''Did you put on a swimsuit?''

Ramona did not wear the things, not in public at any rate. ''No way.''

''You aren't going to swim and let me ogle you in an itty-bitty bathing suit?''

She blushed. He really had no clue at all. He was used to model-slim women. Not in a million years would she let him see her even in her modest maillot. ''Trust me, bathing suits and I are not a match made in heaven. This is better.''

He cocked his head again, making the light dance on his crown. Then he shrugged. ''Whatever you say. Don't blame me when I'm in the water, all cool and refreshed, and you have to sit there in your clothes.''

''I won't,'' she said serenely.

He grinned. ''Let's go, then.''

Chapter 8

Jake loved sailing. He liked being on the water in the quiet, with pine trees arrowing up into the neon blue sky, and the furry deep purple knuckles of mountains embroidering zig-zags down to the horizon. He liked the sound of water lapping against the boat, and the cry of gulls, and the mingled scents of wax and fish and the faint notes of leaf mold from shore.

He didn't ordinarily take anyone with him. He liked to sail alone, to fall into the vastness of nature in complete solitude, but his brothers and mother had nagged him so often about the dangers that he'd begun to feel a twinge of guilt about it.

Propped with her back against the bench, Ramona was an excellent companion. One of the things he liked about her was her singular lack of the need to chatter. She didn't fill up quiet spaces with a lot of meaningless chitchat, like Lance would have, or most of the women Jake dated. When she spoke, it was to point something out or share an observation or muse aloud. It left Jake free to drift along without thinking, which was, in his opinion, the whole purpose of sailing.

There were just a few boats out. Red Creek was usually crowded with tourists all winter, but in the summer, it was really only busy on holiday weekends. There were camping areas near one end of the reservoir, but at the other was a wilderness as yet undeveloped, a landscape dotted with coves and small beaches. Jake headed for that end and, in a calm stretch of water, let down the anchor.

"Do you fish?" he asked Ramona, baiting a line.

"Not really. If you catch something, I'll cook it, but you have to clean it first."

"Hey, I cook my own fish, remember?"

"I forgot, oh mighty chef." She stretched her legs out over the edge of the bench and tipped her face up to the sun. "What's your favorite fish recipe?"

Jake cast his line into the quiet noonday waters, little expecting anything to bite. "Lemon bass," he said, "baked with peppercorns and lemon peel."

Ramona opened her eyes. "That sounds wonderful."

"It is."

"How did you get involved in cooking, anyway? It seems like a strange profession for a man like you."

"A man like me?"

"Yeah, a macho man." She grinned unapologetically.

"Are you stereotyping again, Dr. Hardy?"

She raised her brows. "Did I or did I not correctly name your favorite music?"

"Ah...yes."

"I rest my case. Answer the question. How does a soldier boy like you end up cooking like that?"

"It's not a profession, it's a hobby," he said. "And you know, all the best chefs are men."

She chuckled. "So are most of the best hairdressers."

Jake shot her a grin, but she had already leaned back again, perfectly comfortable with her eyes closed, her legs extended to the sun. He wondered if she had any idea how sybaritic she looked. Her face and throat were dewy, and a bar of sunlight slid down her chest in a curvy line. The sheer pleasure she took in the sun and fresh air made him feel lusty.

For one moment, Jake let himself remember how lovely her breasts had felt, heavy and warm against his palms, the tips eager for his touch. She hadn't known how she looked then, either, had no idea how her nipples had pearled when he kissed her palm, how her eyes had gone limpid and sensual. She just didn't have a clue how sexy she was.

Amazing. He popped the top of a beer and shifted his focus to the undulating surface of the water. He'd promised not to come on to her, and he'd stick by it. It was a lousy idea anyway. As powerful as the physical attraction was between them, she was right—they really weren't the same kind of people at all.

And he liked her too much to indulge his usual hit-and-run sex with her. He wanted her friendship and respect. He didn't have many friends.

Following Ramona's example of undiluted relaxation, he stripped off his shirt and balanced his fishing pole on his knee. He stretched out to let the sun warm his body, sink into his chest and limbs and knit all those little wounds. Nothing ever felt quite as good as the warmth of the sun bathing his body.

The boat rocked gently, and Jake closed his eyes. Sunlight stung his burn and he used his shirt to cover it. He was surprised how well the aloe had worked, actually. What had looked at first as if it would be a raw, blistered burn was only red and angry-looking. It would heal fine.

He dozed, the sunlight red against his eyelids. Sunlight, bright and blazing…

With one of those abrupt, alarming shifts, he was in the desert. The endless, dun-colored desert. The air was filled with the sound of guns and tanks and cries. He couldn't tell who was screaming until a soldier behind him said, "Mary and Joseph, we've hit a village."

On his sloop in the middle of the lake, Jake bolted upright. His movement rocked the boat a little, and he dropped the fishing pole with a clatter. He swore under his breath and reached for the pole with a hand that shook ever so slightly.

He glanced at Ramona. She had opened her eyes and simply looked at him with those infinitely patient, velvety eyes. He saw compassion and understanding and acceptance, and they made him hate himself even more. If she really knew everything, all that gentleness would be wiped away.

"Do you want to tell me about your bad dreams, Jake?"

"I don't have bad dreams," he said gruffly. It wasn't a lie. Dreams were manufactured of dust and fantasies and fears. His were memories.

He expected that she would now pose her question, the question he had promised to answer. His throat dried and he took a long swallow of cold beer to wet it. He had promised. He would answer.

But she only pointed to a bluff. "Look! Isn't that Make-out Point?"

Her simple acceptance of his obvious need to avoid the subject was a little unsettling. Had he *wanted* her to probe those raw wounds? With a mental shake, he looked over his shoulder. "I believe it is."

"Only 'believe'?" she teased. "The Jake Forrest I remember had a string of girls as long as the I-70. My guess is you had your own parking space, with a little plaque nailed to a tree."

In spite of himself, he grinned. "Well, it didn't have my

name on it, but I could usually count on the spot below that ponderosa pine up there on the left."

Her laughter rolled out, husky and sexy. "I don't imagine you had much time to appreciate the view."

"Not the view of nature anyway." He raised his eyebrows rakishly. "Sounds like you know more than a good girl should about the Point. Did we all have you pegged wrong?"

Lazily, she shifted her head, and her hair scattered loosely over the seat. "Is that how the guys pegged me? As a good girl?"

"I don't know about them, but I did."

She gave an exaggerated sigh. "Well, I was. Didn't have a single date in all of high school."

Jake inclined his head. "Really?" What could they have been thinking? How had he been so blind to the charms of this woman all those years ago?

"Really." Her expression was droll. "Think about it. Who was going to ask a dumpy, scholarly girl out on a date? I mean, I probably wouldn't even have known what to talk about. I would have been petrified."

"I bet I could have found a way to make you talk," he said lightly, shooting a grin her way.

"You?" She snorted. "You wouldn't have given me the time of day, Jake Forrest. You liked them then just as you like them now—tall and elegant."

If that was true, he wondered why he spent most of his time with Ramona in a state of near arousal. "Well," he responded guardedly, glancing toward the lake, its surface sparkling with sunlight, "teenage boys are notoriously obvious."

The oddest hint of despair flickered over her eyes. It piqued Jake's curiosity. Had she loved and lost someone important to her?

"How about college?" he asked, hoping for clues. "Did the guys find you there?"

But when she answered, her voice was even and calm. "I had dates in college."

"Anyone important?"

She gave him a womanly, enigmatic smile. "One or two."

Just that fast, he wanted her. Wanted to leap across the small cockpit and cover her body with his own and kiss her senseless. Breathless. "And since then?"

"Mind your own business, soldier boy." With a languorous gesture, she lifted her hair off her neck. "How about you? Why aren't you married? Isn't that part of the up-and-coming officer scenario?"

"I was married for a while. We divorced when she snagged a more powerful officer."

"I'm sorry."

Jake shrugged. "Don't be. It wasn't even a big deal when it happened."

"How long were you married?"

"A couple of years. We were both in our twenties. There were no children, and I lost track of her. Wasn't meant to be."

"I can't imagine sharing a big part of your life with someone and then just losing touch."

He thought about Linda, his ex. Tall and slim and beautiful, she had been exceedingly efficient, bossy and ambitious on his behalf. Truthfully, he'd been relieved to have the marriage end. "Does that mean you keep in touch with those one or two important college boyfriends?"

"Yes."

A twinge of—jealousy?—twisted in him. It surprised him into a smile. "Any regrets on your part?"

"None at all."

Jake thought about pushing a little further, but at that

moment, she slid down on the bench so she was lying flat. Her long hair spilled almost to the floor beside her. Against her body, the gauzy shirt settled and clung to her breasts, and she bent up one knee. She looked utterly trusting, utterly relaxed, and utterly unaware of how delectable he found her.

He stood up. "I'm going to take a dip. Be right back."

Ramona was relieved—at least for a moment—when Jake decided to go for a swim. She could not bear one more moment of his naked, gleaming chest staring her in the face.

It was unfair that a man should be so perfect. His shoulders were broad and neatly muscular without being pumped. His stomach showed washboard strength—likely he still did sit-ups every morning—and his skin was warmly tanned.

The detail that intrigued her the most was the exquisite scattering of hair from nipple to nipple. Not too much. Not too little. Just right—a virile dusting of silky black hair that tapered to a tiny little line that furred his belly below the navel.

She had pretended not to notice when he shucked his shirt, but a woman would have to be dead not to care about all that smooth brown skin. She had the most peculiar picture of the way that single line of hair would feel against her naked stomach.

Yeah. Like she'd notice the feeling of a quarter-inch wide line of hair if Jake Forrest's naked body was pressed to her bare skin.

Sunbathing had always made her feel slightly aroused. It was so luxurious to soak in all the warmth, especially at the start of summer, when the bones had been chilled all winter. The sun worked loose any lingering tightness, softened all the tense muscles.

The combination of the sun, the softly rocking boat and Jake's bare chest made her feel dangerously languorous and hungry. It would be so easy to reach out a hand to beckon him to her. So easy to let him stretch himself over her and kiss her and then make love in the sunshine.

So easy.

With a sigh, she sat up and peeked in the cooler for something to drink. Not beer, she decided. That would probably be the last straw. If she drank a beer, she wouldn't wait for Jake to make a move—she'd probably attack him the minute he came back aboard.

Selecting a can of juice, she stretched and watched Jake swim with the smooth, athletic grace she would have expected him to display, his arms cutting the water with barely a sound. For a single longing moment, Ramona wished she hadn't been so shy about her suit. She liked swimming.

Instead, she drank her juice and idly picked up the fishing pole he had wedged between the cooler and some kind of gadget on the sloop. It was obvious he was not terribly serious about actually catching anything today, so she began to reel in the line, thinking to cast once more.

A shiver went through the line and Ramona halted instantly, afraid she'd done something wrong. Although he might not mind if she played at fishing, it might annoy him if she caught the line in something and broke the whole pole.

She moved to put it back down, but it gave a sudden fierce jump and she closed her hands around it reflexively, holding tight. "Jake!" she cried.

The line rushed out, making the handle on the reel spin crazily. Ramona had no idea what to do, so she just hung on. It occurred to her there was a *fish* on the other end of the line. It was weirdly exhilarating.

She glanced over her shoulder to see if Jake had heard,

and he was swimming quickly back toward the boat. Knowing he would be able to take over in a minute cleared her head, and Ramona gripped the pole more firmly. What did she know about this? The spinning reel slowed, and instinctively, Ramona caught it and reeled it back in a little. The fish pulled it out again, and she let it swim. When the line went slack, she slowly reeled it in a little at a time.

She laughed in delight. Behind her, Jake called out, "Hang on, I'm coming aboard," and she braced her feet to keep her balance in the rocking boat. The fish, seeming to sense a good moment to make a break, suddenly pulled hard.

Ramona drew the pole into her stomach and grabbed the reel. "Oh, no, you don't," she said to the fish, and slowly reeled back again.

Jake came up behind her and put his cold, wet hands over hers. "Oh, he's a big one! Hang on. You're doing great."

The fish and Ramona played tug-of-war for five minutes, with Jake murmuring encouragement and helping her hang on. At last, he said, "Do you want to reel him all the way in?"

"I think I do," she said. "Do you mind?"

"Good for you." His voice was close to her ear, and Ramona noticed with one part of her mind that he was dripping all over her. A rivulet of water tickled its way down her shoulder, then spilled into the valley between her breasts, and his body made the back of her blouse and shorts damp. "Get ready."

"Okay." She braced herself, rocking a little to be sure she had good footing, then following Jake's lead, pulled hard.

The fish broke the water, fat and silver and fighting. Jake cried, "Reel him in now!"

She did. The fish sailed over the side and landed at their

feet, stunned. Ramona felt a twinge, then laughed aloud. "He's big!"

"He sure is, sweetheart." With a reverent hand, he held the flapping body to still it, then before Ramona knew what he planned, slit the creature's throat with a sharp knife. "Thank you, my friend," Jake said quietly.

Suddenly, tears sprang to her eyes, and she stared at the fish with a painful sense of regret and the joy of accomplishment warring in her breast.

"I've never caught a fish this size in my life!" Jake said, and looked up. "Oh, honey." He put his hand around her ankle. "Haven't you ever caught a fish before?"

She blinked, trying to clear her vision. A tear escaped her eye and slipped down her cheek. Mute, she shook her head.

"My dad taught us to thank them. Try it."

Ramona knelt. Jake put her hand on the cold, slick body of the fish. "Thank you," she said.

"Did it help?"

Ramona looked at him. His hair was slicked back from the water, giving his face a strangely exotic look. "Yes," she said. "Thank you."

He was very close. Close enough that she noticed individual bristles on his chin, close enough that she realized one of his front teeth had come in at a slight angle. Close enough that she saw individual minute creases on his rugged, beautiful face. "For what?" he asked softly.

She didn't know exactly. She gestured toward the sky and the lake and the fish. "For all of this. It's wonderful."

With one finger, he touched her cheek. "My pleasure." He stood briskly and put his hand on the anchor. "The only thing that will make it better is to cook him for lunch. What do you say?"

"Where?"

"On shore." He pointed to the isolated beach nearby,

sunny and inviting, with tall trees in a semicircle around it. "I have everything we need."

Ramona eyed the private, inviting stretch of sand, and a voice told her it was a bad idea. But her lips moved of their own accord. "Okay."

Jake made a fire while Ramona spread a blanket on the soft sand and unpacked the lunch she had put together—a good chunk of sharp cheddar, red grapes, a couple of apples, an assortment of crackers and cider.

While Jake gutted the fish and waited for the fire to die to the right level, Ramona took a handful of crackers and wandered to the edge of the lake. Leaving her shoes on shore, she waded in up to her thighs, admiring the glitter of sunshine on the water, the soft sound of wavelets lapping on the shore, the eternal whisper of wind through the pointed tops of evergreen trees. The air smelled of wood smoke and forest. Against her legs, the water was deliciously, bitingly cold. In contrast, the sun made her hair almost too hot too touch.

Glorious, she thought, gazing to the far distant shore and the tumble of the town of Red Creek spilling down the opposite mountainside. From here, it looked tiny and quaint, an old gold-mining settlement turned glitzy little village.

The splash of water warned her Jake was coming. "Penny for your thoughts," he said as he joined her, a half-eaten apple in hand.

"I was thinking I'm glad to be a native of Red Creek. How many people can claim the blessing of being born in such a beautiful place?"

"I can." His eyes crinkled at the corners. "My dad, too, I guess."

"I didn't realize he was a native."

Jake nodded. "He was." He flung the apple core hard, deep into a stand of trees. "Did you know him?"

"Sure. He was one of my patients, too." She lifted her brows in resignation. "Not a good patient, obviously, but when he felt sick enough, I treated him."

"Stubborn old dog."

Ramona sighed, remembering Olan's plethora of life-style health problems—everything from his gall bladder to gout to the clogged arteries he ignored until they killed him. "He might have been around a long time if he'd made a few small changes. Walked a mile a day. Cut about half the fat in his diet."

"Really?" Jake reached into the water and emerged with a handful of pebbles. "I thought his heart was pretty bad."

"His heart was stressed," she said slowly. "But it was a treatable condition."

Jake expertly tossed a rock, and it skipped cleanly over the surface of the lake for a long way. His face had a shuttered look.

"Do you miss him?" Ramona asked, plucking a flat stone from Jake's palm.

He sighed and skipped another rock. "I wish I could say yes. But Lance was the only son my father had time for, and he was even an a—" he glanced at her, grimaced "—a jerk to him. But still Lance pretty much worshiped the ground my father walked on."

Tentatively, Ramona tried to skip a rock, but it clunked into the water. "He was hard on you?"

"I guess." He handed her a smooth, flat stone. "Use a Frisbee motion." He illustrated.

She tried it, and the rock moved in perfect arcs, five times. Ramona laughed. "You're just full of interesting bits of knowledge, aren't you?"

Jake lifted one dark brow. "A man of many talents." A lock of dark hair, now dried from his swim, fell over his forehead, giving him a rakish look. He bumped her playfully with his shoulder. "And you haven't even uncovered my true area of giftedness."

If he had not glanced at her mouth suggestively, Ramona might have been able to toss off this snippet of banter, but that lingering, promising glance gave her a hot, heavy sensation, and her mind went blank. She suddenly became aware of his naked chest, the damp shorts clinging to his taut buttocks.

"Honey, if you could bottle that look, you'd be a millionaire."

Heat crawled up her neck and edged the tips of her ears. She shifted her gaze away to the water. "What look?"

"Miss Innocence," he said with a low chuckle. "Look at me again, Ramona."

"No." Stubbornly, she stuck her hands in her back pockets. "As it is, you think you're irresistible."

"Ah." The single syllable was deep and rich and full of knowledge. It slid down Ramona's spine like a moist tongue. "You have to prove you can resist." Laughter edged his words as he added, "It must be very difficult if you can't even look at me."

As he meant her to do, Ramona laughed. "You're such a bad boy, Jake Forrest."

He grinned, and the expression no longer looked odd on his lean face. Mischief reached all the way to his sapphire blue eyes and shone there like stars. "I am that," he agreed. "Wouldn't you like to find out just how bad I can be?"

Oh, yes. She looked at his mouth, then back to his eyes. "You're too much of a heartbreaker," she said. "I never was one of those girls who wanted to tame a James Dean."

"James Dean?" he echoed incredulously.

"You know the type." She shrugged.

"So what type did you want?" he asked, then held up a hand. "No, let me guess. David Cassidy?"

Ramona laughed. "No way."

He narrowed his eyes in thought. "I would have guessed you to have a crush on Donnie Osmond or...who was that other guy? The one in that Western show?"

"Bobby Sherman. My best friend was wild for him."

"But not you?"

"No." Ramona trailed her hands in the water. "I was wild for Cane, in 'Kung Fu.'"

"What?" He laughed, and Ramona loved the easy sound of it coming from his chest, deep and rich and full of honest enjoyment. "Miss Earth Mother? Miss I-Put-My-Jelly-Up-By-Hand liked 'Kung Fu'?"

"Never missed a single episode."

He cocked his head to look at her. "Unbelievable."

"Stop laughing at me," she protested, and splashed him a little. "Did you ever watch it?"

"Sure. My brothers and I had a date with Y Chang every week." He held out his hand. "'When you can snatch the pebble from my hand, grasshopper, you will be a man.'"

"That's the thing everyone remembers, like it's some big joke, but it was a lot more than that. It was spiritual, in a way television usually isn't. Especially not then," she added, thinking of the other offerings at the time.

"So you weren't watching for the fight scenes?"

Ramona lifted a shoulder. "I didn't say that. I loved the fight scenes."

"Really?"

"Why is that so hard to believe?"

He looked puzzled. "I'm not sure. You're just so—" He broke off. "I guess it's like the doctor and nurse business. I expected you were a nurse because I figured women doctors would usually be so driven or tougher or something."

She smiled. "I guess we both have a lot to learn about stereotypes."

"I guess we do." He splashed her. "And that was very neatly done, grasshopper."

Ramona danced away from him. "What?"

"Avoidance of my devilish talents." His grin was pure male. "But you know what they say. You can run, but you can't hide." With another quick, playful splash at her, he turned toward shore. "Come on. I bet that fish is cooked by now."

As they waded back to shore, Ramona admired his long, tanned back and tried to remember exactly why she was running. In his present mood, it seemed as silly to resist him as it would be to resist enjoying a field full of wildflowers.

So beautiful, she thought. If only he could get well.

Chapter 9

The fish was excellent, and in combination with the fruit and cider, Ramona could not imagine a more perfect meal. She licked the lemony juice from her fingers with a sigh. "I'm afraid I'm going to have to cut our friendship short this very minute, Jake."

"Oh, really? Why's that?"

Falling back on the blanket, she gave a sated sigh. "You feed me too well. I'll be as big as a house before you know it."

He stretched out on the other side of the blanket, the decimated piles of food a safety wall between them, and propped himself on one elbow. "I wish you liked your body more."

With a grin, Ramona spread her fingers over the plumpness of her belly. If the truth were told, she really did like the way it felt. "I like it fine. I just wish I could eat like everyone else and not turn into a Reuben."

"I think you'd be better as a French dip."

She laughed. "Very funny."

"Yet another of my many talents." He moved the plates to one side, then the grapes.

She sat up. "Oh, no, you don't, Mr. Wonderful."

"What?" He gave her a wolfish grin.

Ramona's heart flipped. Dappled sunlight fell upon his face, making him look boyish and approachable. "Don't you start teasing me again."

Undeterred, he put a long, elegant hand on her leg, just above her knee. "We could just make out," he said. "Pretend we were in high school."

"I knew I shouldn't have come out here to this isolated spot with you."

His hand moved a little higher up on her thigh and then a little farther down, curling around the sensitive back of her knee. "So why did you agree?"

Ramona took refuge under her hair, bowing her head so it fell forward and obscured her face. "I don't know."

"Can't hide from me, grasshopper." He moved to duck under her hair and made an exaggerated kissing sound with his lips. "Come on, give me some sugar."

Ramona laughed and pushed at his shoulders. "Ick!"

They tumbled together, wrestling playfully, Jake making kissing sounds and tickling her, Ramona holding him off in mock horror. Their bare legs tangled and slid, and one of his hands got caught in her hair, and they fell back onto the blanket, laughing. It was only then that Ramona realized he was aroused. She felt him against her thigh, and the vision of that heavy sex covered in soft cotton came back to her, flooding her senses with the swift, biting swell of desire.

As if he realized she noticed, Jake pressed ever so slightly into her. "I've been aching for you since this morning."

"Jake..." she protested weakly.

He was braced over her, his face only inches away. Black hair fell around his face and against her palms; his skin was warm and silky. "Can I kiss you, Ramona? Just for a little while?"

Her hands betrayed her by sliding down his back in exploration.

"I'll take that as a yes," he murmured, then bent his head and claimed her mouth.

The kiss was exquisite. His lips were full and hot and moist and he knew what he was doing—that much she had learned at the reception. He had perfect lips, firm and pliant and knowledgeable, and Ramona made a small sound of pleasure at his touch. He slanted his mouth and Ramona opened to him, inviting his tongue to explore as she explored in return, and there was no awkwardness, no confusion, only total and complete harmony.

Dipping, playing, seducing, drinking, he kissed as if the act was an end in itself. He teased her lips with his tongue and suckled lightly. Ramona liked best the light dance of tongues. He seemed to sense that and indulged her, fencing and tantalizing until every bone in her body turned to pudding.

"I love your mouth," he said, lifting his head. "You have great lips."

Ramona pulled him back to her, dizzy with the sensation of kissing him, wanting more. He rolled to her side, then they tangled their legs together and kissed and kissed and kissed just like teenagers. Ramona's blood heated and flowed through her in a tingling rush, alerting every nerve to be ready. When he brushed a hand down her back, she shuddered, and when she explored his ribs, he groaned. The weight of her clothes seemed constricting and safe all at once.

Finally, he lifted his head, and Ramona saw reflected on his face the same slightly dazed expression that summed up her feelings. Equal parts wonder, desire, and contentment. In a rough voice, he said, "I have to stop now."

Ramona nodded. But she couldn't seem to move away. With one finger, she touched his lower lip. "You have a pretty nice mouth yourself."

"Thanks." He swallowed, and his hand moved on her waist, then stilled. "I'm not feeling very resistant, Ramona. Distract me."

She wasn't feeling very resistant, either. Some instinct of preservation prompted her to ask, "How about if you answer my question now, then?"

His vivid blue eyes sobered. "That might be more of a distraction than you bargained for."

"I'll take my chances." The boil had to be lanced.

"All right. Do it now, so I can think about something besides coaxing you out of your clothes."

"Do you want me to move?"

His hand tightened on her side. "No." He closed his eyes. "This is nice."

Nice. A very small word for what she felt lying next to him in a patch of shade from tall pines, in the silence of a summer afternoon in the mountains, his long legs tangled with hers, his member a low thrust against her thigh. She lifted a hand to his dark hair and brushed it away from that vulnerable temple. "Okay. I want you to tell me your dream. The one that keeps you from sleeping."

His eyes flew open. "No."

"You promised," she said quietly. "Any question of my choosing."

Abruptly, he rolled away, turning his long, tanned back to her. "Not that one. Think of something else."

Her body felt cold where he had been, and Ramona drew her knees up to her chest. It would be so easy to let it all go, to pretend he was on the mend and he'd get better on his own.

But Ramona knew he wouldn't, not until he released the bitter memories that were causing him so much pain. Still, discretion was the better part of valor and all that. "Okay," she said, and mulled over a second choice. "Why did you resign your commission?"

For a long, endless moment, he was silent. Tension radiated from the muscles in his back, gone rigid now. Ramona thought he wouldn't answer this one, either.

Finally, without looking at her, he replied, "I couldn't do it anymore. I found out I don't have what it takes to be a soldier." His jaw was hard. "It's that simple."

Her heart sank. "Is it, Jake?"

"It is." He stood up and started gathering things together. "We'd probably better head back. It's getting late."

Jake stepped out of the car at Ramona's gate. She had dozed most of the way back and looked sleepy and a little sunburned as she collected her basket of demolished supplies.

He could think of nothing to say as they rounded the car, and Ramona did not meet his eyes. A dull ache pounded in his chest, and he couldn't seem to break through it.

"Thanks, Jake," she said casually as she unlocked the gate. "I needed a break like this."

"You're welcome." He wanted to make some light comment about the fish or the kissing or something, but nothing came to mind. He only looked at her, aware of the sludge in his chest. "Thanks for going with me."

Her gaze skittered to his mouth, then to his eyes, and she took a step back. It was only right she should expect a goodbye kiss. After everything that had passed between them, he should want it, too.

And he did. But he couldn't seem to take another step closer, and she finally lifted a hand and gave him a brave smile. "I'll see you."

"Okay." It was all he could manage.

But as she turned and walked down her curving driveway, he still couldn't move. Her loose hair swung in thick golden brown swirls across her back like some beautifully woven cloak, and her bottom swayed very prettily. When her dogs came rushing around a corner, she touched each one, and they greeted her with devotion and eagerness.

Standing frozen on the other side of the gate, Jake imagined himself leaping nimbly over the barrier and running after her. He saw himself pulling her inside to her herb-strewn kitchen, then into the dark recesses of her bedroom. He saw himself making love to her, maybe all night. He saw himself sleeping on her breast....

She didn't turn her head for another look and he didn't leap over the fence. Instead, she disappeared around a bend, and Jake moved on robotic legs back to his car.

The restlessness that had driven him out to the bar last night was back. It rattled on his nerves and danced on his spine. He also knew he was physically tired—the long day in the sun after a night short of sleep had taken its toll. He needed a nice hot shower, a good meal and a long, undisturbed night's rest.

So he tried it. He went back to his condo and showered, then made himself a thick, juicy steak with a baked potato and washed it down with a bottle of honeyed ale. He watched ESPN while he ate. It soothed him a little. Whistling softly, he straightened up the apartment, took a couple of sleeping pills with some water and went upstairs to bed.

Where he stared at the ceiling. And shifted to stare at the wall. Then flipped over on his belly and closed his eyes. Nothing.

With a sigh, he clicked on the bedside lamp and read until he felt very drowsy, but as soon as he put the book away and turned out the light, he was wide awake again.

Slowly, a feeling of panic began to creep over him. He

tried to tell himself it didn't matter if he slept tonight. He didn't have to be anywhere early in the morning—he had a good manager at the restaurant. He tried to tell himself he was a night owl, and it would be okay to get up and watch movies on the cable channels—all night if he wished—and rise at noon.

He watched a movie and half of another one. He paced and avoided taking a drink because he didn't want to mix it with the pills. At 3:00 a.m., he turned the stereo on low and reorganized the few things on his kitchen shelves. At four, he started on the living room, gathering old magazines and the accumulated junk he'd left lying around.

At five, he made some coffee and watched the sun rise over the mountains, bleakly admitting he had no life. There was nothing he believed in. Nothing he cared about except maybe his mother and brothers. Nothing in his life that would ever give him any joy. He felt hollow, empty, useless.

The blank walls of his condo seemed to mock him. He looked at the white painted walls and remembered Ramona's rich, fecund kitchen. You knew the minute you walked into the plant-filled room that the woman who lived there was warm and giving and kind. You felt it.

Once, his home had reflected his tastes. Because a military man had to move regularly, he preferred to keep those possessions to a minimum, but he'd chosen them with pride and care. They spoke of his travels and the passion he had once felt for beauty. He'd collected unusual artworks representing the cultures he'd visited and had once been proud of the painting he'd found of the night skies.

Everything was stored in a closet upstairs. He hadn't bothered to unpack any of it. They mocked him, his things. Mocked his grand dream of being a soldier, the only dream he'd ever had. Now he looked back on the arrogant youth, the fast-track officer, and felt pity for the fool he'd been.

Jake buried his face in his hands and swayed dizzily. Exhaustion. He recognized it and fell sideways on the couch, praying for rest. For peace. For the healthy sleep of a normal man.

And into his exhausted mind crept his dream. His memory.

The village lay in ruins, hit by allied bombers that had flown in earlier, trying to dislodge the last of the Iraqi soldiers fleeing Kuwait as the U.S.-led forces moved in to liberate the land. A row of captured soldiers stood at the edge of the village, hands locked behind their heads. "Poor bastards," someone said. Some of the Iraqis wept in gratitude.

Jake prowled the village, feeling sick. It was sparsely populated. Most of the occupants had fled into the desert when the Iraqis invaded, and it had been bombed as a known headquarters for Saddam Hussein's army.

But not everyone had fled. Toward dusk came a cry, high and thin and miserable. Jake heard it and carefully worked his way from house to house, calling out. He finally located the child in a ruin, a single hand stretching from underneath a pile of rubble. When Jake closed his hand around the small, cold fingers, the child cried out again, a piercing, hurting, lonely cry. Jake yelled for a cluster of soldiers to come over and see what could be done, then asked one of the Iraqis to tell the child they were doing what they could.

The child screamed as they started to dismantle the building, and a medic shook his head. Jake insisted they keep on, the little boy's hand clutching his in a fierce, unyielding grip.

The last scream was the worst. The pressure of the debris that had kept the boy's wounds from killing him also masked his pain, and when the final load was removed, the child breathed his last with the most unholy sound of pain Jake had ever heard.

It tore into Jake's mind, shattering his sleep, and he bolted upright, blinking. His eyes flew to the clock—he'd been sleeping exactly seventeen minutes.

And now the panic attacked in full force. Rushing, he put on a light jacket and grabbed his car keys. He couldn't quite catch his breath as he fumbled with the door. Once outside in the bright, clean light of early morning, he sucked in a deep lungful of air and leaned against the wall.

As his breath returned, despair followed close behind. He pressed his forehead against the rough wood wall. He was losing his mind. Day by day, piece by piece. He felt utterly isolated, the man caught on the wrong side of the movie screen again. Restless and aimless, he got in his car and started driving. Just picked a road and followed it.

A strange exhilaration grew as he made his way around the sharp mountain turns and up and down steep hills. The car responded to his quest for more speed with nary a jump, and he clamped both hands on the wheel. Wind blew in through the open window, cold and light and breathable. The ZZ Top cassette stuck out of the tape deck and he shoved it in, letting *La Grange* blaze from the speakers.

Fear. All he had to face was his fear. The road was as intimate to him as his own body, and he stepped on the accelerator with giddy pleasure, feeling the wild mix of adrenaline and terror and excitement roar together through his blood as his speed increased and the car responded as if it was made for this.

The tires hit leftover winter gravel on one of the passes, and for a blinding, terrifying second, Jake teetered between control and disaster, fighting to save himself from the hundred-foot drop over the edge of the mountain. When the car smoothly regained its grip on the road, he laughed aloud.

His highest speed ever on this same road was seventy-seven miles an hour, clocked in a race with his brother,

Lance—which Jake had won. Their mother, learning of the crazy race, had taken their car keys for a month.

Now he eyed the speedometer. It read seventy-four miles an hour, and the hard turn was coming up. He edged up a mile at a time, loving the giddy thrill of the car hugging the road like a skier on the slopes, steady and easy. Seventy-five and the road began to rise and turn.

He pressed a little harder, focusing utterly on the challenge. Seventy-six, and the wind whipped through the car with a violent noise, tossing his hair in and out of his eyes.

Seventy-seven... Jake grinned and pushed it even higher. Seventy-eight. He roared around the turn, slid on a rock and skittered, bumping the guardrail lightly, then breaking free.

He whooped on the downward side, sticking his fist out the window, and raced downward now, heading for the last turn and then a straight shot into town. Seventy-nine... eighty...eighty-two. He gripped the wheel and leaned close over it, feeling like a racing driver headed for the finish line.

He took the last wide turn at ninety-three, an almost sickening speed in any other vehicle, but the tiny sports car took it as if she'd been raised by mountain goats. He laughed, loving the way his terror had evaporated now and was replaced with pure, almost sexual, exhilaration.

At the foot of the hill, he saw the sheriff's car too late. Plainly marked, it waited behind a tree near the Mallard place. By the time he fully registered the police car, Jake had zoomed by it at an unbelievable ninety-five. Wouldn't need radar to check his speed.

Fast.

The lights and siren came on instantly, and Jake gradually pressed his foot to the brakes, slowing a little at a time. Eighty-eight...eighty-four...seventy-nine.

His undoing was a simple cardboard box, torn by the

wind from someone's trash, no doubt. It danced over the highway on a current of wind, and as Jake approached, it flew up in the wake left by a truck just ahead.

There wasn't time to dodge it. Jake slammed on the brakes and held on to the wheel as the cardboard was blown over the windshield and plastered there by his speed. He shouted a curse and swerved toward the grassy field on the side of the road. The car took it for one minute, and Jake thought he was going to be okay.

It bumped wildly over ruts in the earth, and then he heard a sickening, deep thunk. The steering wheel was torn out of his hands and he was flung to one side. The car veered crazily on two wheels. Then, as if in slow motion, it tipped over out of control and still going way too fast. Instinctively, Jake put his hands over his face as the car went into a full roll. He had an impression of something coming through the windshield, then everything went mercifully, silently black.

Chapter 10

Ramona's beeper went off at 6:02 a.m. She was not sleeping—the alarm had rung ten minutes ago, and she'd smacked the snooze button. In the drowsy confusion of awakening, she thought at first it was the alarm going off again and hit the button twice before she realized it was her beeper.

Instantly, she was on the phone to the dispatcher. "Car accident on Gate Pass," the man on the line told her. "One man. Maybe serious. The ambulance is on its way out."

It took three minutes to brush her teeth and throw on her sweats and tennis shoes. In five, she was on her way down the hill toward town.

For all its recent advancements, Red Creek still had inadequate medical service. The clinic Ramona ran served a population of ten thousand residents scattered over a sixty-square-mile county, a county with an average altitude of seven thousand feet. One other doctor operated in town, and the VA home boasted two resident physicians, with a host of specialists who could be summoned from Denver.

When Ramona had accepted the job heading the clinic, she had insisted the emergency room—the only one for over seventy miles—be upgraded. With the ski slopes so close, she wanted to be able to handle traumatic injuries in case of inclement weather. An emergency medical helicopter was parked in the police department headquarters and could transport cases to Denver in just under thirty minutes, but patients often needed to be stabilized first.

The number of emergencies was no higher than average, but given the combination of the slopes, winding mountain roads and a lot of flatlanders who didn't respect the roads or the weather they way they should, sometimes the emergencies were quite serious.

She beat the ambulance by five minutes. Her nurse, shoving a cap over her head, had beaten Ramona by one. As the siren and lights roared toward the clinic, Ramona said, "Did you hear anything on the scanner?"

Christy shook her head. "Only that it was a rollover at the foot of Gate Pass. Possible head injury."

The ambulance drew up and both women looked toward it. The back doors opened, and the ambulance driver turned to pull out the gurney. Obviously, the patient was alive—and very unhappy. Ramona couldn't see him, but she gave Christy a wry glance at the complaints pouring out of the ambulance. "I'm fine! Let me out of here!"

Jake.

She recognized the voice an instant before he was wheeled out on the gurney. His dark hair was matted with blood. Streaks of blood and dirt marred his face. His blue eyes were startlingly bright. He saw Ramona and swore.

For one brief moment, her heart gave a tight, fierce squeeze. A rollover in his sporty, impractical little car. He could have been killed.

It nearly paralyzed her, and Ramona wondered if she ought to call in another doctor. The paramedic muttered,

"He's mouthy as hell, but his blood pressure indicates shock. Maybe a concussion by the pupils."

Galvanized, Ramona moved forward, feeling the objective and scientific physician take charge as they moved him inside. She gave orders and checked him over. Definitely a concussion, and the gash on his head would require a substantial number of stitches. Dark bruises marked one shoulder and arm. His left cheekbone was scraped and bruised.

He said nothing as she stitched up the cut on his head. Ramona respected his silence until she'd tied the last—the sixteenth—stitch on his scalp. "That's it," she said, putting her scissors on the tray. "We're going to keep you overnight just for observation, but you should be able to go home tomorrow."

"Fine." He didn't meet her eyes.

Ramona looked at her nurse. "I'll take it from here. You can check out if you like."

Christy looked from Jake to Ramona and an almost imperceptible smile touched her mouth. "Will do, Doc." She glanced at her watch. "I've got just about enough time to catch some breakfast at the B&B café. Join me there if you can?"

"I will."

She exited, her rubber-soled shoes squeaking on the highly waxed linoleum floor. Ramona watched her go, then turned back to Jake in the silence left behind.

His eyes were lowered. A bluish swelling marked his left cheekbone, creeping into the vulnerable tissue below his eye. He looked weary and lost and utterly impenetrable. He must have felt Ramona's perusal, but he didn't show it.

"What were you thinking, Jake?" she finally asked.

A studied shrug.

"You were damned lucky not to kill yourself."

He nodded.

Ramona inclined her head. "Was that the whole idea? Just kill yourself and be done with it?"

"No!" The answer was vehement. "I couldn't sleep, so I got in the car, trying to...I don't know. Just..." His jaw tightened. "I don't know. Escape."

Ramona reached for his hand. It was cold, and across the knuckles were a series of small scrapes. "The sleeping pills aren't working anymore?"

"No."

"Maybe we'll try something else, then. Some people develop a tolerance to almost any drug very quickly—and you might be one of them. That was a pretty mild sedative, too. Maybe we'll try something stronger."

Touching her patients was something Ramona did instinctively—a hand to the arm or shoulder, or the clasp of fingers, gave strength and calmed distressed or weary people. Jake's hand lay like wax under hers, and she felt suddenly like a teenager making up an excuse to touch the object of her crush. She stuck her hands in her pockets.

"But, Jake," she said, "I don't really think any sleeping aids are going to help you until you can get to the root of your problems. Think of your trauma as a boil—it's going to cause you pain until it's drained of its poison."

"What the hell do you know about it, Ramona?" Bitterness drew his face into a sharp mask. "You sit here in your safe little world and your safe little life, making jelly and playing Mother Earth. You don't know a damn thing about my life."

She could have sworn he was very close to tears. It was nothing so definite as a sheen in his eyes or a waver in his voice, just a sense that it took everything he had to turn his sorrow to anger. Mildly, she said, "Appearances can be deceiving."

"Yeah."

"They have group sessions at the VA home. You're not

the only soldier to ever experience this problem, and you might find it helps to talk to others."

"Leave me alone, Doc. Get the hell out of here and go preach your love and truth to someone else."

Ramona told herself his anger was only a manifestation of pain, that he was struggling with feelings he couldn't name and didn't dare confront, but his rejection stung anyway. She nodded. "Try to get some rest."

His snort of ironic laughter rang a long time in her ears.

Louise was fixing breakfast when the call came in from Ramona. She had bacon sizzling in a big cast-iron skillet, enough to feed herself and Alonzo, who stayed in the guest house and somehow managed to appear at just the right moment every morning. Weekdays, she got up at six to cook so he'd have something in his stomach before he went off to work, and she'd grown used to the easy, quiet camaraderie of the man these past months.

He came in at seven, his black hair neatly combed away from his face, his work shirt clean and pressed, his hands clean. He smelled of after-shave. "*Buenos días,*" he said.

Louise smiled. "Same to you, handsome. I've just about got everything ready. Sit down and have a cup of coffee." The phone rang, and Louise picked it up without the slightest presentiment of danger. "Good morning!"

"Louise, this is Dr. Hardy. Look, he's okay, but Jake has been in an accident and I'm keeping him overnight at the clinic. I thought you'd want to know."

"What, an accident?" Louise sank onto a chair. "Jake? What happened?"

"He rolled his car at the foot of Gate Pass. He's got a concussion and I put stitches in his head. By tomorrow morning, he's going to look like he was in a brawl, but the injuries are not serious."

A cold fist hit Louise's stomach. She bowed her head

and rubbed the bridge of her nose, trying to take it in. "Rolled his car?"

"Louise, he's all right."

Across the screen of a mother's imagination, Louise saw the sporty car rolling over and over, crushing the body of her son within, tearing his body to shreds. "He was lucky."

There was a pause on the other end of the line. "Yes," Ramona agreed.

Louise straightened. "I'll be over there in a little while."

"Good."

As she hung up, Alonzo asked, "Bad news?"

Her eyes filled with tears. "Not good. Jake rolled that damned car of his. He's at the clinic. I'm sorry about breakfast, but I'm going to have to run over there." With shaky hands, she untied her apron, then moved the skillet from the burner and turned everything off. Struggling for control, she said, "I reckon there's enough bacon cooked and you can scramble some eggs and eat that."

"No, no. I will drive you."

"Oh, you don't have to put yourself out." She blinked. "I'll be fine in a minute."

And then, somehow, Alonzo was beside her, and his arms were around her, solid and strong, and his shoulder was exactly the right height for her to lean her head on. His shirt smelled of after-shave and laundry soap. It had been so long—so long—since she'd had the comfort of a man's arms. Years and years. She let her arms snake around his waist, where he carried somehow comforting love handles made of tortillas and pork.

"I'm so worried about him, Alonzo."

"I know."

"He doesn't care about anything. Nothing. I don't know how to help him."

Alonzo's hand moved on her hair. "Just love him. That is all a mother can do."

She allowed herself to lean on him for a few minutes longer. Since he had moved into the guest house last fall, Louise and Alonzo had become good friends. Both widowed, in their late fifties, it had been only natural. Alonzo missed home cooking, and Louise missed cooking for others. It had been a natural and companionable relationship.

But as she rested in his arms, Louise felt something else stir, something she could have sworn was nearly dead. Against her breasts, his chest was smooth and hard, and his hands moved gently on her hair. A sudden surge of heat swept through her body, and embarrassed, she made to step away.

He didn't let her. He caught her arms just above the elbows, and Louise looked up at him in surprise. He was not a great deal taller than she, and his face was very close. The warm brown eyes did not twinkle just now, and his mouth under the thick black mustache was serious. Caught in her strange rush of emotion, Louise only looked at him, sure it couldn't be desire she saw on his handsome face. Not for her—a plump matron who never remembered to get her hair cut regularly, a woman who'd not been able to keep her own husband at her side even when she was young and slim and attractive.

But it looked like desire. His gaze, so rich and warm, touched upon her lips, and against her arms his thumbs moved in that restless, unmistakable way that meant a man wanted to put his whole hand somewhere a lot less proper than her elbow.

Suddenly, he stepped back, letting go of her. "We should go, eh?"

Flustered, Louise only nodded. Of course he wasn't attracted to her. How ridiculous.

In her office, Ramona gnawed a pencil distractedly. She had about three dozen different items of paperwork to be addressed, but she couldn't focus. Her mind kept straying to the clinic's single patient.

Just after Louise and Alonzo had left, the sheriff had come in and cited Jake for reckless driving, careless driving and speeding. Ramona grew dizzy when she saw the speed the sheriff had recorded: ninety-six miles an hour.

On the downward stretch of Gate Pass.

It made her feel ill to think of what might have happened. Not only to Jake, either. If he'd lost control when there had been other cars around, he might have killed someone else.

Jake showed no emotion when he was ticketed. No remorse, no fear, not even resignation. He simply accepted the tickets, put them in the drawer with his wallet and lay back on the pillows. Ramona, watching from the hall, experienced the fear on his behalf.

In her office, she leaned back in her chair and looked out the window toward Mount Gordon. Noontime sunlight cast a harsh brightness over the landscape, washing away details and giving the scene the slightly unreal look of a postcard.

Ramona's conflict was growing. Besides the ethics of the situation with Jake, there was genuine risk to him if she could not keep herself emotionally unattached as his physician. By necessity, she knew many of her patients—she was even good friends with some of them.

But she had never doubted her ability to make objective, clear decisions about their care. It had always been easy to keep her personal life and professional life separate.

With Jake, the line had blurred. And sitting in her quiet office, she had to admit it was because she was sexually attracted to him. He was not simply a friend or a colleague or an acquaintance. Of all the things he aroused in her, the strongest was pure, undiluted sexual desire.

No, even that wasn't quite accurate. The truth was, she felt a dizzying combination of things with him. Desire was certainly a major ingredient, but so was respect and genuine pleasure in his company. Curiosity, admiration, even a pleasant feeling of challenge went into the mix. She liked his mind and his irony and his sense of humor.

Idly, she doodled on a scratch pad. The bottom line. She had to remove herself from treating him. Her objectivity as a physician was compromised and she couldn't trust herself to treat him properly.

Before she could change her mind, she called Dr. Richards at the VA hospital, then stood up and took a deep breath before she marched down the hall to deliver the news to Jake. He appeared to be sleeping. Knowing what a precious commodity it was to him, Ramona hated to wake him, but given the concussion, he had to stay awake. Ironic.

As she entered the room, he stirred and opened his eyes. "If you're planning to deliver another lecture, please save it till later. I'm sure I've already heard it at least three times this morning."

Ramona shook her head. "No lecture. I just want you to know I'm not going to be your physician—I've referred your case to Dr. Richards at the VA hospital. You know him?"

"Big black guy?"

"Yes."

"Do you mind if I ask why?"

She hesitated, folding her hands in front of her. Then she simply spilled out the truth. "I'm having trouble being objective about you and your care."

He lowered his gaze. "I see." As if weighing the switch, he nodded. "If I remember, this Richards is a Vietnam vet, right?"

"Yes. He lost a leg in one of the major battles—I forget which one."

Again Jake nodded, his face closed tight. "Is that why you're resigning from my case—because you think some vet might have a better chance at getting me into some kind of treatment program?"

"Partly," she admitted. "Maybe a man who's experienced some of the same pain you're feeling will be able to help you drain that boil better than I can."

The blue of his eyes—that rich, deep, incredible color—intensified, as if the blue had been heated by some internal and very hot flame. "It won't work, Ramona. All those guys, the World War II veterans, and the ones who fought in Korea and Vietnam—they're real soldiers. Some of them spent years in the field."

"Jake, that doesn't have anything to do with—"

"Listen to me, Ramona!" he broke in, sitting forward in the bed, wincing even as he did it. He put a hand to his bruised temple and held it there as he spoke. "You know how many soldiers we lost the summer of 1944?"

She wanted to make him lie back down, wanted to get him a cool cloth for his headache. But she only shook her head in answer to his question. "How many?"

"Almost one hundred thousand. In three months. There wasn't a town or a family in America that wasn't affected. In Vietnam, we lost nearly fifty thousand over nine years or more, and those poor bastards had to come home to a country that spit on them. It was a hellhole, Vietnam." His voice roughened with emotion. "In the Gulf War, we went in, kicked butt and got out. It was over in minutes, practically—and we were heroes when we came out. Parades and the whole nine yards for some stupid two-bit conflict with a petty dictator who didn't even get captured."

Ramona didn't dare move, and she barely breathed, so as not to interfere with this sudden, unexpected disclosure. He almost seemed to forget she was there.

"All I ever wanted to do was be a soldier, like Harry and your dad. It seemed like the ultimate—to fight for your country and keep it safe, and protect all the women and children.'' Another man in such obvious pain might have wept. Not Jake. His eyes only grew hotter, more vivid, until Ramona thought they would turn into pure blue flames. ''One tiny little battle. I couldn't hack it, Ramona. I didn't have the balls.''

She didn't believe it. Not for one single, tiny second. He might have been sickened by things he had seen, or felt he hadn't measured up to some heroic standard in his mind, but she felt certain he had never lacked for courage. She kept silent.

''So, you see, I'm not in that class of soldiers you want me to spill my guts to. I can't do it.''

''I understand,'' she said quietly. ''I won't ask anymore. Just let Dr. Richards treat your physical ills, then. He's a good guy. You'll like him.''

He nodded wearily.

''You look like hell,'' she said. ''I wish I could let you sleep. You want me to call one of your brothers to come sit with you, maybe play cards or something to help pass the time?''

A voice came from behind her. ''Not necessary, Doc. A brother has come to the rescue.''

Ramona turned. Lance Forrest, hair streaked even blonder than usual, his skin a rugged tan from his honeymoon trip, stood in the door. ''Hi, Lance!'' Ramona said, moving forward to give his cheek a kiss. ''How was the honeymoon?''

He wiggled his eyebrows wickedly. ''Just fine, thank you.''

Lance looked at Jake. ''What, you couldn't wait for me to come kick your butt, so you let your car do it instead?''

Jake gave his brother a wan, reluctant smile. ''Yeah, that's it.''

''He can't sleep for another six hours,'' Ramona said.

"Jake, Dr. Richards will be around sometime this afternoon."

"Gotcha, Doc," Lance said with a salute.

Ramona spared one last glance at Jake, but he didn't meet her gaze. With a strange hollow feeling in her chest, she left the brothers alone.

Chapter 11

Ironically, because they said he couldn't sleep, Jake wanted nothing more than to slip into oblivion. All day, his eyes felt grainy and dry, and a thudding headache pulsed at the base of his skull. By evening, he was so exhausted he could barely focus on anything, a state that was not unfamiliar. He'd had maybe four hours sleep in the past forty-eight. In that time, he'd gone dancing, got drunk, gone sailing, been burned and crashed his car.

Dr. Richards came in just before dinner, a tall black man with a half-moon of head showing between wings of salt-and-pepper hair. Jake didn't miss the slightly awkward gait of a man with a false limb, and he wondered which battle had claimed the real one.

"Hello, Jake," the older man said, holding out an enormous hand. "I guess Dr. Hardy has told you she referred you to me."

"She told me." Jake shook the offered hand and tried to struggle into a more dignified sitting position. It was hard. Every damned muscle in his body screamed a protest over any kind of movement.

As if he understood Jake's need to be more than an invalid, the doctor smoothly bent and cranked up the bed. "Better?"

"Thanks."

"Nasty accident, I hear."

"Yeah." Jake looked away from the knowing eyes behind sturdy glasses. He wanted to add something, but couldn't think of what it might be.

"How does the car look?"

"Haven't seen it yet." He lifted a shoulder. "It's probably totaled."

Dr. Richards pointed to a chair. "You mind if I sit down a minute?"

"Go ahead."

"I won't keep you long, but I want to get an idea where you are, so when you're feeling better we can figure out how to treat you."

Jake grimaced. "I'm not sick or anything."

"No, Ramona said the trouble is insomnia, which she believes is related to posttraumatic stress."

"That's what she says."

"You disagree?"

The man had a great voice, Jake thought idly. James Earl Jones deep. That made it easy to listen to him. With great effort, Jake swam unsteadily through the fog of his exhaustion to consider whether he thought Ramona was right. The effort was too much. He felt a rising irritation and a piercing kind of pain through the middle of his solar plexus. "Look, Doc, I have no idea. I only agreed to take the sleeping pills because my mother was fussing over me day and night. I thought it would get her off my back."

"Did they help?"

He nodded. "For a while."

"Are you willing to try something else?"

"I guess." At the moment, he felt like he could sleep a couple of million years with no problem.

"All right, then." The doctor stood up. "When you get to feeling a little better, call me at the VA home and make an appointment, and we'll see what we can work out."

Jake nodded wearily. Couldn't hurt. Suddenly, he remembered Harry and swore aloud. "Doc, is Harry Goodman one of your patients?"

"No, but I see him nearly every day. Is there a problem."

"Yeah." Jake couldn't very well ask the man to smuggle in beer and cigarettes. "Would you just let him know what happened? I'm usually in to see him every other day and I don't want him worrying."

"No problem. Get some rest and I'll see you in a few days."

After dinner, they finally let Jake sleep. And sleep he did: a deep sleep. Dreamless and quiet. No ghosts screaming.

When he awoke, he was parched and achy, but the blurring fog over his mind was gone, and he knew he'd genuinely slept for a good long time. Groggily, he reached for his watch on the nightstand. Five a.m.—which meant he'd slept for almost ten hours.

When he moved, he could feel the strain of the accident in every muscle of his body—across muscles in his shoulders and down his back, in his neck and stomach. He couldn't be sure, but he suspected the soreness came from trying to keep control of the car.

His car. Damn. They'd hauled him out of the wreck and into the ambulance so fast, he hadn't had a look at it, but he was fairly certain there wouldn't be much left of it. It pained him. Aside from the inconvenience of not having anything to drive until he bought something new, he'd never had a car he'd liked as well.

With slow, painful movements, he sat up until his legs were hanging over the side of the bed and rested while the black dots in front of his eyes slowly disappeared, then put his bare feet on the cold, clean linoleum and hobbled into the bathroom.

The greenish fluorescent light did him no favors. One eye was purple and red from the eyebrow all the way down to the middle of his cheek where it ended in a raw scrape. It was puffy and sore. Together with the cut lip and two-day beard, he looked like a skid-row bum.

"Nice, man," he told his reflection, then leaned forward and lifted his hair in order to look at the stitches along his scalp. They were as neat and tidy as he would have expected of Ramona. The mirror reflected the cut on his knuckles and he lowered his hands to look at them, unable to remember how those particular injuries had happened. He flexed his fingers. A little stiff, but not bad. "Frankenstein's the name," he said wryly. "Self-destruction is my game."

There was a small shower cubicle and Jake chanced it, careful not to get his head wet. Wasn't there some rule about keeping stitches dry for a day or two? He couldn't remember—better not to risk it. The water stung the burn on his thigh, and he had to grit his teeth until he got used to it. Weird that the most painful injury was not from the accident, but from a spilled cup of coffee.

In spite of the stinging burn, however, the hot water and soap made him feel marginally more human. He found his clothes in the small closet. The sweats were dotted with blood, the T-shirt soaked with it. He was stuck with the hospital-issue gown, but he'd be damned if he'd go wandering through the clinic with his rear end hanging out—and he desperately wanted some coffee. He smelled some brewing somewhere. Probably too much to hope for that it was French roast, but a man could dream. Actually, a cup of instant would probably be ambrosia at the moment.

Taking the blanket from the bed, he wrapped it around his waist and tucked in the edges. Maybe some kindly nurse would lend him some scrubs to wear home. Surely they'd let him go this morning.

Thus attired, Jake wandered down the hall, following the scent of the coffee. It was quiet in the clinic, but he knew they kept a nurse on when there were patients overnight. His feet made no sound on the linoleum, and he kept a hand on the blanket to make sure it didn't slip off.

The smell of brewing coffee became stronger at the desk. "Hello?" Jake called. No answer.

He rounded the counter and followed his nose into a small room in the back. Or it looked like a small room from the desk. When he got inside, various little rooms unfolded like a maze. Storerooms with locked cabinets and different kinds of equipment, a shadowy room with a bed, another with lockers along one wall. In the middle of everything was a room with a kitchenette. The coffeemaker sat on the counter near a sink and the pot was full. It had just been brewed, going by the sound of the slowing gurgles and the steam coming from the basket. Heaven. Jake hastily opened cupboard doors in search of a cup.

As he poured the steaming liquid, he heard footsteps approaching and suddenly felt guilty. Making sure his thin blanket was still tucked tightly around his waist, he turned.

Ramona came through the door, her hair caught up in a loose knot at the top of her head, a lab coat draped around her lush figure, her glasses perched on her little nose. She had a lollipop in her mouth and a chart in her hands, and she didn't see him right away. Jake felt the strangest twist in his gut at the sight of her—she looked healthy and comfortable and solid. Everything he wasn't.

She didn't look up until she was nearly upon him. "Jake!" she exclaimed. "What are you doing out of bed?"

He lifted his mug. "The coffee coaxed me out here. Hope I'm not breaking any rules by helping myself."

She chuckled, and putting her chart in a rolling file, she poured herself a cup. "I'll let you slide, just this once." She sipped a little and eyed him carefully. "How are you feeling?"

Was she being a doctor this morning, or asking as a friend? Jake wondered if it was possible for her to separate the two, really. "I got the best night's sleep I've had in several months. Makes a big difference in a person's attitude."

She grinned. "You look like you've been brawling with a biker gang."

"Kinda feels like it, too." He rotated his shoulders. "I'm pretty stiff, but it's the kind that will go away in a few days."

"Good. You should be able to go home this morning, then."

Jake nodded idly, then somehow found himself adrift in those velvety brown eyes. So much compassion in those eyes, in that face. He thought of his behavior the day before when they'd brought him in. "Ramona," he said suddenly, reaching unconsciously for her hand, "I'm sorry about yesterday. Said some things I shouldn't."

Her fingers lay in his, and for a moment, he thought she'd draw them away. Instead, she curled them around his lightly. "There's nothing to be sorry for, Jake."

"Yeah, there is. Bad manners, at the very least. Adolescent sulking. Embarrassed by the accident, I suppose. I was a fool on that road." As he pictured what might have happened, his stomach clenched painfully, then eased. "When I think of what I might have done to some innocent person on the road, I feel sick."

"The same thought crossed my mind, but I also thought of your being smashed into bits in that little car." She took a breath and smiled wryly. "I'm glad to hear that you recognize the error of your ways. It might be too little, too late, however. Considering the violations, you might very well lose your license."

He scowled. "I hadn't thought about that. Damn." Still, he followed her lead. "What a fool I am sometimes."

"Jake," she said quietly, moving closer, "look how much clearer things are for you after one good night's sleep. If you can get to sleep on a regular basis, I think everything else might be fixable."

He kept his head down, feeling the familiar, almost panicky resistance rise in his chest. "Don't, Ramona," he growled. "Please."

She gently touched his unmarked cheek, just a soft brush of her fingertips over his face, then away. "Okay. But you have to promise to try whatever Dr. Richards suggests, or—"

"Or what?" He looked at her with a smile, knowing she would not offer any real ultimatums. "You'll beat me up?"

Her expression sobered. "Or I won't be able to stand watching you kill yourself, and I'll just have to avoid you."

He narrowed his eyes, stung. What made her think she was so important that a threat like that would make any difference to him? That plump little wren figure in her plain white lab coat, spectacles perched on her nose, her hair all piled up on her head, she was hardly the kind of woman that could launch a thousand ships. It annoyed him.

But in his hand, her small fingers curled with trust and curious strength, and he knew she did mean something to him. Without Ramona to hang on to, he thought he might drift off into the ether completely. He swallowed. "Deal," he said.

A vulnerable expression crossed her eyes then, a softness

Jake should have seen before this. In a flash, the past few days replayed themselves in his mind—the moments in her kitchen with his hands on her breasts, in the sloop and on the shore, kissing like kids.

Then the strange, awkward moments in her driveway, and his sulking when they brought him into the clinic. Now he was acting as if they were simply friends again, and it wasn't true. Not for either of them.

Standing there with her trusting hand in his own, she had more dignity than any woman he'd ever known. She gave freely, without expectation, and Jake in his selfishness just took and took and took. What had he given her except a lot of hassle and too much temptation?

He bowed his head, ashamed, words sticking like dry crackers in his throat. He wanted her. In his bed. But a woman like this wasn't capable of giving her body without giving her heart. He knew it, and she knew it. All the talk of just being friends and keeping their distance was designed to keep her safe from that painful ending.

And what did he do? He kept pushing, kept needing, kept wanting her. He himself was perfectly capable of giving only his body, because he had no heart or soul left. They'd been bled out of him these past few years. He was as hollow as a straw man.

On a sudden swell of regret, he lifted her hand to his mouth and kissed it fervently. "Thank you, Ramona."

It unnerved her. He could see it in the quickly hidden flare in her eyes. "For what?"

He closed his eyes and kissed her strong, capable fingers once more. "For being there for me when I can't give you anything in return."

Her smile was unexpected and oddly knowing. "Oh, you've given me a lot, Jake Forrest. A woman can always use another friend."

Jake said nothing. A true friend would leave her alone

now that he could see traces of genuine caring creep into her smiles. A true friend would run away as fast as he could and give her some peace.

Instead, Jake said, "Do you have time to drive me to my apartment? I can call Lance to take me to the restaurant."

"Sure. I can bring you back to town on my way back to the clinic, if you hurry. We need to do it right now, though." She glanced at her watch. "I have a patient at seven."

He smiled. "Pretty early office hours."

"She can't get in any other time—she's a teacher." She stuck her lollipop back in her mouth. "Go get dressed and I'll take you home."

Ramona wasn't sure what she'd expected to find in Jake's apartment. Something militarily neat, maybe, with a huge stereo and few chairs and an enormous bed. No food in the cupboards, except maybe some instant coffee and an old box of crackers.

As she walked into the condo, however, she realized the vague picture she'd imagined was all wrong. For all his present self-destructiveness, he was a man who cared about beauty, about fine things, and it showed in his apartment. The rooms were large and clean, with cathedral ceilings that opened onto a bank of windows giving a bright, unbroken view of the mountains and a creek running through a meadow. The furniture was not merely serviceable, as she'd vaguely supposed, but an artfully chosen Santa Fe style, the fabric a pleasing stripe in muted hues of turquoise, sienna and mauve. Instinctively, she brushed a hand over the polished cotton.

"I'll just be a second," he said, going up a set of open stairs to a loft. "Make yourself comfortable."

That was pretty much impossible, Ramona acknowledged, perching on the edge of the couch. The room smelled of him, of that heady cologne and male skin and shaving cream, and the scent made her skin feel oddly sensitive. Restless. She was aware of the small sounds of his moving upstairs, just out of sight beyond the rail that separated his bedroom from the downstairs, and she tried not to imagine his shedding the sweats he'd worn home from the hospital. Tried not to think of his long, hard thighs all bare, and the hips that would be as lean and well muscled as the rest of him....

She closed her eyes, but it didn't help. After a moment, she jumped up and paced into the kitchen. Onions and peppers and apples, neatly sorted, hung in a three-tiered basket near the stove, and a good set of cutting knives clung to a magnetized bar over the counter. The coffeemaker and a grinder were high-end and sat in the midst of plain white, heavy ceramic jars she assumed held coffee. Curiously, she lifted the lid of one and inhaled the aroma of some very dark beans. A wine rack in the corner held several bottles—Ramona looked at them without really knowing what the labels meant. Some were in German, some obviously French. One or two were American labels she recognized.

Jake came back down the stairs whistling, his step light and free. He carried socks and a pair of tennis shoes in one hand, and Ramona saw that he'd taken the time to shave quickly. His jaw gleamed. In spite of the bruises, he looked hale and strong and—judging by the sudden melting of her hips—utterly edible. "Do you know anything about wines?" he asked, seeing her interest.

Ramona put her hands behind her back. "Not really."

The kitchen was tiny. When he stepped closer to take a bottle from the rack, they were practically breathing the same molecules. He'd splashed on a little of his cologne, and it filled Ramona's head, sensual and mesmerizing. She found herself gripping the counter behind her, amazed at the sudden swell of awareness and arousal that poured through her limbs.

Whoever he was, whatever his problems, Jake Forrest was an astonishingly sexy man. Lean and a little rough, that dark hair brushed back from his gorgeously angled face, his hands a work of art...

She took a breath and let it out slowly, trying to focus as he told her about the pale green bottle of wine he'd pulled out. She nodded in what she hoped appeared to be an intelligent manner, even though she hadn't heard a word he said.

But her senses were on overload. Her gaze drifted over the line of his jaw, down his neck to the triangle of tanned skin at the collar of his shirt. Down his lean waist, down taut hips and thighs clad in worn denim, and her nose was filled with that sexy scent, and there was just no room for listening.

He put the bottle back carefully and Ramona shifted, thinking now they'd leave the kitchen, and she could pull her wits together. Once they were out of this tiny little space, cool and dim with only the light from the big window coming through the pass-through bar, she would be able to put some space between them. She could turn her attention to something else, and his scented skin wouldn't be so overwhelming.

"I just have to put my shoes on," he said, lifting them up to show her, as if she hadn't realized.

Blankly, she nodded.

He turned to lead the way out, and Ramona concealed a sigh, carefully focusing on the floor so she wouldn't think lecherous thoughts about his rear end.

Thankfully, he didn't seem to notice her distracted state. In that lazy, loose-limbed way he moved—so at odds for a man who had once been a soldier—he wandered into the living room, sat in a chair and dropped his shoes. Ramona followed him, feeling as shaky as if she had actually had sex. She perched on the couch, right at the edge.

Silence thundered through the room. She struggled to look anywhere but at him. Struggled to come up with a line of conversation that might help keep her mind off his body. It suddenly seemed to her that this must be how it was for adolescent boys. They were probably flooded with visions of sex twenty-four hours a day, poor things. The notion surprised her into a grin.

"What's so funny?"

Ramona pressed her lips together. "Nothing. I was just, um, thinking it was too quiet in here." An idea popped into her head. "You need a pet."

He chuckled. "Right."

"I'm serious. Maybe a cat to curl up on your lap. Purr you to sleep."

An instant before he gave her that slow, sensual grin, Ramona realized how leading that sounded. "Purring is nice," he said. "Come on over anytime and I'll get you purring."

"Jake!" she protested. A blaze of color reddened her cheeks.

He laughed softly. "Couldn't resist."

She looked at her watch. "You'd better hurry up or I'll have to leave you behind."

"You wouldn't do that."

"Try me." She'd do just about anything to get out of this apartment before she humiliated herself. Anything.

The rest of the day, Ramona couldn't stop thinking about his apartment. Something nagged at her, just out of reach. It hadn't been the bachelor pad she had expected, but there was something missing anyway.

Finally, it dawned on her. There were no pictures on the

walls, no plants, no little creature comforts at all, except in the kitchen.

It wasn't really a home. No wonder he couldn't sleep. It was as impersonal as any hotel room. Ramona figured she might have trouble sleeping in such a place herself.

She trusted her instincts in most things, but when she found herself at the local animal shelter, face-to-face with a dozen meowing cats, she had to seriously question her motives. It wasn't the smartest thing in the world to make a gift of a pet. She didn't know if Jake even liked cats. She didn't know why she picked a cat instead of a dog. He seemed more like a dog person after all. She couldn't remember if he had even seen her cats at her house that other morning.

She nearly backed out, but just as she was about to leave, a half-grown gray tiger came up to the bars and butted his head against them. His meow was ragged, one ear was torn, and his tail had evidently been run over.

And his purr was so loud it could be heard in three states.

She put her hand against his big head and rubbed with vigor between his ears. The purr intensified, and he rolled his back against her outstretched fingers. "What's this one's story?" she asked the attendant.

"Stray. A lady on Fifth Street said some folks left him behind when they moved. He hung around the neighborhood for a month before she brought him in."

With a sinking feeling, Ramona knew she was doomed. If Jake didn't want him, she'd take him in herself. What was one more cat, really?

As golden evening moved in, Ramona drove back to the condo complex. Thick bars of deep rose and yellow light cut through the valleys to fall over the verdant landscape and pinken the white bark of aspens. The mountains with their coat of dark trees looked blurred, soft as fur.

Ramona pulled into the lot and parked. Walking on the

sidewalk was a beautiful young woman, maybe twenty-five, perfect in the way of a model. Gilded hair, gilded skin, long limbs and upthrust breasts—just Jake's type. She gave Ramona a friendly, open smile so Ramona couldn't even hate her.

"What am I doing here?" she said to the cat, who leaped to the dashboard curiously, nosing at the edges of the window. "What in the world am I doing?"

Making a fool of herself. She was armed with a tattered, half-grown cat, three jars of chokecherry jelly and a loaf of sourdough bread from the bakery. Could she be any more Mayberry RFD?

Unfamiliar embarrassment rushed through her. She had it bad for Jake Forrest—real bad. Somehow, he had broken through all her practical, even-tempered calm defenses and stirred up emotions she hadn't even known she was capable of feeling.

And what did she do about it? Dress up and put on lipstick like any normal female? Invite him out dancing where things might take their natural course? No, she brought him homey presents. She hadn't even remembered to put on a clean blouse or wash her face. She'd just wanted to get over here and give him something, make an offering.

In sudden panic, she reached for her car key. Then hesitated. Stupid as it was, she really had felt earlier that these simple gifts might make a difference to him. A cat purring at his feet could soothe a lot of sorrows, as she well knew. Chokecherry jelly, made from the fruit of these very hills, could ease his hurt by giving him pleasant memories of childhood. And the bread—well, it just seemed like it went with the jam.

No. She closed her eyes and started the engine. No, she couldn't do it.

Chapter 12

From his loft bedroom, Jake had seen Ramona pull up. In spite of his optimistic start to the day, he'd lasted only half the morning at the restaurant. Just long enough to make schedules for the next two-week period, scribble his name on the payroll checks the manager put in front of him, and review kitchen orders. There was a feud going on between two waitresses over some man both of them wanted, and it gave him a headache. Barking orders for them to solve it or get out, he called Lance to give him a ride home.

He ached more than he would have admitted aloud, and stiff muscles plagued his shoulders and neck. He'd gone upstairs to fetch some analgesic ointment when he glanced out the window and saw Ramona's car. All day he'd been aware of that weird sense of distance—he couldn't seem to make more than superficial contact with the rest of the world. He spoke and listened, but everything seemed like a dream or a movie. Not real. Twice at the restaurant, someone had tried to talk to him, and Jake knew they were talking. He watched their lips move, but he simply couldn't hear them.

That scared him. There were times lately when he wondered if he really was going crazy. Maybe his mother wasn't too far off the mark to worry about him—maybe it ran in the family.

Ramona had pulled into the parking lot of his apartment, but although he waited for her to get out, she didn't. Long minutes passed, and he thought maybe she was gathering things out of the seat or something.

But how long could it take? Frowning, he went downstairs and to the front door—just as her engine started. He bolted down the steps. "Hey!" he called. "Don't go!" She hadn't started to pull out yet, and with relief, he saw her reach for the key. The engine stopped. Jake jogged up to the window. "Did you forget about some other appointment?"

"No." She shook her head. Her hair was loose, and it made a gossamer web over one shoulder. "I just wasn't sure I should bother you after all."

"You could never be a bother." She looked good to him. Vividly colored, solid, flesh and blood, as if she'd walked out of the movie to join him. "I was just about to make some supper. I'll cook for you and we can drink some wine."

She lifted one shoulder and looked away. With an odd expression, she said, "You might not feel that way when you see what I brought over."

"What? Amulets to ward off bad dreams?"

"No." She reached over to one side for something he couldn't see. "Guess again," she said, and turned back, her arms full of something...

"A cat?" Instinctively, he reached for the animal so she could get out of the car. It was an appealing gray-and-white-striped tiger with long fur. Big. "Hi, there," Jake said, scratching him under the chin. The cat crawled up on his shoulder, nosing his ear, and purred loudly. Jake laughed. "Hey! That tickles."

Ramona got out of the car, holding a basket. "So you do like cats?"

"Well, I hate to ruin my macho image, but I always had a cat as a kid. I love them."

Her relief was almost palpable. "After talking about it this morning, I decided a purring cat might be just the thing for your insomnia. And even if he doesn't cure it, he'll be good company in the middle of the night."

"I thought you weren't going to be my doctor anymore," Jake said. The cat felt warm and comfortable in his arms, and Jake suspected she might be right. A cat. Such a simple thing, but he hadn't even considered getting a pet.

"Just a friend."

Standing there looking slightly abashed, her hair tumbling in long strands down her back, her face devoid of any makeup she might have worn earlier, she looked like the ultimate earth mother. Jake didn't like the type. He didn't like short women. He didn't like guileless simplicity or country ways.

But he liked her. He liked the fathomless depths of those velvet brown eyes, her healthy, clear skin, her beautiful, lush breasts and her tiny hands. He liked her hair, free and shiny, caressing her shoulders and the open way she looked at him. Just the sight of her eased the tension he'd been feeling, that edgy restlessness.

Impulsively, he bent over and pressed a light kiss to her mouth. "Thank you."

She swallowed. "You're welcome."

"Come inside. I'll get you some wine."

"No, I don't want to keep you. I just brought you the cat and some cat food and things like that."

He gripped the animal with one hand and took her arm with the other. "Let me feed you."

For one more moment, she hesitated, and Jake saw with a start of surprise that she wanted to come in. It was the first time she'd come to him, and a strange emotion curled in his belly over that. Dimly, he recognized it as happiness.

Firmly, he locked his arm in hers. Her breast pressed softly against his forearm, and it was a powerfully erotic sensation, just that small movement of firm flesh. Desire unfurled through his loins, thick and golden. He smiled at her.

He let her go once they were inside. "What do you have in the basket?" he asked.

She held it in front of her with one hand. In the other was a plastic grocery bag. "The bag is cat supplies."

"And the basket?" he repeated.

"People supplies." A faint blush edged her cheeks. "Now I see it was silly, but I brought you some jelly and a loaf of bread from the bakery. Seemed a good idea at the time."

Jake put the cat down to explore and took the basket out of her hand. He didn't move away, taking simple enjoyment from the closeness of her small round body and the glow of her complexion. "Why was it silly?" he asked in a low voice.

She shrugged, and her gaze darted away. "I don't know. I'm sure you are used to more glamorous presents."

He touched her arm with one finger. "I am. Glamorous and shallow presents that could be given to anyone. Impersonal presents." He traced a line up her arm and pushed her hair back over her shoulder. "Nothing was ever heartfelt."

Her eyes darkened, turned to those dark, still pools that so drew him. Feeling himself thicken with desire, he wondered if she knew her nostrils flared slightly when she was aroused, or that her nipples visibly pearled. The sight lured him, made him want to unfasten that simple buttoned shirt and put his mouth to those aroused, hungry points. For a moment, he thought about it and even felt himself swaying forward the slightest bit.

Abruptly, she ducked her head. "I hope you like everything."

Jake respected her obvious need to put some distance between them. He stepped away casually. "Let's see what we can put together." He cocked his head and moved into the kitchen. On the radio in the living room, he heard the DJ announce a triple play of the Allman Brothers. "Hey! Will you turn that up for me?"

"Sure." She grinned, and the slightly saucy Ramona was back, just that fast. "Now, why am I not surprised you like the Allman Brothers?"

"Don't you?" Through the pass-through bar between kitchen and living room, he watched her lean forward, her hair swirling over her shoulders as she studied the various knobs. "The one on the right." Her derriere stuck out at the most appealing angle, and he inclined his head, admiring it. "You have a sweet little rear end, Doc."

She gave him a wry glance over her shoulder as the music came up, playing "Jessica." "You're a skirt chaser, Mr. Forrest."

He cocked his head in acknowledgment, grinning as sweet Southern guitar music filled the room. Together with Ramona's gifts and the sheer pleasure of her presence here, the music made him feel hopeful. Even cheerful.

"Let's see what we've got," he said, taking quilted glasses of ruby-colored jelly from the basket, along with the loaf of sourdough. "Bless you," he said, and gave the package a little kiss. "Mmm, sourdough. I love this stuff."

"What can I do?"

"Just stand there and let me admire you. Or—" he gave her a wicked grin "—admire me."

She crossed her arms. "I can stand here and be beautiful. You, however, look like a boxer who came out on the wrong end."

"True enough." He turned to switch on the oven, then opened the fridge. "Ah!" He pulled out a wedge of Brie, still in the wrapping, and a bowl of ripe strawberries he'd bought this afternoon. He put them on the counter and swiveled around to the wine, his eyes narrowing. "Montrachet?"

"If you say so. You're the expert."

He winked. "Elegant, with a pretty band of pear."

"I can only have one glass, though—I have a mom-to-be about to go into labor any moment."

"Understood." Deftly, he opened the cheese, wrapped the bread in foil and put them both in the oven. "Now," he said, opening the dry white wine, "we have to do this right." He poured a little of the Burgundy in each of two glasses and gave her one. "Swirl it like this." He gently demonstrated. "Now lift it to your nose and sniff. What do you smell?"

Ramona closed her eyes. "Forest?"

"Good. Now sip just a little and swish it over your tongue." Again he demonstrated. Imitating him, Ramona swished, her pretty mouth pouting nicely. He swallowed. "What do you taste?"

Ramona cocked a brow. The earthiness that was so much a part of her glinted now in her dark eyes. "Elegant with a band of pear."

Jake laughed. "Quick learner."

"Mmm." She held out her glass and let him fill it to the brim. "It really is wonderful."

"Yeah." And she was wonderful. Summer-light air poured through the open door to the balcony, scented with pine and mountain and meadow. From the oven came the mingled richness of Brie and sourdough bread, and in the living room, a bluesy guitar danced as if intoxicated by the heady fragrances.

And to his amazement, Jake was fiercely glad to be alive, to be experiencing this moment. He bent over and pressed his mouth to hers, touching only her lips, nothing else. Just for a moment, a moment when he tasted wine and summer on her pretty pink mouth, a moment when he smelled sweetness in her hair. She kissed the way she did everything, with full, sensual awareness, and her slow, savoring responses made him dizzy.

Swallowing, he straightened. "I'm really glad you came over," he said, and brushed a finger over her cheek.

Her smile was womanly and warm. "Me, too."

The cat, having made his rounds, wandered back into the kitchen and rubbed against Jake's legs. "I guess I need to feed you, too, huh?" He took a slightly chipped ceramic bowl from the cupboard, put it next to the wall and filled it with the food Ramona had brought. The cat nibbled delicately, settling in. Jake stroked the long, pale gray fur, and the cat purred softly, almost continuously. "I'm really touched, Ramona," he said. In fact, it was hard to remember the last time he had been so moved by anything. "What should I name him?"

"He's your cat."

"Okay...how about Plato?"

She snickered. "Beep. Boring."

Jake smiled. "Look at those tufts of hair around his ears. He looks like those pictures of Einstein. How about Albert?"

"How about Mr. E?"

The cat looked up curiously. Jake and Ramona both laughed. "Mr. E it is," Jake said.

"I think so." She looked up at him, smiling.

Jake was suddenly filled with a fierce wish to touch her, to put his hands under that thick hair, against her neck. He found himself staring at her mouth, pink and full. She looked away.

A new song came on the radio, and he felt his foot tapping in time to "Midnight Rambler." "Come on, Miss Hen," he said, taking her glass and setting it beside his on the counter. He grabbed her hand. "Time for another dancing lesson."

"There isn't much room," Ramona said, nevertheless allowing herself to be led.

He tugged her into his arms, lacing his thighs with hers. "We don't need much for this kind of dancing." He put his hand flat on the small of her back and pulled her into him, the position intimate and suggestive. "Put your hands on my shoulders."

She looked vaguely alarmed, but against his palm, her spine softened. Her hands landed on his shoulders. "Like this?"

"You got it." Looking down at her, he started to move. "Now let yourself just swing a little, back and forth."

He closed his eyes to let just the music and Ramona come in, nothing else. He could feel her heat, the swish of her hair against his arm and the exact moment she let go.

They flowed together as one swaying branch of a tree, swirling and turning in perfect accord. "You've got it," he said, and bent his head to touch the side of hers. He clasped one of her hands in his own and let his other hand slip lower, cupping her bottom and pressing her even closer to him.

And Ramona, sweet and shy, moved with the sensual abandon of a Gypsy, arching her back, letting her body brush his, their thighs slide and tangle. He turned his head and kissed her neck and she sighed against him.

The slow, erotic, thudding notes of "Whipping Post"

came on, and Jake groaned, pulling her closer yet. "I love this song."

"Mmm."

He let his hands rove over her body, sliding them up and down her sides in time to the music, skimming the outer curve of her breast, the plumpness of her hips, the channel of her spine. Quietly, he hummed along with the music, feeling part of it, part of her, part of the golden late-afternoon summer sunlight that warmed his lids.

Her nose brushed his throat, and Jake pressed his cheek to her hair. "You feel so nice," he murmured as the song wound down.

The DJ broke in, shattering the mood. Jake realized his thumbs were stroking the sides of her breasts, and her mouth was on his throat. She pulled away a little, lowering her head.

"Wow," she said, and looked up. An earthy laugh rolled out of her, husky and sexy.

Jake cupped her chin and kissed her, sliding his tongue into her mouth in an urgent, heated demand. She met it breathlessly, then pulled away. "The food is going to burn."

"Damn!" He jogged into the kitchen, smelling scorching cheese, and pulled out the metal sheet. "We're safe," he reported. "Just in time." With a towel, he retrieved the bread and put it on the counter next to the melted cheese.

Ramona came in behind him. "Good. I'm starving." She leaned over the counter and grabbed her wine. The action made her breasts swell over the top of her shirt, giving him a lovely view of the creamy curves. Her hair was slightly tousled from the dance, and her cheeks were ruddy with color. She reached for a strawberry, swirled it through the cheese and popped it into her mouth.

Jake watched her, mesmerized by a kind of desire he'd never experienced in his life. He'd wanted women before.

He'd even fancied himself in love once or twice, but never had he felt this need to make love so fiercely, not only in his hands and mouth and aroused organ, but also in his feet and knees and throat. He wanted to turn her to oil, so he could spread the essence of her all over him, turn her into food and eat her, make her smoke so he could inhale her.

She sucked softened Brie from her finger, seemingly oblivious to his condition. Then she lifted her eyes, those big brown eyes, and they were heavy lidded with desire and invitation, and he understood that her sweetness was only one side of her. She knew exactly what he was thinking.

Jake dipped his finger in the warm Brie and held it out to her. Without looking away from him, she swayed forward and took his hand to hold it steady, then took his finger in her mouth and sucked the cheese off.

His control snapped. With a growl, he grabbed her arms and stretched them above her head. "You're making me crazy," he said, trapping her between his body and the wall. She made no protest, only lifted luminous eyes to him. Pressing his whole length against hers, he kissed her. Fiercely.

And she kissed him back, her mouth and tongue meeting his every thrust with a kind of wild eagerness. He released her arms and put his hands on her shoulders, sliding them down to touch her breasts, her waist, her hips, tugging her against him. "Damn, Ramona, I want you."

Her hands pulled at him and roved over him, sliding open palmed over his buttocks, down the back of his thighs, upward again to his waist. She kissed him greedily, then pulled his shirt out from the back of his jeans, and Jake felt the tingling brush of her fingers on his naked skin with a force like a hurricane.

Turning slightly, he lifted her to the counter and settled her there so he could reach her more easily. She didn't break the kiss, only settled on the counter and wrapped her legs around him. Her hands went to the buttons of his shirt, and Jake pressed his hips closer as he in turn unbuttoned her blouse.

Shoving the fabric away, he touched her breasts above her bra, nipping at her lips lightly as he did so. She moaned with pleasure, low in her throat, and her fingers dug into his shoulders as he spread his hands over the thin, silky bra. Her nipples nudged the heart of his palm, and he moved lightly, teasing them to harder points. And all the while, their tongues meshed and danced and swayed together, exploring, delving, drinking.

It seemed as if he'd been waiting to do this for an eternity, since that day of the wedding, and now he found himself almost mad with the need to touch her and hear those breathless, pleased sounds coming out of her as he stroked her aroused nipples through fine silky cups, and plunged his tongue deep into the heat of her mouth, and felt her tighten her thighs around him, pulling his arousal closer to the heated core of her.

Jake put his hands on her shoulders and lowered his head, kissing her throat, her collarbone, and finally closing his mouth around her nipple, nibbling a little through the fabric. She made a sound somewhere between a sigh and a groan, and Jake did it again on the other side.

He rocked his hips against her, feeling her response, and finally he simply reached up and pushed her shirt and bra off her shoulders, trapping her arms at her sides. He couldn't catch his breath, looking at her luscious pink-and-cream breasts, firm and supple and oh, so ripe. He opened his mouth on her, feeling his breath come from him in ragged, hoarse gasps. The taste of the pebbled flesh against his tongue nearly sent him over the edge.

He lifted his head, dazed and awash on a wild current of need. He took her face in his hands and kissed her, mouth open. "You're wonderful...and real...and beautiful," he whispered, kissing her between words. He tasted her lips and her chin, touched her breasts, then slid his hands lower.

She stared at him, her eyes wide and wanting and wary all at once. "I keep trying not to want you," she said. "But it isn't working."

"And I keep telling myself you deserve a lot more from me than what I've given you. I keep telling myself if I was any kind of honorable man, I'd just leave you the hell alone." He drew a line down her face, over her lips and down her neck. He wanted to touch every inch of her, to kiss her and know her. He wanted to please her, satisfy her. "Touch me, Ramona," he said in a raw voice. "I want to feel your hands on me, too."

She swayed forward, that earthy, knowing smile on her face, and kissed his mouth, his chin, his throat. She traced a cross over his chest, throat to belly, then nipple to nipple. She moved without haste, and he loved the richly sensual slowness, the way she savored the act.

He closed his eyes with a groan, burying his hand in her thick hair. "I somehow knew you'd be like this, Ramona, so full of passion."

Lingeringly, she pressed her lips to his chest. "It's you, Jake," she murmured. Her hands moved surely to the top button of his jeans.

Jake found he could scarcely breathe for anticipation. In a haze, he looked at her, so pagan and beautiful and sexy, and knew it wasn't him at all. Like the herbs in her kitchen and the plants tumbling from every surface in the house, this was but another element of her lusty zest for living. For being.

In the background, the radio still played on, something quiet he didn't know, and it seemed perfect for this moment, for Ramona. For a heart-stopping moment, the strange sense that he might be falling in love wove through him, alien and exhilarating and terrifying.

And then all thought fled as she unbuttoned his jeans and slid her hand inside to close on his hardness. He gripped her shoulders as she caressed him, breathing encouragement, even as he tugged at the shirt that still clung to her. She resisted his efforts to take it off, and he closed his hand around hers. "Why?"

She only shook her head—but with a flash of insight, Jake thought he understood.

He deliberately put his hands on her belly. It was not slim. It was not flat. It was plump and soft and white, and he wanted to press his face into the comforting flesh. He lifted his head and caught her eye. "You're incredible," he said, "and beautiful."

And to his amazement, they were not just words to make her feel better. He'd never realized how soft a woman like this would feel. He'd never understood that the planes and angles of an elegantly thin woman would never cushion or comfort the way her body did. He kissed her deeply, gratefully, hungrily, and slid his hand down between her legs to caress her there, urgent need growing in him by the second.

Suddenly, a shrill electronic sound burst into the moist sound of their breathing and kissing and gasps. Jake, delirious with kissing her, did not immediately lift his head. Her tongue was a sin all its own, agile and daring, wanting more.

But the noise came again, and Ramona pushed him away. "My beeper!" she cried, looking wildly around for it. Shoving her hair from her face, she said, "Hand me my purse." Reluctantly, Jake did. "I have to call," she said seconds later, and Jake handed her the phone. Tugging her shirt around her, she slipped by him and reached to punch in the numbers.

Jake gave a quiet, disappointed curse and marginally readjusted his clothes. To distract himself, he lifted his glass and took a sip of wine, but even that could not compare with Ramona. He eyed her hungrily as she rang the number. From where he stood, a generous view of breast was visible at the opening of her shirt, and he knew he'd never again see her wear anything with buttons without imagining that sight.

"This is Dr. Hardy," she said into the phone. "I was paged." She listened, then, "How far apart are the pains?"

Jake's mood crumbled. Even he knew enough to realize a baby was on the way. With a groan, he struggled to refasten the buttons of his jeans, wondering if he'd lost his only chance to have her, or if she could be coaxed back.

As she spoke, he approached her, slid his hand into the opening of her shirt, then pushed her hair out of the way so he could kiss the back of her neck. She closed her eyes, but her voice was steady as she said to the person on the other end of the line, "I'll meet you at the clinic in ten minutes."

She hung up and Jake groaned, burying his face against her neck. "Can't you call another doctor?"

"It doesn't work that way," she offered reluctantly.

She ducked to elude him, but Jake caught her against him, clasping a naked breast in each hand as he pressed his mouth to her shoulder from behind her. "Don't go, Ramona. Please."

For a second, she softened against him, sighing. Jake pressed his hips into the fullness of her bottom. She trembled slightly and surrendered as his hands moved restlessly, urgently, on her body, his teeth against her shoulder. Fiercely, he sucked at a tender place at the base of her throat, and she groaned, her hands gripping his thighs behind her.

"Jake," she whispered, "I have to—"

He opened his mouth and wildly planted kisses to her

ear, to her neck. "No," he growled, and turned her gently in his arms. He picked her up and put her against him, holding her bottom until she wrapped her legs and arms around him. The position was exactly right for the marriage of his mouth and her breasts. She gripped him in a swoon of shuddering passion, straining against him for a long, delectable minute. Jake felt mad with want of her.

But she pushed him away again. "Jake, stop. I have to go. I don't want to any more than you do, but this woman is counting on me." She put her feet down and pushed away gently. "You have to let me go."

A dark emotion rushed through the blur of his desire. He dropped his arms. "Fine. Go."

Silently, she dressed. "Jake, this is part of my life. You have to understand that."

He closed his eyes, recognizing the emotion roiling inside him as jealousy. "I do," he said. "I'm sorry."

Her smile was lightning bright, and she sailed across the small space between them to press a fervent kiss against his mouth. "Good. I'll see you soon."

Then she was gone, and the room was suddenly too quiet. Jake sank down into a chair, feeling deserted, and horny and very depressed.

Chapter 13

The baby came fast and without much trouble, but when Ramona was finished, she did not return to Jake's condo. It had been in her mind to do so when she left him, but after a few hours of cooling off, she decided it would be unwise.

In her own bed, with a cat purring and warm on her tummy, Ramona stared into the darkness and replayed the evening with Jake. She wanted him, heaven knew. He aroused in her a passion she had never experienced, never even really believed existed.

Miraculously, he wanted her, too. But alone and clear-headed now, without the narcotic presence of the man himself to distract her, Ramona wondered about his motivation. Why was he drawn to her in particular?

And the only answer she could come up with was that he needed healing. She didn't think he knew that, didn't think he even had the faintest idea of what impelled him, but Ramona could taste his need when he kissed her. He was almost—driven. She really wasn't the sort of woman to inspire that kind of blinding passion in a man.

Traitorously, she liked it. She liked the sense of power it gave, the flush of feminine exhilaration it made her feel.

More, she loved the way she felt when he touched her. As if every cell in her body were filled with a moist, honeyed light. A single finger dragged along the inside of her elbow, the brush of his lips over her tummy, the whisper of his hair brushing her chin and neck and breasts—all of it made her feel hungry and alive. In Jake's arms, privy to his skilled and ardent caresses, Ramona had become someone new.

She liked touching him. He was sexy and responsive and sensual. She liked the sounds he made—low growls, slow, throaty sighs and murmurings of fervent longing.

Restlessly, she turned to her side, aware of a heaviness in her groin, a weighty need in her breasts and lips and palms. She wanted to throw on whatever she could find, jump in her car and roar over to his condo to take up where they'd left off. Even the thought made her ache with desire.

Why had she come home instead?

Because, quite simply, tonight Ramona had realized that she was falling in love with him. And he was wounded, and he wanted her for reasons he didn't understand, and once he healed, he would take up the life he'd deserted. A life in which a simple country doctor had no place.

When it came right down to it, Ramona didn't think she could bear having him, then losing him. Far better to avoid the temptation and save her heart. Whatever the clichés said, she didn't believe it was better to have loved and lost than never to have loved at all. She didn't want that kind of sorrow in her life.

Which didn't mean she was afraid of risks, or afraid of love. She wasn't. But foolish risks, risks that were almost certain to hurt her, those were better left unexplored. She wouldn't jump out of a plane without a parachute, she wouldn't ride a motorcycle without a helmet and she wouldn't sleep with Jake.

Wincing, she knew he wasn't going to take kindly to the news. He'd be annoyed. He was a man who was used to getting his way, and if for no other reason, he'd be all the more set upon getting her into his bed for whatever amount of time she held his interest. Ramona would have to prepare herself for that. She wouldn't bother to be reasonable or calm. She'd give him a simple, clear explanation—and leave him to his irritation.

And as much as it pained her, she would have to avoid him after that. Since Dr. Richards had taken his case, it shouldn't be hard.

She ignored the pang of regret she felt. These past few weeks had been very pleasant. Already she would miss him.

But Ramona didn't have a chance to tell Jake anything. The official Fourth of July weekend would start Friday, two days away, and the usual crowd of campers and tourists were flooding into town. It was worse than usual, since the Fourth fell on a Monday, making it a three-day weekend.

The morning after she delivered the baby, she had her first two cases of a summer flu that had nasty respiratory manifestations. By the next day, she decided most of the townspeople had come down with the virus, along with a good percentage of the tourists. The small clinic was soon bulging with victims, including two asthma cases and four elderly patients whose flu shots hadn't protected them against the mutated strain and they'd developed pneumonia. A hoard of preschoolers who had picked it up at day care, among them Curtis and Cody, Jake's nephews, were afflicted, as was Tyler. She dispensed medications and cough syrup and nasal sprays and inhalers in numbers that made two pharmacists call her in alarm.

To make matters worse, the usual Fourth of July burns started appearing. Fireworks were strictly outlawed in Red Creek except for the carefully controlled display given in the town square every year, but the law never stopped anyone. The townsfolk were as stubborn and independent as Westerners came, and by hook or by crook, they'd have their fireworks. They could drive into Denver for mild sorts of sparklers and snakes and smoke bombs, or drive another hour and a half across the Wyoming border to buy anything they wanted—including Roman candles, bottle rockets, and a whole menu of shooting stars.

And with fireworks came burns.

The teenage boys were the worst. They lit bottle rockets in their hands or pointed Roman candles at each other. One boy, involved in just such an incident, had come very close to losing his eye. Instead, the fiery ball had skimmed his temple and seared away the hair in a line above his ear. Treating him, Ramona commented, "You're lucky your hair didn't catch fire. I'd hate to see a boy your age bald."

He blanched.

Twice Jake called her house and left messages on her machine, but by the time she got home at night, it was too late to call him back, and she was too exhausted anyway. He appeared once at the clinic, but Ramona didn't even get a chance to talk to him. Every time she headed in his direction, someone else rushed toward her with something urgent she needed to address that very minute. Finally, giving up, she waved and gave him a rueful smile, and he seemed to take it in good grace, giving her a smile as he waved farewell.

By Saturday, the patient load was down a little, but Dr. Richards called from the VA home to tell her that some flu cases had begun to appear there. Ramona swore under her breath. It was a nasty enough virus among the young and healthy—but it devastated the elderly. She told him she'd get over there as soon as she could.

She didn't make it until evening, and by then, the past few days had begun to take their toll. Dr. Richards, dressed in green scrubs, took one look at her and shook his head. "You're too old to play intern, Ramona. How much sleep have you had?"

Wearily, she rubbed her forehead. "Precious little. This flu seems like it's about to run its course, however, and once we get through the weekend, most of the tourists will go home, and maybe most of the burns will stop, too." In reality, the truth was that she had not slept more than three hours at a stretch since Tuesday, and she wasn't twenty-four anymore. She felt the exhaustion in her shoulders, at the back of her neck and in her grainy eyes.

"Take tomorrow off," Dr. Richards said. "I'll cover for you."

Ramona frowned, shaking her head. "I appreciate the offer, but you have plenty going on here yourself." She took a chart from the hanging files along the wall. "How is Mr. Redfeather?"

"No, you don't," he said, and plucked the chart out of her hands. "You can't treat patients when you can't even see straight. The VA is sending a couple of residents up to help, and we can cover you."

Ramona knew he was right. "Let's make a deal." She grabbed the chart back. "Let me look in on my patients tonight, and I'll take off until morning."

"No deal. You take off till Monday morning and I'll let you go visit the old codgers."

"Monday!"

"Come on, woman. You're young and healthy and you need to do more than work. Get some sleep, then head over to the picnic and watch some fireworks." He smiled. "Doctor's orders."

She pursed her lips. The truth was, she was exhausted and fed up with the crisis. If she took a day off, her humor would surely be restored. "Are you sure?"

"Yes."

"And you'll call me if you need me?"

He held up three fingers. "Scout's honor."

"Then we have a deal." She took out another chart to add to the pile, then as casually as she could, asked, "How is Jake Forrest doing?"

A flicker of a smile crossed Dr. Richards's face. "Well, there's no question he's got a classic case of PTSD, but along with that goes the classic resistance. I haven't had any luck getting him to talk to a counselor or go to a group."

Ramona shook her head. "Too bad."

"You know, just out of curiosity, why did you refer him? You're one of the best with cases like this."

She lifted a shoulder, carefully training her gaze on the charts. "I was becoming personally involved." She took a steadying breath. "I also thought he might respond better to a man and a soldier, instead of..." She paused. "How did he put it? 'What can a woman know about any of it?' Or words to that effect."

"Ah. Macho man."

Once, Ramona would have agreed with him, but now she wasn't sure the label fitted. Still, maybe she shouldn't be the one to judge. "Something like that."

He moved toward the door. "Do your rounds, then I want you to go home and sleep. Got it?"

"Yes, sir!" Ramona saluted smartly, drawing from him the chuckle she'd hoped she would.

Jake hurried down to the sun-room, his stash for Harry hidden in his coat. A light rain was falling outside, making the room seem even gloomier. It was empty.

Frowning, Jake went to Harry's room. The old man lay in bed, covered by heavy blankets. His complexion was waxy and his hair hadn't been washed. "Hey, old man," Jake greeted, pulling up a chair. "What did you do? Go and get sick on me?"

Harry gave a raspy cough. "What the hell happened to you? Were you brawlin', boy?"

Jake winced. Harry had been a cop after his years in the service, and he wouldn't take kindly to this story. "I had a little accident in my car."

"Little?"

"Well..." Jake cleared his throat. "I totaled it."

"Damn, boy. You haven't got the sense God gave a monkey. Didn't I tell you sports cars are bad news?"

"You did, Harry. I didn't listen."

The old man looked disgusted. "Crank me up so I can sit straight. This bed is driving me crazy."

Jake complied. "I brought your stuff. Sorry I haven't been here, but it's been hard to get a ride."

"I told you before not to worry about it when you can't come. I get along all right."

"I know," Jake said. "You want me to stash everything in your closet?"

Harry looked at the door. "The cigarettes you can put in my coat pocket there. Close the door and give me the ale. I'll hide it under the covers."

Jake grinned. "You got it." From beneath his jacket, he took the single bottle of ale, and walking across the room, he hid the cigarettes and closed the door. On the way back, he noticed the other bed in the room was empty. "Where's your roomie?"

Harry sipped his ale and sighed deeply. "Damn, that's good. One of life's finer things." He settled back, the bottle hidden under the covers. "George died last night. Cold as ice when they tried to wake him up this morning."

"I'm sorry."

Harry shot him a glare through rheumy eyes. "Man couldn't speak, and every minute he was awake, he was in pain. Death was a blessing, boy."

Jake lowered his head. Obviously, Harry was put out with him, no matter what he said. "Well, how are you feeling? Did you catch this flu?"

"That's what they said."

In the corner, the television news played a clip of tanks moving in the mountains somewhere, maybe Bosnia or Croatia. Jake felt a sharp, stabbing pain and looked away.

"You sleeping any better?" Harry asked.

"Sometimes." Jake folded his hands. "Ramona brought me a cat. She said it might help."

Harry chuckled. "Now there's a woman. Pretty little thing, and plenty of meat on her bones. I like a woman like that."

A vision of her naked breasts and round tummy flashed in Jake's mind, and he sighed. "Yeah. Me, too. Too bad she's so damned busy all the time."

"She still your doctor?"

"No. I'm with Dr. Richards."

"Yeah? Why?"

Jake shrugged, but he thought he knew. "I yelled at her one night. Told her she didn't have a clue what was bothering me. I mean, really—" he spread his hands "—what can a woman like her know about all this? She's the most protected, cheerful little thing I ever met."

"You got it wrong, Jake."

"What do you mean?" Harry had gone very still, and on his face was an expression of fury and sorrow Jake had never seen. "What is it?"

"I got something to tell you, boy, but if you tell another soul, I'll haunt you till the day you die."

Perplexed, Jake leaned forward. "Tell me."

Harry settled, then lifted his ale for another sip before he began. "That woman has seen plenty of pain, pain like a man will never understand. You know what I'm getting at?"

A prickle of foreboding moved through Jake's chest. "Maybe."

"It must have been that winter after you went to West Point. I was on duty. A winter afternoon, nothing much going on. We were playing poker in the squad room, waiting for the shift to be over so we could go home."

The prickle grew stronger. Jake wasn't sure he wanted to hear this. This was starting like one of Harry's war stories, the stories that had so enthralled him as a boy. Harry had a talent for starting slow, relating normal, everyday details that served to illuminate horrors in a way nothing else could. "Harry, maybe if it's a secret—"

"You need to hear this."

Jake took a breath. Nodded.

"There we were, this boring afternoon. Nothing to do, and in walks this little girl." Harry swallowed, his eyes focused on that long-ago day. "She was beat up pretty bad. Had these marks on her neck and mouth, and she didn't have on any shoes."

Jake found his breath coming too fast, like a panic attack was coming on. He fought the urge to cover his ears, to block the terrible thing he knew he was about to find out.

"You see that look one time, and it stays with you forever. It was plain she'd been raped. But there she was, shivering and no coat. She walked all the way out of the mountains like that. She didn't shed a tear, either, just came up to us and said real calm, 'Some boys raped me, and I left them passed out up near Henrietta Pass. They'll freeze if you don't go get them.'"

Horrified, Jake stared at Harry, his mind almost unable to grasp Harry's words. "They...raped her?"

"Yeah. We kept it real quiet, so she wouldn't have to deal with people staring and calling names, you know, like they do. I was half-tempted to just let them freeze to death up there, but we called the rangers, and they fetched the bastards. Kids from college, out on a break. Drunk and stupid and mean."

"Why are you telling me, Harry? I'm sure she'd rather people didn't know."

"I'm not telling people, boy. I'm telling you. She knows what she's talking about when she says people can make peace with things. She knows how to help you, if you'll just let her."

Something very like tears gathered behind Jake's eyes and clogged his throat. He bowed his head, pressing his palms hard into his eyes. "Damn."

"Jake."

He raised his head.

"I'm worried about you, son. You need help."

Panic welled up in him and then Jake stood suddenly. "I gotta get out of here. Sorry, Harry. I'll be back tomorrow or the next day."

Harry only nodded. "You do what you have to do, son."

Jake left the VA home on foot, walking aimlessly in the light drizzle, along sidewalks cracked since his childhood, past homes with wide porches and tall trees grown up to shade the lush green lawns. Through the windows, he glimpsed families sitting down to dinner and waved to people rocking on porch swings. He walked through downtown, past the B&B café and the old honky-tonk his father had favored.

And still his chest ached and his head roared and he couldn't seem to catch his breath. Over and over he saw violent images of Ramona being so brutally violated. Walking through the snow to town. *Without her shoes.* Bruised and ravaged and hurt. He shoved the pictures away, but they kept coming back. Ramona without her shoes in the snow, walking back to town with bruises and sorrows and pains he didn't want to imagine.

Rage swelled and choked him. Brutality was everywhere, creeping into everything, staining the world. In his memory, he heard a boy screaming, and the sound became mixed up with Ramona crying.

No, Harry said she hadn't cried.

Blindly, he ducked into a little bar and ordered a Scotch, straight, and drank it in a single gulp. It burned through the thickness in his throat and he ordered another. The ache dulled a little, and the images finally halted. The bartender suggested he quit after four and cut him off at six, then called him a cab. The cab. There was only one. That struck Jake as slightly absurd.

Outside, the rain had stopped. Reflected light shimmered in spots across the wet blacktop, blue and red and white, and it made him sad for some reason he couldn't name. Inside the cab, he couldn't breathe and rolled down the window to suck in a gulp of rain-scented air.

Abruptly, he was sober. Or nearly so. More than he wanted to be. Fury welled in his chest and roared through his mind, and he knew where he wanted to be. He gave the cabbie the address.

Ramona took a long, hot bath and washed her hair. Padding around the house in her nightgown and robe, she made an omelet for supper, with toast and jam and a big mug of hot chocolate. Outside, a light rain pattered in the pines and against her windows, and the sound was relaxing. Her dogs, deprived of her attention the past few days, arranged themselves in a half circle around her, and if she moved, they followed. It became annoying after a while. "Come on, you guys,'' she finally said in exasperation. ''I swear I'm not going anywhere tonight.''

She was wiping off the stove and thinking gratefully of her bed when Manuelito jumped up and started barking furiously at the back door. Startled, Ramona looked at the clock and saw that it was nearly eleven. Who could be out there? Quickly, she went to get her gun and cocked it. The other two dogs took up the intruder alert, and Ramona waited, rifle at the ready.

When the knock sounded on her back door, she nearly swallowed her tongue. She'd been half hoping it was a bear or some other mountain creature making its way over her property, but no animal knocked.

''Who is it?'' she called out.

''Me, Ramona. Jake.''

She flung open the door with equal portions of relief and irritation. ''This is the second time you've nearly gotten yourself shot. Have you ever heard of a phone?'' He simply stood there, framed by the screen door, his dark hair damp and brushed back from his face, his hands loosely tucked in his pockets. Ramona finally registered the utter misery that shadowed his blue eyes. ''God, Jake, what is it?''

''Can I come in?''

''Yes. Yes, of course.'' She pushed open the wooden screen. ''Are you all right?''

He came into the kitchen, not taking his hands out of his pockets, and turned to face her. The hollows under his eyes were deep and dark, and his jaw had that gaunt look of sorrow. He hadn't looked this haunted since the first time she saw him at the wedding. ''No,'' he said finally. ''I'm not all right.''

She smelled the Scotch on his breath. ''Sit down. I'll make you some coffee.''

''I don't want coffee.''

Ramona halted. ''What do you want?''

He closed his eyes, and it made him look unbearably weary. He seemed to sway on his feet, and she wondered just how much he'd had to drink. Quite a bit. Putting the gun away on its rack, she moved around him to the sink. Water would be best under the circumstances. Plain old water to wash the poisons out of his system.

Gently, she put her hands on his shoulders, intending to steer him to a chair. But he grabbed her fingers and kissed them, and Ramona was—for a moment—lost. "Ramona..." He cursed softly, profanely. "I can't stop thinking. I can't turn it off. It's killing me."

"What is, Jake? Tell me about it."

He lowered his head, closed his eyes as if to shut out the visions that tormented him. "There's no peace, is there? Not anywhere." His voice was ragged.

And Ramona, who'd been tending strays and patching up soldiers for most of her life, could do nothing but reach for him. He swayed forward dangerously, his hands catching around her waist, his head falling to her shoulder.

"There is peace, Jake," she whispered. "Right here. Right now." She put her hand against his hair, stroking it to soothe him. Against her body, she could feel the bone-deep trembling of a man resisting his pain. "Let it go, Jake. Let go of that pain."

He only moaned, a quiet howl of grief, and his fingers dug into her side as he pressed his face harder into her neck. "I want to be in you, Ramona," he said.

Now it was her turn to close her eyes. To resist. His soul was bleeding, and so was his heart, and he needed her. She ached to give him what he thought he wanted, but her instincts told her it would be wrong. "No, Jake. Not like this. Not drunk."

He lifted his head, and in his eyes she saw he was lost in a wilderness of pain and bewilderment. "Then just let me hold you." As if his head were too heavy to hold up, he lowered it slowly, putting his forehead against hers. "Please."

In that single instant, Ramona knew it was too late for her. She wasn't falling in love; she'd already fallen. All the way. Way, way over her head. In this tortured man who had nothing to give her, she had found the one man she wanted for all time. It wasn't logical or reasonable or even possible, but the fact remained. She loved him.

And because she did, she cupped his cheek tenderly with her hand. "All right," she whispered. "Come lie down with me."

She led Jake to her bedroom, redolent still of patchouli and roses from her bath. He sank onto the bed and kicked off his shoes, then lay down in all his clothes. Ramona turned off the light and went to stretch out next to him, leaving on her robe. She covered them both with the quilt. Jake put his arms around her, pulling her tightly into his embrace. Ramona nestled her head in the hollow of his shoulder and put her hand on his chest, over his heart.

In moments, he was sound asleep. And Ramona, pierced, lay a long time in the darkness listening to his heart beat and his breath move in and out of his lungs before she, too, fell prey to her exhaustion and slept.

Chapter 14

In his dream, it was bright and hot. A furnace blast of wind, eternally laden with sand, tossed grit in his face. Mirages shimmered on the horizon and mingled with the black smoke from burning oil wells. Jake sat, his gun on his knees, and viewed the scene with a vast sense of hopelessness. They had been victorious. They had vanquished the invaders and freed the beleaguered people of Kuwait.

But the grit battered his sunburned face, stinging like biting gnats, and the air stank of death and oil and he wished only to be somewhere far, far away. He hated himself for it, but he also knew he wasn't alone. They all wanted to escape.

Into the quiet came a cry. Thin and weak, but distinctly a cry of pain.

And then in his dream, his hand was clasped tightly around the small, dirty hand of a child, and an agonized sound of unimaginable pain ripped through the blinding desert noon, ceaseless and excruciating.

As he had a thousand times, Jake started awake, half-sitting up with a cry on his own lips, a hand tightly wrapped in his own, horror in his throat and belly, torn by an anguish he could never escape.

This time, he was not alone. This time, a woman's soft form flowed around him, smelling of soap and sweetness and honor, her hair a gliding silkiness brushing his arms, her breasts full and giving against his arm. "Shh," she whispered, and stroked his brow. "Shh. I'm here. It was only a dream."

Her hand was cool against his forehead, her body a comfort he could never have imagined. Jake pulled her close to him, tucked her next to his heart and let himself be soothed, let the trembling seep away, let the horror glide on flapping bat wings into another man's dream.

A miracle. A miracle. He breathed the word as she stroked his head and his temples, and somehow, somehow, he drifted away into sleep again.

A miracle.

There was light in the room the next time he awakened, and Jake was alone. Disoriented and dry mouthed from the copious amount of Scotch he'd consumed, he was lying in a four-poster. A Siamese cat with a white mustache was curled next to his head on the pillow, shifting only a little when Jake moved his head to look at her. "Did I take your place, sweetie?"

He felt a stab of guilt. Mr. E had been alone all night. Jake had fed him before going to the VA home, but he had probably been lonely.

Through the open door of the room, Jake heard Ramona humming and the faint clink of utensils. The smell of coffee and something cooking wafted into the room, and the combination struck him as powerfully harmonious. Comforting. Of course she would hum when she cooked. Of course she would cook a breakfast. Of course she would have a bed like this enormous four-poster with its patchwork quilt and a big fern hanging in front of the window. Of course the walls would be polished pine, and the artwork scenes of gardens and nature that soothed the eye and the spirit.

Slowly, he sat up, amazed to find his head wasn't too bad. His mouth felt like a sewer, and he didn't like to think of his appearance, but maybe the morning wouldn't be so bad. As he stood up, he had the sense that something terrible had happened and he tried to remember what it was. Why he was in Ramona's house at all this morning—

It rushed back, the terrible story Harry had told him. Stunned all over again, Jake sank back onto the bed. He bowed his head, fighting the new rage the memory brought, the rage that made him wish to be armed with his rifle.

In the kitchen, Ramona's humming became a song. It was a beautiful sound. Her voice was a surprisingly strong soprano, the song something exotic and lilting. Maybe a folk song.

He lifted his head. He looked again at the bed. At the picture of a purply red geranium in the rain that hung over the trunk in the corner. He inhaled the aromas of coffee and soap and the meaty smell of cooking. And remembered her holding him in the night, taking him to her bed with a heart full of love and trust.

How had she done it? How had she weathered such a monstrous act? Urgently, he stood up again, meaning to go in and ask her, then he stopped. Instead, he went to the bathroom first and washed his face. He heard her song coming closer and then her gentle knock on the door. "There's a toothbrush in the linen closet. Towels, too, if you want a shower."

Suddenly, he did. He wanted to wash away the howling of the night before, the shame of coming to her in his pain when she had borne so much herself. He wanted to wash away four years of cowardice and be the man he once had been, that strong, proud soldier who might have—

Standing under the spray, he left the thought unfinished. Might have what? Saved her? Protected her? Wreaked vengeance?

All of it. For his whole life, he had believed a soldier did just that. Noble things. Good things. Made the world safe for women like Ramona, for boys like Curtis and Cody, for the innocent and helpless. Soldiers were heroes who fought and got bloody and died so no one else would have to. And it was all such a lie. There was no such thing as a hero. No such thing as keeping anyone safe.

It made him breathless with sorrow. He put his head against the cool tile and forced himself to take in a deep breath, to suck it all the way to the bottom of his lungs. One thing he could do for Ramona was stop hassling her, dumping his pain on her. Stop making an ass of himself with drink and reckless driving, or at least do it where she wouldn't see him.

Carefully, he combed his hair, realizing it was way past his collar. In a fit of self-loathing, he stared at his face, at the yellowing bruises, his unshaven jaw, his hollow eyes. He looked like he was dying. Maybe he was.

Before he opened the door, he halted and squared his shoulders. Show time, as Bob Fosse always said. One thing he would not do again was burden Ramona Hardy. Not for another single second.

She was stirring something in a big cast-iron pan on the stove when he came in. She still wore her robe, but she'd pulled back her hair from her face. The light was dim and cool, and he realized it was raining, giving a musical undertone to the morning.

Against the tumble of plants and the quiet light, Ramona looked like one of her pictures—fertile and motherly and sensual and beautiful. Halted in the doorway, Jake could only look at her, feeling helplessly ensnared as desire washed over him, filling his every cell with a potent, powerful yearning.

She glanced up and smiled. "Good morning."

He swallowed and stepped into the room, almost dizzy. "I'm not drunk anymore," he said.

Carefully, she put down the big spoon she was using. "I can see that."

He crossed the floor in his bare feet and stopped in front of her, lifting his hands to put them around her face. "You're so beautiful," he said, gazing deeply into her velvety brown eyes. He smoothed her hair from her face. "So sweet."

She looked at him wordlessly, her hands on either side bracing her against the counter.

"Last night," he said quietly, "Harry told me what happened to you." He paused. "He told me about the rape."

Disappointment washed over her face, disappointment and something else, maybe despair or sorrow. "And so you came here to ask me about it."

"No. No. I don't remember why I came here." He put his hands on her shoulders. "I was so angry, thinking of it. I can't even breathe whenever I let it come back into my mind. I wish that hadn't happened to you."

She didn't meet his eyes. "So do I."

And now a hundred questions did crowd into his mind. A thousand. He grabbed the first one. "How can you be the way you are after something like that?"

"How am I, Jake?" For the first time since he'd met her, there was an edge to her words, a hardness in her face. "What exactly do you mean?"

He hated himself for doing this, but he ached to know the answers. "You're one of the most sensual women I've ever known. You make sex feel like a joy. How can you be so free?"

She lifted her eyes, and Jake glimpsed the wariness she tried to keep hidden, the core of strength and courage deep within her. He saw the fierce stubbornness of a survivor. "Those boys..." she began, then stopped. Taking a breath, she tried again. "Those boys took a lot from me. They stole my innocence, and for a long time, my ability to trust. I was afraid all the time, I couldn't focus and I had nightmares." She swallowed. "I still have nightmares. I still have scars on my body. I won't ever be able to put on a pair of cross-country skis again." She smiled bitterly. "My hands shake so badly I can't fasten my buckles."

Her voice was very calm, very matter-of-fact. Jake felt sorrow rise in him, sucking away the heat of his rage. His throat grew thick.

She looked away, and now her voice was not nearly as steady. "For years, I carried a terrible burden of hatred—" she paused, her gaze focused on some distant spot "—and rage. You can't imagine what it's like to be overpowered that way, to be so helpless." Her voice quavered. "They hurt me a lot."

Jake didn't trust himself to speak. His eyes felt hot.

She took a deep breath. "But when I finally started to want to get well, to really heal, I knew one of the things I had to take back was sex. I couldn't let them take that from me, on top of everything else. I couldn't let one day define the whole rest of my life. Do you understand?"

"Yes," he whispered, rubbing her shoulders.

"And I haven't. My life belongs to *me*." Her voice broke. She gave a little cry and put her head against his chest.

He clutched her close, as close as he could, while she wept against his chest. And his own hot tears fell, where she could not see them, where she would not know how he ached for her. How he wished he could take that burden and carry it for her! "You're so brave, Ramona. You'd be a good soldier."

She choked a little, almost a sound of laughter, but only clasped him tighter. "I never told anyone all of that. How mad I was. How it hurt. How much I hated them."

He rocked her and kissed her hair and smoothed his hands down her back. "I'm sorry to make you think about it."

"Sometimes it's good to bring it out. It loses power that way."

Against his body she was soft and warm and comforting, and he felt as he had last night. Whole for as long as she touched him. Maybe it was that, or her willingness to share her story, but he found himself shutting his eyes very tight and pulling her as close as he could. "There was a little boy in a Kuwait village. The village had been bombed ahead of our arrival, and there wasn't a lot of it left."

He halted, unsure he could go on with it, even with Ramona holding him. As if she sensed his conflict, she pressed into him, and her hands moved on his back.

And he found he could go on after all. He told her the reality behind the dream, of the boy crushed in the rubble and his endless, endless scream. "Whenever I go to sleep, that scream returns to haunt me. I feel like I'm never going to stop hearing him scream."

She pulled away a little and took his face in her hands, stood on her tiptoes and kissed him.

Something in him just gave way. Jake groaned, hauling her roughly to him. He opened his mouth and she met him in a deep, searing kiss, their bodies pressed into a tight, almost breathless embrace. He grasped her head, his fingers lost in her thick, glorious hair. Tilting his head, he plunged his tongue into her mouth, needing to taste her, feel her, love her. His whole body yearned for her, and he could feel her hands on him, roving, exploring, clutching. Needing.

He touched her neck with his open palms, absorbing the fragile delicacy of the skin, and slid his hands down to her collarbone and shoulders beneath her robe. His fingers stumbled on the slim straps of her nightgown, and he pushed them away, all the while kissing her and kissing her and kissing her.

A sense of urgency flooded him, an unstoppable and furious need to be with her, to touch and taste all of her, to be buried in her and absorbed by her. He unfastened the belt of her robe and pushed it away and off her arms. She cried out softly and helped him shrug it free. He surfaced momentarily for breath, and with a swift movement, he skimmed the simple, silky gown to her waist, exposing her breasts to his gaze. Reverently, he touched her and kissed her again, whispering her name in a chant.

And then there was no time, no thought, only her hands on his skin, and her mouth against his, her lush body against his palms and his mouth and his raging member. His shirt came off and fell to the floor, and he groaned aloud as she slid her torso against his and touched his sides with the tender skin of her inner arms, their bodies brushing and colliding and settling into a swaying, dizzying motion. She lifted her head and gasped, "My bed," and somehow they backtracked to the cosy, pine-paneled room with its four-poster.

As long as he lived, Jake knew he would never smell roses or patchouli without thinking of Ramona falling to the bed, clad only in her panties. Ramona holding out her arms, her hair spread around her, her eyes smoky and dark as he shed his jeans and came to her, flowed over her. His thighs and hers, his groin pressed to the heat of her, her lips and her breasts and her hands all over him, hungry and eager. Low, pleased sounds came from her as he tasted her and slid against her. He would never forget the way she knelt over him, her hair and breasts sweeping forward to brush his excruciatingly aroused skin, to put her mouth on him as if she loved the taste of his flesh.

He would never listen to the rain pattering against the glass and the trees without remembering Ramona beneath him, waiting as he poised himself above her, Ramona so hot and close around him, making him whole as she took him into her, wrapping him with her arms and legs, breathing against his neck a soft, loving litany of encouragement, Ramona as she rocked and clutched him.

They became liquid, flowing together. He was no longer aware of where he ended and where she began. When he spilled into her, it was not only his seed, but his heart and soul and life and body, all pieces and shreds, and he felt her spirit fill him in return, felt the flow of their union go between them like some ethereal, unseen ribbon born of the colors they made, wrapping them, binding them. He kissed her and felt her pulse around him, and with a cry, he buried his face against her shoulder and let her love him, hold him.

And for a moment, in Ramona's arms, he was alive and whole and saved.

Love washed through Ramona on waves of pleasure and desire and wonder. Jake lay heavily against her, his great dark head buried in her shoulder, and she held him close, within and without, wanting him to be with her always, never to part from her again. She would lie in this bed with him for as long as she lived, never leaving it, as long as he would stay.

His mouth moved on her throat, infinitely gentle, so much sweeter than she would have imagined of him.

Then he was kissing her jaw, and her face, and her mouth and her eyes. His hands wound around her head, his palms over her ears, and he kissed her as if she was some precious, long-wished-for being, as if she was his most sacred love.

She touched his hair, the dark, thick strands tangling around her fingers, and let him kiss her, and she kissed him in return. So precious. So vulnerable. So full of pain.

But here in her arms, he had found peace for a little while. In her arms, he had slept all night. Once he had awakened, crying out, and instinctively, Ramona had known it was the same dream that had haunted him, the dream that pinned him to the past. But holding her hand so tightly she'd feared her fingers would be crushed, he had fallen asleep again. It seemed a very large victory.

The intense intimacy had to end, and it did, all too soon. Jake moved, first to pull the quilt over them, then to lie on his side facing her, his head cradled on his arm. With one big, dark hand, he reached out and covered her breast. "Are you okay?"

Ramona had not been sure. She felt as if the whole world had shifted in those rain-colored moments of their love-making, as if nothing would ever be the same again. It frightened her. But his hand felt right, and his voice was the voice she had waited for, and she turned to face him, to put her hands on him. She smiled. "I'm wonderful, thank you. Are you okay?"

He chuckled, and Ramona felt the sound in her palm, held against the silky dark hair that glazed his hard chest. "I've been a lot worse."

In the low gray light, his eyes were a blue so clear and bright they were almost painful to look upon. Long black lashes and his deeply tanned skin increased the contrast. "You have beautiful eyes," she said. With the tips of her fingers, she lightly touched his cheekbone, rubbed the prickles of his unshaved beard. Soberly, he let her, and Ramona touched his beautiful, unsmiling mouth.

Everything *had* changed, Ramona realized. Everything.

Somehow, Jake had turned her life upside down, making her feel things, wild things. Until he had come into her life, with the roar and intensity of a tormented lion, she had been very careful. She had created for herself a safe and comfortable environment, had put up walls of kindness and goodness. And within that secure and beautiful world, she had lived without fear or worry, serving as well as she could and living out her dreams within a walled garden.

But like a wild creature, Jake had scaled those walls and stalked her among the flowers, tempting her from the first to stroke his dangerously beautiful hide. And even knowing she could be mauled, the temptation had proven too great to resist.

Now, as she let her eyes feast on his masculine form, she felt desire creep up her spine and fill her body, and she rose on one elbow and pushed away the quilt that covered him, pushed it down to his waist. A brilliance burned in his sapphire eyes and he fell back as if he understood she wanted to look at him. Without shyness, she admired his lean, long torso, tracing the dark line of hair over his belly. He was too thin, his body showing only the muscles he must have gained as a soldier and the fine elegance of bones. "You don't eat enough," she said.

Her hair had fallen over her shoulders, to half cover her breasts, and Jake reached out to lift it away. "I want to look at you, too." His fingers lightly brushed her nipples.

It aroused her to have him admire her, to look at her body as if it was beautiful, and she wondered if he felt the same way. She pushed the quilt lower and exposed his member and his thighs and his knees, then she pushed it all the way off him so she could admire his ankles and feet, too.

She rocked back to rest on her knees and looked at him, all of him. His hand stroked her thigh, but he said nothing as she continued to admire his splendid form. She felt marvelously pagan dressed only in her hair, unashamed of her plumpness as she always had been before.

"You look like some mythical goddess of nature," he said quietly, moving to touch her. "All hair and eyes and breasts. I think that must be what you are." He curled toward her, putting his lean thigh over her legs as he kissed her ribs. "You're magic, I know that."

Ramona clasped his head and pressed her mouth to his hair, feeling heat and hunger rise up in her again as his mouth found her breast, as his tongue flickered over the aching tip. "Oh, no," she whispered, "you're the one who's magic."

He tumbled her sideways, and they fell into a lazy exploration, seeking the tender spots and the ticklish ones, touching and kissing and stroking. A long time later, they made love again, very slowly, in contrast to the furious heat of their first joining. Slowly, he entered her, and slowly he moved, and slowly, easily, Ramona met him. Easily, slowly, gently, they kissed and touched and drifted, lost in one another for a long, long time in the rain-swept morning.

And as he moved within her, and over her, and became one with her, Ramona knew it had been worth whatever happened later. Whatever happened when she lost him, she would always have this morning to remember, this morning when she had made Jake forget his sorrows and his pain, this morning when she had been beautiful and whole.

She had held the lion.

Chapter 15

"Much as I hate to do it," Jake said, "I'm going to have to get home and take care of Mr. E. I'm sure he's lonely by now."

They were lingering over second cups of coffee, the remains of a very late breakfast scattered over the table. Ramona felt replete and content. "I understand. I guess you need a ride, too, don't you?"

"That I do." Under the table, he covered her bare foot with his. "Then I think I'm obligated to go to my mother's house for what was supposed to be a picnic, a little pre-Fourth celebration."

Ramona glanced at the still-gray skies and chuckled. "Cancel the picnic."

"She'll just move it inside." He hesitated. "Don't suppose you'd want to go with me?"

A strange little stab pricked Ramona's heart. Go with him to his mother's house? Where everyone would take one look at them and know exactly what was going on? "I don't know if that's a good idea, Jake. It might be... uncomfortable."

"I won't be uncomfortable. And you know the whole family. It isn't like being around a bunch of strangers."

"I know." Still, her gut told her it was a bad idea. This thing between them was new and precious and private, and she didn't know how it would change when it was reflected back to them from the eyes of his family. "They'll all be able to tell we've..." She almost said, "become lovers," but that made it sound like an ongoing thing, and Ramona suspected quite the opposite was true. "We've been lovers."

He reached for her hand. "'Been,' Ramona?" His thumb moved over her wrist. "Does that mean we won't be anymore?"

It was hard to look straight at him, at that face full of elegant planes and sensual angles, at the vivid blue of those eyes, and think anything at all. "I don't know. Will we?"

Her question hung uneasily in the room. Ramona heard her need for reassurance in it and hated herself for it.

Jake bent his head and kissed her inner wrist very gently. "Please come with me today."

Light caught in his dark hair, glossing the crown, and Ramona touched it, glorying in the heavy, silky feeling of it against her palm and in the shape of his head beneath. Her heart ached with the wonder of him, with the sheer pounding force of her love for him. And even though she knew it wasn't wise, she said, "All right. I'll go."

Louise was totally in her element. The refrigerator bulged with potato salad—made with mustard seed, her secret ingredient—pasta salad with olives and fresh tomatoes and green onions, and gallons of sweet tea, brewed in the sunshine all day yesterday.

In the oven were baked beans and her extraspecial, to-die-for barbecue chicken, which would have been better cooked over the grill, but tasted just as fine coming out of the oven. It was the sauce that made it special.

In the living room, playing a game of Chutes and Ladders with her grandsons, were Lance and Tamara, still newlyweds enough to want to be touching all the time. Tyler had delivered Curtis to the house last night, but had begged off himself, pleading a need to sleep off his flu. Louise had taken one look at his red-rimmed eyes and pasty skin and excused him.

In the dining room, Alonzo entertained two of Louise's museum friends with tales of the Mexican revolution, in which his father had ridden with Pancho Villa. Both women listened, rapt, as he described a dangerous mission across the desert, his words lilting and falling in musically accented English. Louise smiled. She never tired of the sound of his voice and evidently she wasn't alone.

Dinner was almost ready, and she glanced at the clock with a frown. Jake still hadn't shown up. It worried her. She hoped he hadn't gone out and gotten himself in more trouble. He'd pretty much managed to avoid her since her visit to the hospital, and she wondered if maybe she'd been a little harsh in her lecture.

Taking the huge roasting pan of chicken out of the oven, she set her mouth in a firm line. No, she hadn't been too hard on him. He'd acted the fool, driving down that mountain like he was sixteen and stupid. By now, he ought to have learned he was mortal.

A slim young woman came into the kitchen. "You need help with anything?" she asked. She, too, had an accent, but it was decidedly less lyrical than Alonzo's. Anna Passanante, the new curator of the museum for which Louise worked part-time, was a native of Queens.

Louise straightened. "Well, let's see. You can chase that

chatty Alonzo out of my dining room and we can start setting the table."

Curtis, her son Tyler's boy, ran into the kitchen and flung himself around Anna's legs. "Tell me a story, Miss Anna! Pleathe?"

Anna patted his head. "Right now I'm going to help your grandma set the table. After we eat, okay?"

"The dragon story?"

"Absolutely." She gave him a stack of napkins. "You can help me if you want. You want?"

Curtis nodded happily, and Louise felt a pang. Curtis ached for a mother. Although Louise spent as much time as she could with the boy, it wasn't quite the same. His own mother had died in childbirth, so Curtis had never known her, but his father showed no signs of ever getting over her.

As Curtis rushed off to put the napkins on the table, Louise said, "You're sweet to be so good to him."

"He's a good boy. I feel sad for him."

A commotion arose at the front door. Louise peeked around the corner, and relief rushed through her when she saw Jake come in. To her surprise, someone came in behind him, a woman bundled in a raincoat and hat. Louise frowned, hoping he hadn't brought one of his bubbleheads around for her to be nice to.

But the woman took off her hat, her long, pretty hair spilling out over her shoulders, and Louise smiled broadly, cutting a glance toward Alonzo, who winked. It was Ramona Hardy, looking a little shy and flushed. And if Louise was not mistaken, the woman had that slightly blurry, dazzled look about her that meant she'd been recently and thoroughly loved.

Louise couldn't help chuckling quietly to herself. Alonzo joined her in the doorway, putting his hand on her arm. "The doctor, no?"

"Am I good?"

Alonzo looked at her soberly. "Do not meddle today, do you hear?"

"I never meddle."

He snorted. Taking her hand, he pulled her back into the kitchen. "You meddle," he said. "Always thinking about everybody else. Think about you, today, hmm?"

"Alonzo, this whole day is for my family. Let me enjoy giving it to them."

"Okay." He nodded, and his mustache wiggled. "But then, let me give you something, okay?"

She frowned. "Like what?"

Before she could blink, he pressed a kiss to her mouth. He held her arm loosely, right above the elbow, and his mustache tickled her lip. Louise didn't even have time to close her eyes, so she was looking deep into his eyes with those starry lashes while he kissed her.

Just as quickly, he straightened. With a wink, he said, "You want to think so much about romance, maybe you should think a little about me, hmm?"

He left her standing there in the middle of her kitchen. Louise lifted her hand to her mouth, and for a brief, wild moment, she felt about fourteen. *He kissed me!*

It was a very good feeling indeed.

Jake knew it was a mistake the minute he walked into the house and saw his mother's expression. It was the cat-that-swallowed-the-canary look—a suppressed grin, a shine in her eyes. And he wondered how he had forgotten her faked sprained ankle. Had she been matchmaking?

The notion that he'd somehow been manipulated caused him to feel a suffocating sense of pressure in his lungs. He didn't want to *think,* not about Ramona or his future or anything else. He just wanted to keep this sense of warmth and satisfaction she gave him. Thinking would mean facing everything—not only his own wounded psyche, but what had happened to Ramona and how that made him feel.

No.

He slid a glance at Ramona out of the corner of his eye, wondering if she sensed his panic. Maybe she had been right—this was a mistake. And he didn't want her to feel uncomfortable or strange or—

Covertly, she squeezed his arm and moved into the room. "Tamara!" she cried, and crossed the wide living room to give the woman a hug. "You look gorgeous!"

Even Tamara, who was somewhat shy and reserved, couldn't resist Ramona. She jumped up to accept Ramona's embrace.

Curtis and Cody rushed forward, chasing away gloomy thoughts. "Uncle Jake!" they cried.

"Give uth piggyback ridth!" Curtis pleaded, jumping up and down.

"No, I want to play alligator!"

Relieved to have a distraction, Jake dropped on all fours. "Hop on, guys."

"Oh, boy! Horsie!"

But the respite didn't last long. The boys were called to wash their hands, and Jake was left to sit down in the living room with Tamara and Lance, who sat side by side. Holding hands. Tamara had a sunny glow from their trip to the islands, and Lance looked—Jake frowned—happy.

Ramona sat in a chair near Tamara. Jake sat in a chair across the room. He couldn't imagine himself all tangled up with her the way Tamara and Lance were sitting, holding hands and making eyes at each other. Not all the time—Tamara wasn't like that. But every so often, they'd look at each other and something would flash between them. Rich and hot and deep.

Jake felt a little pang. He glanced at Ramona. Her hands were folded neatly in her lap, and she appeared to be perfectly comfortable. Along her jaw was a faint reddish mark, and he frowned, then realized it was a whisker burn. A sudden flash of her beneath him, holding him, washed through him, heating his blood. Following that came a sense of embarrassment. She looked as if she'd been well loved. Would everyone see that?

Did he care? Could be. But maybe not for the reasons he might have in the past. He didn't want them to think anything about Ramona. He wanted her protected from speculation.

She didn't talk much and carefully avoided his eyes. In a little while, she excused herself to go say hello to Louise.

The conversation ground to a halt. Tamara slid her hands over her thighs and gave a bright, false smile. "Maybe I'll go see if I can help set the table. Or something."

Jake shifted. "Where's Ty?"

"He's got that flu," she answered as she headed toward the kitchen.

Jake nodded.

"So." Once they were alone, Lance leaned forward and lowered his voice. "What's up with you and the doc?"

A dozen responses rushed into his head, were considered and rejected. Finally, he said, "None of your business. Between me and her."

Unaccountably, Lance smiled. "Cool."

"What's that supposed to mean?"

"Nothing, man." Lance raised his hands, open palmed. "I always liked her."

Jake suddenly wondered if Lance knew about the rape, if he knew everything Ramona had overcome to be the woman she was today. Then he remembered what Harry had told him—everyone involved had kept it quiet so Ramona wouldn't have to face the speculation and suspicious looks that inevitably went along with such cases. He was suddenly, deeply grateful she hadn't had to endure that along with everything else.

"Hey," Lance said quietly, "chin up, man. I'm just kind of surprised. She's not your type."

"That's the whole problem," Jake said. She was way too good for him. And he would just drag her down. He'd already started.

"You ask me, it's an improvement."

Jake looked at him, and just like that, the sense of separateness kicked in. Lance didn't seem real. The room seemed like a stage set. He felt as if anything he said would echo out of him for a long time before anyone could hear him, and it would take just as long for anything they said to reach him across the vast gulf of distorted reality.

He closed his eyes, his heart racing with the knowledge that he was losing his mind.

From a great distance, he heard Lance say, "Are you all right, Jake?"

"Just a headache," he replied, lifting his head. He had plenty of practice appearing to be normal, after all. "I drank a lot of Scotch last night."

Mercifully, the boys rushed into the room just then. "Time to eat! Come on!"

Around the big dining-room table, everyone gathered. Ramona sat next to him, real and solid, and Jake was absurdly grateful. He reached for her under the table, taking her hand hard in his own. She felt like a lifeline, like the one thing he could count on to hold on to. Only her voice, chiming in with the others, seemed to reach him without that weird delay, like a film with the audio slightly out of sync.

He couldn't really eat. The beans and bread were tolerable, but the chicken in its thick sauce seemed too rich, too heavy to even look at closely. So he drank the tea and kept his hand on Ramona's leg and let the conversation wash around him, distantly observing that they all seemed to be enjoying themselves. Alonzo entertained them with his usual wild stories and slightly ribald jokes. The boys picked at their food in between rushing to the windows to see if it had stopped raining.

He did notice his mother. She sat at the head of the table, slightly mussed from the day's cooking, and practically glowed. He didn't remember ever seeing her look so happy—and surely not when his father was alive. Jake sat up a little. While he was growing up, this room had rarely been used for meals, and it had never rung with this much laughter or good feeling.

In his strangely disconnected state, it was easy to slip back into the past, to remember the rare nights Olan had made it home for supper. When he was there, the family ate in the dining room. All three boys dreaded it. Joining them at the table, he spent the meal barking out criticisms of their manners and their posture and the rare comments or stories they might venture to tell about the day. When it was just Louise and the three boys, they sat in the breakfast nook overlooking the mountains, and she invited each of them to tell one bad thing and one good thing that happened. Bad thing first, so it was canceled out by the good one. Usually.

Looking at his mother, Jake was fiercely glad that she was free at last. Free to be the happy woman nature had intended her to be, free to be round and rosy-faced and sweet-tempered, full of silly puns and robust laughter. His father had never liked the way Louise threw her head back and guffawed. Thought it made her seem common.

Picking at his plate, Jake realized his father would also have had plenty to say about Alonzo, who looked at Louise as if she were a ripe melon he couldn't wait to devour. Olan would have had plenty of critical comments about Jake's present life—he'd have jeered over Jake's choice to give up the army in favor of running a restaurant, sneered over Ramona, shaken his head knowingly when Jake wrecked his car. He'd always been so sure they'd all amount to nothing.

But his death had freed Louise. As well as Lance, who'd always played the good-time Charlie more for his father's approval than out of any real aptitude. And Jake was now free to screw up his life with abandon and totally self-destruct if he wished.

That notion made him frown, and he narrowed his eyes, wondering if his twisted brain had some agenda related to his father, if that was also playing a part in all this. A fresh wave of panic welled up, pressing the air from his lungs. He took his hand from Ramona's leg and put it against his chest. He didn't want to think.

"Jake, I wish you'd shut up," Lance said. "Person can't get a word in edgewise with you yammering all the time."

It took a moment for the words to penetrate. Jake stared blankly at his brother. Next to him, Ramona put her hand on his leg, and he jerked away, startled. Almost immediately, he understood how she would take that, and he reached for her hand, but she put it on the table. A red stain crept up her neck.

Damn. A circle of faces looked at him, waiting. Jake leaned forward and lifted his glass of tea. "Happy Fourth of July," he said, and there was only a faint trace of irony to the words.

"It isn't going to be Fourth of July if it doesn't stop raining!" Cody protested.

The phone rang, startling all of them. Louise got up to answer it and came back to point at Jake. "For you. Someone named Red Dog."

"What?" Jake found himself smiling. In relief, he went to the kitchen to take the call. "Red Dog—is it you?"

The liquor-roughened voice came clearly through the line. "Who else?"

Jake laughed, and it was a real laugh. "Where are you?"

"Well, I'm here in town. Seemed to me a Red Dog had to see a Red Creek. I'm in some little dive called the Wild Moose or somethin'—this army buddy of mine said he ran it."

The familiar rusty sound of his voice gave Jake a sudden sense of relief and brought him back to reality. "I'm kind of in the middle of something, but I can be done in a hour. Can you amuse yourself that long?"

An earthy cackle reached his ear. "I'll make friends with Jack. We'll be waitin'."

Ramona drove Jake down to the Wild Moose without saying a word. The rain had stopped and Ramona expected the weather would soon clear—long-term rain wasn't something that happened much in the mountains.

Next to her, Jake was as quiet as he'd been all day, and she didn't feel inclined to make small talk herself. There wasn't any ease or comfort in this silence, however. It roared with unsaid things, with unmet expectations and uncomfortable realizations. Ramona would be glad just to get away from him. But when she pulled into the parking lot, he didn't get out.

Trying not to look at him, she wrapped her hands tightly around the steering wheel and focused on the wet scene beyond the windshield. Thick gray clouds hung low over the mountains, and the ground shimmered with arcs of reflected light. Raindrops still pattered down steadily from the pine trees all around.

She felt him looking at her in that hard way he had, as if he could see through her skull and into her brain. After a moment, he said, "I'll call you, okay?"

The words pierced her. She closed her eyes. "Please don't patronize me."

"What does that mean?"

She looked at him, and the sight of his blue eyes in that handsome, rugged face sliced her anew. "Don't insult me by giving me one of your standard lines." She paused, wishing she could be blasé, that she could offer some witty little parting comment, but she couldn't. The past twenty-four hours had gone too deep for her, and she wouldn't pretend for his sake that they hadn't. "Just go."

He reached for her, putting his hand against her hair. Ramona winced and ducked away from his touch. "Damn you, Jake. Do you have to make this so much harder? I've been trying from the beginning to be honest about all of this. I tried to tell you—"

"Tell me what?" His voice was dangerously soft. "That you've fallen in love?"

Ramona raised her eyes. She let him see, just this once, what was in her heart. "Yes," she said simply.

He stared at her fiercely, and Ramona saw a myriad of emotions flicker across his face. Each one made him more haggard. "Ramona, you deserve so much better."

She made an impatient noise. "Just go, Jake."

"Ramona—"

She raised a hand to ward him off. "No. Don't kiss me and don't charm me and don't give me that poor-wounded-boy nonsense. I tried to be your friend and you wouldn't let that be, and now you have to deal with the consequences."

He looked stunned. And confused. For a single moment, that genuine perplexity almost moved her. Then she stiffened her resolve. "What's the matter, Jake? Hasn't anyone rejected you before?"

His face hardened. "I didn't mean to hurt you, Ramona,'' he said, and she thought his voice sounded a little rough. He opened the car door. ''I swear.''

And Ramona had to give him that. ''I know you didn't. Take care, Jake.''

He closed the door quietly. As she drove away, she saw him in her rearview mirror, watching her car disappear. He was still there when she turned the corner and lost sight of him.

It was only then that she pulled the car over into a deserted street by a park. And she put her head down and let herself cry. He really had not meant to hurt her. He hadn't intended to take anything from her that she wasn't willing to give. He had come to her instinctively, a wounded creature who needed healing, and she'd been unable to resist his need. She had given herself to him in hopes that he would somehow find that solace.

But it hadn't been enough. He was still bleeding, might still bleed to death. Even the sacrifice of her heart had not stanched the flow. She would lose him—not to some other woman or some realization of the value of his life—but to those festering, dangerous wounds.

There in the gloomy afternoon, Ramona prayed. Prayed that heaven would watch over Jake Forrest and at least keep him from killing himself. She prayed for an army of angels to guard him and tried to imagine their surrounding him in flowing robes and swift, strong wings, swords in their hands.

''Please,'' she whispered to the heavenly beings she hoped could hear. ''Keep him safe.''

Chapter 16

Sgt. Robert "Red Dog" Martinez was comfortably ensconced at the bar of the Wild Moose when Jake came in, and the very sight of his old friend made the tension in Jake's chest ease away. The waitresses who'd been fighting yesterday were now companionably bent over Red Dog's tray of wares. The man leaned on his elbows on the bar, one foot propped on the bar stool next to him. Long black hair was caught back in a leather thong, and he wore a long black raincoat and a pair of snakeskin boots.

Red Dog was, to put it mildly, crazy. He could drink more Jack Daniel's and remain standing than anyone Jake had ever seen, and he had a wild sense of humor undercut with a fierce irony that had saved morale more times than Jake could count. A good soldier. A good friend.

"All I had to do was look for the women," Jake said dryly, taking the stool next to him.

Red Dog laughed, the sound as raspy as his voice. "I was just showin' them some of my work."

On the bar was a wide, flat acrylic case lined with dark blue velveteen. In the slots cut into the foam below the fabric were silver rings, bracelets and earrings, all worked in a distinctive style with turquoise, coral, abalone and lapis lazuli. "Nice," Jake said, tugging out a pair of earrings worked with a bright turquoise inlay. The color made him think of the dress Ramona had worn to the VA home—that filmy thing that looked so pretty on her. When he realized the direction of his thoughts, he put the earrings back, his mouth tightening.

"One hundred percent American Indian made," Red Dog said, tongue in cheek. "Can't get that just anywhere."

The darkness building in Jake disappeared. He'd forgotten how Robert could do that—make everything seem like a joke. Everything in life.

"How much for this bracelet?" one of the waitresses asked.

Red Dog cocked his head and gave her a crooked smile. "For you, darlin', forty."

The woman almost visibly melted. "I'll have to come back. I don't have that much on me."

"He'll be around for a couple of days," Jake said. "I promise I'll bring him back."

Red Dog closed his case and put it beside him. The waitresses moved away reluctantly, casting glances over their shoulders. "So, how are you, man?" He lit a cigarette. "You look like hell."

"It's been a rough couple of days." Jake fingered the lingering tenderness around his eye. "Wrecked my car."

"You, too, huh?" He laughed. "I fell asleep on the way to Albuquerque a few weeks back." A frown flitted over his forehead. "Car's totaled."

"Yep," Jake said. "Mine, too. I'm not entirely sure I'm going to have a license when I'm through."

Red Dog narrowed his eyes. "You weren't drunk?"

"No." Jake lifted a shoulder. "Just stupid." He grinned and lifted his hair to display the cut. "Sixteen stitches."

Red Dog whistled softly in an appreciative manner, then stuck his cigarette in the corner of his mouth, shrugged out of his coat and tugged up his sleeve to show a long, still-raw scar that ran snakelike from his wrist to his elbow. "Forty-six."

"Beat me again."

"It was my cattlelike reflexes." He grinned wryly.

At the reference to a big, dumb soldier they'd both known who had slaughtered every cliché he heard, Jake laughed. It was the first time in days, and it shook something loose in his chest. "Poor Jared. Didn't have a single brain in his head."

"Good quality in a soldier."

"Yeah." He gestured to the waitress. "You want another drink?"

"Sure. Same thing." He pushed his empty glass toward her. "You ever miss it?"

"Not the war," Jake said. "Not even the army. Not anymore."

"Me, neither."

They both fell silent, watching Pam pour a Scotch for Jake, a bourbon for Red Dog. Into Jake's mind there came a memory of a harsh blue sky stretched over a flat, endless, dun-colored desert.

Next to him, Red Dog swore and pinched the bridge of his nose. "I don't think it's ever gonna go away, man. Not ever."

"No, I don't think so."

"Hell of a thing," Red Dog said, and drank deeply.

"Amen." Jake lifted his own glass, downed it and stood up. "Step over to my office and let's play some pool."

Ramona went home to the solace of her animals. They seemed to sense her distress and padded along behind her from room to room, singly and in groups. She settled herself in the kitchen, thinking she would make a cup of tea. Manuelito sighed and lay down by the back door, while Pandora and Venus wove around her legs, politely taking turns. Guinevere the terrier mutt and Arthur the Lab sat by the door to the living room, ears up, watching her carefully.

She put the kettle on the stove to boil, but the dishes from her breakfast with Jake were in the drying rack, and the sight gave her a pang. "Damn you, Jake," she said quietly. "I really didn't want this."

Guinevere whined sympathetically and shifted from foot to foot. Ramona knelt to scratch the dog's ears and allow her chin to be daintily licked, one tiny touch of the paper-thin tongue. Another to the cheek from Arthur's thick one. Venus tripped over and rubbed along her thigh, her tail drawing a line on the underside of Ramona's arm, and Pandora, not to be outdone, rubbed her ears on Ramona's left ankle, then fell in a plop with her paws in the air, offering her white stomach just in case Ramona had an urge to rub it. From his post by the back door, Manuelito muttered softly in his eerie wolf voice, a half whine that had always sounded very close to words.

Ramona, surrounded by furry beings, laughed and sat down on the floor with her back to the wall to make room for all of them. "Come on, Manuelito, you, too." Happily, he trotted over, gently nosing Venus aside to put his chin on her knee. The two cats curled up in her lap, back to back, while Arthur took her right side, Guinevere her left, leaving Manuelito's huge body to guard her front. It made her feel weepy again. "Why can't a man be more like a dog?" she asked, scratching Arthur's muzzle. "Simple, loving, uncomplicated." She chuckled. "Not to mention devoted."

They did make it rather difficult to feel sorry for herself.

She had understood the risks inherent in loving Jake. She'd known from the very beginning that he would not be the kind of man who could make a commitment of any kind. Even if he did, she wouldn't be able to accept his offer, not when he had so many problems he had to solve. In his present state, he couldn't function alone, much less take on the responsibility of a family.

A family. Surely she had not been so foolish as to imagine such a thing with Jake. Surely she was wiser than that.

But with two purring cats in her lap helping her reflect, she had to admit the thought had wafted through her mind a time or two. She had come to know what kind of man he was capable of being, what kind of man he was underneath his pain. A good man, a strong man, one who had the capacity for great love, honor and commitment. But until he came to terms with his sorrow and the loss of his dream, commitment would be impossible.

And she had understood that right from the beginning. She had lectured herself about her need to offer him healing. She had tried to be logical, clear-minded and honest with both herself and Jake. In the end, however, love was not logical. It didn't follow any rules.

Now all she could do was continue to try to be honest and forthright. She loved him, but she could not heal him. She had to put him out of her life, cleanly and without regret. Especially without regret. A soft, fleeting vision of him in her rain-dimmed room shimmered in her mind. No, she would not regret that. Not for a single moment.

When the kettle started to whistle, Ramona put her face against the head of each one of her animals in turn. "Thanks, you guys. I don't know what I'd do without you."

She rescued the kettle and poured the boiling water over a tea bag. A crisp, light lemon scent rose on the steam, and she inhaled. The little things made life good. She had to remember that.

The phone rang, and for a moment, Ramona simply looked at it, hoping with a traitorous part of her heart that it was Jake calling, that somehow, she had misunderstood what was happening at his mother's house and on the way to the Wild Moose. The need for it to be him on the other end of the line made her stomach turn over, and she briefly considered letting it ring. She need to be stronger before she talked to him again, strong enough to be clear and honest and reasonable. Reasonable.

She grabbed the receiver on the third ring. Her voice was altogether too breathless when she said hello. And for an endless beat of a heart, Ramona waited for the sound of Jake's resonant voice on the other end of the line.

"Hi, Ramona."

It was the voice of a man. The voice of a man with a beautiful, deep, rich voice of his own: Dr. Richards. "John! What's up?"

"Well, I have some bad news. Harry Goodman, the old vet Jake Forrest was so fond of, died about half an hour ago."

The news was not unexpected. Ramona had lost another elderly patient to the virulent bug, but a plucking pain touched her heart anyway. She'd been very fond of Harry. "The flu, I assume?"

"Yeah. He slipped away in his sleep. Very peaceful." He paused. "I thought you might be the best person to break the news to Jake. He's not going to take it well, I guarantee it."

"No, he won't. Thanks, John. I'll get in touch with him right away."

"Harry left him a letter. I'll put it on your desk."

"Thank you."

Ramona hung up, feeling an uncomfortable sense of impending disaster. Not over Harry—heaven knew the man was a medical anomaly. He should have died five years ago, but somehow had managed to squeeze out an enormous number of extra days. And he had deserved a quiet, uncomplicated death.

But Jake was devoted to the old man. She dialed Jake's home number. It rang four times before the answering machine took over. She hung up without leaving a message and instead called Louise. No answer there, either, and as a last resort, she tried the Wild Moose. Embarrassing to have the waitress answer and sound faintly pitying. "Sorry, hon," she said. "You just missed him. He left here with an army buddy of his not ten minutes ago. I think they were headed out to the Tick Tock."

Ramona thanked her and hung up. *Hon.* As if she were one of the dozens of women who chased Jake, only to be forgotten in the wake of the next one. She shuddered inwardly.

Crossing her arms, she wondered what to do next. Chasing him from bar to bar around town was out of the question, but a sixth sense told her he had to hear this news gently.

She redialed his home phone and left a simple message. "Jake, this is Ramona. It's very important that you call me as soon as you get this, no matter what time it is." She left her home phone and beeper numbers, just in case. It seemed odd that he'd never called her, considering everything, but he hadn't. He might not know how to reach her.

To be safe, she left a message on Louise's machine, as well.

All day long, Louise had been waiting for her family to clear out of her house. Contrarily, they lingered, playing games with the children and telling tales. Curtis begged to spend the night with her, and she was stunned to hear herself refusing. "Not tonight, sugar. Grandma's tired."

Lance and Cody looked at her in astonishment. "Are you sick, Ma?" Lance asked.

"Don't be silly," she said. "I'm just not in the mood for company tonight."

"Hey, Curtis, you want to spend the night with us instead?"

Curtis flopped down on the floor. "No. I wanna be here."

Annoyance pricked Louise. "Get up off that floor, boy, and quit acting like a spoiled baby."

His blue eyes showed astonishment. "I'm a big boy," he protested.

"Not when you act like that, you aren't. If you want to spend the night with Cody, you do that, otherwise, I'm going to call your daddy to take you home in just a few minutes."

"Come on," Cody said, squatting beside his cousin. "We'll build something with Lego blocks."

With a last, censorious glance at his grandmother, Curtis nodded.

It should have made her feel repentant, but it didn't. At least not until the family had finally gone, leaving her alone in the house. Alonzo had gone to the store for her to get some coffee for breakfast.

And only then, as she put the last bits of the feast away, did Louise realize how it all must have looked to Alonzo. Her face flamed. Did he think she expected him to come here later? And what if he did, only meaning to share a cup of late-night hot chocolate with her as he often did, and Louise acted in some way that told him what she'd really hoped for?

It was just too humiliating. Bad enough to go through it as a young girl with something to offer. So much worse at fifty-something with a body she wouldn't let a man see on a bet, and the smell of garlic clinging to her hands.

The kitchen windows opened to a distant view of the valley, smoky blue today with the rain. Louise put down the bowl she was holding and looked out at it, cursing herself for her foolish hopes and shaking her head at the twittering lunacy of a middle-aged woman who had really only learned how not to ask for things for herself. Until a man with twinkling eyes and a soft, musical voice had moved into her guest house. Even then, she hadn't allowed herself to want more than he gave so generously. His companionship and his charm at her breakfast table were more than she'd had in many years.

A hand fell on her shoulder, and Louise started violently. She turned, knowing it had to be him, and now she had to face all the silliness she'd built up over the long hours of the afternoon.

"So long a face!" he exclaimed. "Is there some trouble?"

Louise shook her head and briskly reached for the bowl. "I reckon I'm just a little worn out from all this."

One strong hand, work gnarled and sun darkened to a rich pecan, closed on her wrist. "You have done enough."

Afraid he would somehow read her thoughts, Louise kept her eyes down. "I only want to wash this up right quick."

"No," he said, and those hands closed around her face, cupping it tenderly and firmly. "Not today, hmm?" In the dim, quiet kitchen, his dark eyes were sober for once, sober and deep and full of meaning. "I am so glad," he said, "that you no want to be Grandma tonight."

"You must think I'm—"

"Beautiful," he said softly, and kissed her. And this time, Louise had time to enjoy it. Time to savor the hunger that pulled her closer, that gripped her more tightly, and let him kiss her deeply in a way she only vaguely remembered.

His thick mustache was a delicious counterpoint to the sensual play of his lips, and then—oh, merciful Minerva—his tongue asked admittance, and Louise gave it.

It made her dizzy, kissing Alonzo, and she let him put his arm around her and pull her into his body, against the shape that had become so familiar and dear to her these past months.

And finally, Louise let herself go and put her arms back around him, and let herself touch his strong back and the love handles over his belt, and when he whispered that he'd like to take her to his house, to his bed, she tripped down the hill behind him in the rain like a girl, holding his hand. The guest house had only one big room, with a kitchenette at one end and a small bathroom behind a door at the other. His bed was covered with a beautiful Mexican blanket, and his clothes were hung neatly from pegs. He turned on the radio to a Spanish station playing ballads and didn't rush her. They danced for a long time before the fire swelled up hot enough between them that he began to take off her clothes and touch her bare flesh, and she touched him back.

And after all her worry, there was no embarrassment when he looked at her and caressed her. It wasn't a sober or frightening thing at all. He made love the way he did everything else, with much good humor, his musical voice teasing her and whispering, his fine mouth and strong hands chasing away her worries. Afterward, he made a cradle of his shoulder and pulled her into it and kissed her hair.

Content in the wonder of the moment, Louise fell asleep in his arms.

Chapter 17

Jake and Red Dog hoofed it between a couple of honky-tonks in town, but neither of them had the heart for the banter required to impress women. Still, it was after mid-night before they caught a ride back to Jake's place, making jokes about two grown men who didn't have a car between them. It wasn't particularly funny, and Jake suspected it caused Red Dog as much discomfort as it did Jake.

Mr. E padded toward them eagerly as they came in, and Jake scooped him up. "Hey, guy. I came home just to keep you company. How about that? I also brought you some-thing." He laughed as the cat nosed in his pocket, where he'd tucked a plastic bag of shredded crab from the restau-rant.

In the kitchen, Jake got out a dish and put the crab down for the cat, who gulped it looking over his shoulder as if he was sure someone would take it if he didn't eat it right away. Jake impulsively reached down and stroked his back. "You're safe now, bud. I promise."

"Hey, Jake," Red Dog said from the living room, "where are all those paintings you had? The ones with stars."

They'd been together in Germany before Desert Storm, and in Texas before that. Jake had forgotten Red Dog would remember. "I've never put them up."

"How come? I like those paintings."

Jake lifted a shoulder. "Never got around to it, I guess."

Red Dog paced the room, rounding the periphery as if he was on patrol. "Too bad." He suddenly halted in the middle of the room. "Who was the woman who dropped you off today? I saw her through the windows."

Jake hesitated. The pinch came back to his chest, the pinch put there by her wounded eyes. "Her name is Ramona, Ramona Hardy. She's one of the local doctors."

"Not your usual type."

He wished everyone would quit saying that. "Yeah, well, she pretty much told me to get lost this afternoon, so it doesn't matter anyway."

"Women," Red Dog commiserated, shaking his head.

"Yeah." Jake frowned, rubbing the weary place between his brows. "But she's different. You ever get that feeling that you're watching a movie? Like the whole world is going on around you and you can't quite connect?"

Red Dog's face closed. "Yeah."

"When I'm around Ramona, it stops being a movie. She's real." Jake shook his head, remembering again, with a pang, how she had felt around him this morning. Flames of rage licked his gut when he thought of what had been done to her. His jaw tensed automatically and his hands itched for a gun. "She's been through a lot. It makes me want to kill someone."

"That's the part I don't like, man." Red Dog started pacing again. To the long glass doors at the end of the room, then back. "Wherever you look, there's all this violence, and you can't do anything.'' He paused, his back to Jake. Quietly, he added, ''I don't like the violence in me.''

Jake nodded.

''Hey, your message light is flashing,'' Red Dog said.

Kind of rare these days. Jake wandered over and pushed the button. Ramona's voice, sounding tight and worried, came on.

''That her?'' Red Dog asked.

''Yeah.'' Jake rubbed his solar plexus.

''Sexy voice.'' He finally flopped on the couch and kicked off his shoes. ''I'm gonna crash, man. It's been a long day.''

''Take the bed upstairs.'' Jake could tell he wouldn't sleep. Not tonight. ''I'm going to stay up awhile.''

''I don't want to kick you outta your bed. I'll be all right here. You know me. Close my eyes and I'm out.''

Jake envied him. ''You won't be kicking me out. I'm wired.''

''It's your house,'' his friend said, and ambled up the stairs.

Alone, Jake stared at the phone, wondering what it was that Ramona wanted. Wondered if he wanted to hear it tonight. She didn't seem like the kind of woman who'd use that kind of message to get him to call, just so they could hash things out some more. But you never knew.

He played the message again. Call her, whatever time it was. Important. Could someone be sick or something? He picked up the phone. Put it back down.

The bar scene had depressed him tonight. Noisy and tinsel bright, hollow as a drum, it had made him feel lonely and out of step. The women were too young for him and had no frame of reference for his life—why hadn't he seen that before? He didn't want to talk about rock bands and concerts and trips to Saint Petersburg.

Women old enough for him had no use for such a scene. They had lives, had made connections to the community and with loved ones. They had realized life was finite and not to be wasted.

Like Ramona.

Jake leaned back in his recliner and turned off the lamp. Mr. E, spying the open lap, immediately filled it with soft fur and a low, rumbling purr. Staring out the patio door to a sky washed with rain, Jake finally admitted to himself that Ramona had changed him. Until the day they had met again at the wedding, he'd been drifting as aimlessly as a tree trunk caught in a river current. She was the tree itself, strong and rooted in the earth, and she made it seem like the right thing to be.

Weary, he closed his eyes and imagined her standing with her feet on solid ground, her hair floating out branch-like, her body the healthy, stalwart trunk. It made him smile. She'd probably hate that image.

Somehow, he slept all night. From midnight right through to dawn with a cat in his lap, his shoes still on his feet and no dreams to bother him. Blinking awake in the purpling morning, he tried to remember if he'd taken a sleeping pill, but he hadn't. And although he and Red Dog had certainly downed a few drinks, Jake had been a long way from being drunk.

Amazing. In the past, his episodes of insomnia had ended like this, abruptly and without warning, and he was simply able to sleep again. This time, at least, he'd have enough sense to realize it would be back.

Meanwhile, he felt as clearheaded as he had in days. He made a pot of coffee from freshly ground beans, showered and left a note for his friend. Red Dog wanted to see some of the vendors in town about carrying his jewelry, but nothing would be open on the Fourth of July. He'd have to stay another day.

The morning air was cool on Jake's face, smelling of pine and rain and that subtle scent peculiar to the mountains themselves. Walking toward town, Jake wondered about hiking this afternoon. Might be a lot of tourists around this weekend, but he knew a few back roads no one bothered much with.

At a convenience store, Jake bought a pack of Winstons and a can of Colt 45, which was about the closest thing he could find to Guinness at seven-thirty in the morning. Probably Harry wouldn't want a drink this early, but Jake wanted to be prepared. He had some questions to ask the old man, and he wanted to apologize for being such an idiot a couple of nights ago.

Briefly, his mind swirled around Ramona, and he pushed the thoughts of her away. She was something he had to think about when he—

With a sudden sense of dread, he remembered her phone call of last night. Damn. He'd fallen asleep without calling her back. At the pay phone outside the store, he looked up her home phone and dialed, framing an apology in his mind.

No answer. She'd left her beeper number, too, but he didn't have it with him. With a frown, he hung up. He'd call her when he got back. If something had happened to his family, someone else would have called him by now.

The VA home sat on a wide, green acreage surrounded with several parking lots for visitors and the handful of residents who could drive. Few cars were in the lot this morning, but Jake saw Ramona's. It gave him a sense of unease. She didn't do rounds till later.

He stopped outside, his skin prickling. Sometimes in battle, a soldier got that warning, just a hint of it, before something went down, and Jake knew enough to respect it. More than once it had saved his butt.

But there could be no danger in a VA home. He shook off the premonition and went inside, waving to a nurse he didn't recognize as he continued past the desk toward Harry's room. The door was open and he approached it quietly in case the old man was sleeping.

Just inside, he stopped. The bed was empty. Not just covers-tossed-back empty, but stripped clean, as the other bed had been Saturday night. The mattress, Jake noticed, was not a very good one, cotton ticking covered with striped canvas. He wished he had known that before—he would have seen that Harry had a decent mattress.

Jake put the Winstons and the Colt 45 on the bed and walked from the room. Later, he would find out what was being done with the remains, where the funeral would be held, all of that. For now, Jake couldn't breathe, and he had to get outside.

Twenty minutes later, Ramona happened by Harry's room and spied the red package of cigarettes lying on the mattress. She let loose an earthy curse, then with a sigh, entered the room. Next to the cigarettes was a big can of malt liquor, still ice-cold. A bittersweet pang went through her as she picked it up. Who knew how long Jake had been smuggling contraband in to the old man? She smiled. How like him.

Suddenly, she dropped it, ran out to the hallway to look for Jake, then out the front doors of the home. She saw him walking down the hill at a fairly brisk pace, a tall, too-lean figure in jeans and a plain corduroy shirt he managed to make look elegant. His black hair shone in the sun.

Ramona stood there for a moment, watching him. Once, she opened her mouth to call after him, then decided against it. He knew she was here. If he needed her, he would have to make the first move. A man sometimes had to fight his own demons alone.

With a heavy heart, she went back inside, unable to prevent herself from again imagining that army of angels following along beside him, swords and strong arms at the ready.

Jake felt numb all day. As if from a great distance, he went on with his life, going with Red Dog to a picnic in the town square, where he automatically engaged in banter with his brother and helped entertain his nephews, who were anxious to get to the highlight of the day—the fireworks. Red Dog set up his case of jewelry on a picnic table and sold a healthy smattering of mostly earrings. Equipped with a collection of bone and tiny stones, he carved tiny, intricate feathers between customers, and Jake watched idly.

"Where did you learn to do that?" he asked finally.

"Nowhere, really. My grandpa used to do the silver, and he taught me when I was little, but the feathers are kind of a new craze. Do 'em right, and they sell for a pretty penny." He pulled out a pair already finished. "The trick is to find the right stones and bones, look for the pattern in them, so they tell you what feather they want to be."

The pair he held was a reddish brown, with little white spots on them. Along the edges were exquisite, delicate feather marks. "What did these tell you they had to be?"

Red Dog shook his head. "Poor Anglos gotta be told every little thing," he said tongue in cheek. "Red-tailed hawk."

Jake thought the color would suit Ramona, and for a brief moment, he imagined how they would look swinging against her neck. "How much?"

"For you, G.I., five dollar."

Jake shook his head. "Real price."

Red Dog turned his mouth down and shook his head. "No way, man. I'm crashing at your place. Consider them payment for the introductions tomorrow."

A woman Jake didn't know stopped by the table and asked the price of a bracelet. Red Dog stood up to talk to her.

Jake fingered the earrings, then in a single explosive rush, his grief came crashing in on him, hard. Harry was dead. Feeling an unmanly swell of tears rage up behind his eyes, he turned abruptly and walked away from the crowd, fighting to hold on until he could hide. Behind an old oak, alive with squirrels making food raids on the picnic crowd, he sank to the ground.

A hundred pictures of Harry passed through his mind. Harry as a trim policeman in his uniform, bringing flowers to Jean after a fight, as an irate homeowner when Jake had tried to slide by with less than his best work, as a good listener when Jake had a problem.

Jake couldn't believe he was dead. He couldn't believe he was taking it so hard, either. If he let himself think of it at all, he felt he'd be sucked into a black hole that would consume him.

A familiar voice spoke at his side. "I thought I saw you disappear over here."

Jake looked away, hiding his tears. Only then did he realize he still held the feather jewelry. The wire scratched his cheek, and he put the earrings in Ramona's hand. "Red Dog made these," he said gruffly. "I thought they'd look nice on you."

Ramona, her hair loose on the summer breeze, looked at them, then back at Jake. "I'm sorry about Harry," she said.

For a long moment, he wanted only to reach for her, to put his head on her shoulder and weep away the sorrow in his heart. Her eyes, those empathetic, velvety eyes, were calm and knowing, and Jake was ashamed of himself. All he ever did was take. All she ever did was give.

"It was just his time to go," Jake said.

Ramona reached into her bag and took out a white envelope. "He left a letter for you," she said, holding it out.

Jake took it, another swell of grief making it impossible to speak. He nodded stiffly and squeezed one word past the tightness in his throat. "Thanks."

She put a hand on his shoulder. "You know where to find me if you need anything."

Her hand warmed him. Everything in him ached to reach up and hold it there, to draw upon her vast strength to regain his own, but he didn't. He let her go without a word.

On the way back to his condo, Jake stopped by the liquor store for Guinness. Red Dog raised an eyebrow, but said nothing until they got back to the condo and Jake gustily drank one.

"Since when do you drink stout?"

"An old soldier died last night." He paused, swallowing the dark brew. It cut through the thickness in his throat. "I decided I wanted to have a wake tonight."

Red Dog looked at him steadily. "All right. You get drunk, I take watch." It was an old established pattern between them. "Where? Here?"

Jake shook his head, looking through the windows to the dark gray sky and the faint line of mountains below. He suddenly knew exactly where he wanted to go. The name popped into his mind from nowhere. Henrietta Pass. There was a good, wide meadow there and a good view of the sky above town. They could watch the fireworks and mourn the passing of a good soldier.

"Bring a coat. It might get cold up on the mountain."

Outside, there came a booming, thudding sound. Jake ducked automatically, bracing himself. Across the room,

Red Dog did the same thing. In the sky beyond the windows, a brilliant shower of red and blue stars lit the night.

Red Dog swore, then looked over his shoulder with a wry grin, lifting his chin. "Fireworks."

Another boom shook the windows, and a rocket burst high in the sky. "God bless America," Red Dog said, and laughed. His jean jacket had an upside-down American flag on the sleeve, and he put it on, grimacing ironically. "Let's do it."

Jake nodded. He bent down and gave Mr. E a good rub. "Be back in a little while, guy. I won't leave you alone all night again."

"All night?" Red Dog echoed. "You spent all night with a woman?"

Jake didn't answer. That was private.

But as they hiked in the dark, moving sharply upward on a path that led into the mountains from the edge of the condo lot, Jake couldn't help thinking of Ramona. Although he walked with Red Dog through the wet of a pine forest, something of Ramona lingered around him like a wraith, as if her spirit had left her body to hover around him. It made him ache.

It was better this way; that was what he told himself. In the long run, he would spare her pain by cutting things off now. It had been a mistake to show up at her house the night before last. It had been even more of one to make love to her the next morning—but somehow, he couldn't regret it. He thought of her breath on his neck, of her hair brushing over his body, of the sounds she had made as he moved in her.

He stopped abruptly on the path, winded with emotion.

Red Dog halted and turned to look back the way they'd come. He grabbed onto a tree. "Why didn't you tell me it was so steep?"

Jake opened a bottle of Guinness and settled on a boulder

to drink it. "I thought you were raised in New Mexico. A lot of mountains there."

"Yeah. In Albuquerque, which is a city, in case you don't know your geography. And don't believe everything you hear about Indians. We don't all like heights."

"You mean you don't want to build skyscrapers? You don't have fleet feet that can cling to those narrow steel beams a mile above the ground?" Jake grinned across the darkness. "I'm really disappointed."

"If you guys wouldn't make up those lies," Red Dog said, peeking over the edge of a rock to see what lay below, "we wouldn't have to act crazy on you all the time." Seeing the town of Red Creek glittering in a tumble down the hill, he pulled back with a grunt. "That's a cliff!"

"You'll be all right. Just stay on the path. It's not far now."

"No way." Red Dog sat down abruptly. "I'll wait right here. Catch you on the way down."

Jake considered the view from this spot. As if to accommodate him, a burst of starry, colored lights exploded across the sky. "All right. This is far enough. By the way, this is a cross-country skiing path. In the daylight, you'll see it isn't quite as bad as it looks at night. And I know it like the back of my hand." He took a long pull from the bottle, feeling a pleasant warmth all the way down his esophagus. "Spent my childhood here, remember?"

"Yeah, well, bring me back when I can see what I'm doing." More fireworks exploded high above in a shower of red and blue. "Too bad bombs don't go off like that, huh?"

Jake nodded. He glanced at the path and followed its shadowy line up as far as he could see. He suddenly wondered where Ramona had been when—damn. He couldn't even think the word.

He forced himself. When she had been raped. Where had

it been? It seemed as if the violence of such an act would forever stain the air around it, and he wondered if he would feel it if he stumbled over the spot. "I'll be back in a minute," he said, standing up abruptly.

"Feel free."

Jake hiked up the trail a little way. Just a few feet, he told himself. He did know the mountain, but he'd had a few drinks. Enough to throw off his judgment anyway.

Behind him, the fireworks boomed, and their stars illuminated his path for a few moments. He scrambled around a tough patch of rotten granite, then paused. He glanced back at Red Dog, and it seemed he'd gone farther than he thought. He couldn't see him at all in the darkness.

A match suddenly flared—only a couple of feet away. It lit the piercing eyes and high cheekbones of Robert "Red Dog" Martinez as he held it to his cigarette. He waved out the match, inhaled deeply and blew out the smoke. "I still remember how to sneak up on the enemy," he said.

"You get over your little attack of vertigo?"

"Never said I had vertigo. I was just tired." He lifted his chin toward the path. "Even a city boy knows you aren't supposed to hike alone at night. What if you break a leg or something? Then I'd be stuck out here by myself."

They walked up to a more level stretch of ground, an open meadow with tremendous views. Henrietta Pass, named for a woman who'd camped there during a blizzard in the winter of 1902—and lived to tell the tale.

Jake stopped abruptly. What had Ramona said to the police? *Some boys raped me, and I left them passed out near Henrietta Pass. They'll freeze if you don't go get them.* He cursed, then quickly moved forward. The meadow ended a few hundred feet away with a line of trees and a sharp, steep drop to the town. He strode to the edge of it and stared at the glittery scene. The fireworks display was just ending, and the sky exploded in one shimmering spectacle of light after the other, before gradually fading away into darkness.

In his mind, Jake imagined the meadow as it might have been on a late winter day, thick with snow and blazing with sunshine. He saw a trusting Ramona ski into the clearing and pause in admiration of the glorious weather. He saw her realize the danger, saw her take flight.

He cursed and bowed his head, his throat thick with grief. Red Dog joined him and bumped his arm, giving him a bottle without saying a word. Jake drank gratefully, trying to blot out images he never wanted burned on his brain.

It didn't help. And standing there, Jake knew it never would. Harry would still be gone. Ramona would still have been raped. A boy still would have screamed away his last breaths on a blazing desert half a world away.

Next to him, Red Dog spoke, his voice hushed and raspy. "There isn't a single day that I don't think of that boy."

"I know," Jake said. "We're stuck with it."

But in a sudden rush of insight, Jake realized they could *live* with it. They could never make it okay. But it just was. That was how Ramona had done it.

There was no miracle. No thundering revelation. It just was.

"Let's go back and get some sleep," he said heavily.

As he turned, he swayed a little with the stout and the headiness of his epiphany. Quickly, he repositioned himself, and with a sickening, slipping sensation, felt the ground give way under his right foot. Instinctively, he pitched forward, but it wasn't enough.

Silently, he fell.

And fell.

And fell. He had just enough time to notice the clouds had cleared away overhead, leaving a black sky covered with silver glitter. He distantly heard the crash of glass shattering somewhere and had enough time to note it was probably the bottle of Guinness he'd been holding. He even heard Red Dog cry out.

And then he struck rock, landing so hard that his body mercifully couldn't even register the pain. He thought he bounced, then his face struck something hard, and Jake tried to scramble for some hold on the rock, but his body seemed bent on a course of its own, and he felt himself tumbling again—then slammed hard.

He thought with a brief, bright sharpness that he did not want to die, and then blackness claimed him.

Chapter 18

The dogs barking frantically awakened Ramona from a restless sleep, jolting her to heart-pounding wakefulness. She glanced at the clock as she tossed on her robe: 1:17 a.m. She automatically grabbed her gun and cocked it as a fist pounded on her door again and again, sending the dogs into a frenzy.

"Who's there?"

"Ramona, it's Tyler. Open up!"

Tyler? Ramona blinked. The dogs whined and barked and trotted back toward her, then growled at the door. "Just a minute."

She peeked out the curtain, and sure enough, there was Jake's brother, Tyler. With a cry, she opened the door. "What's wrong?"

Ty's face was drawn and his hair was loose on his shoulders, something she'd never seen. "It's Jake," he said without preamble. "He's stuck on a ledge below Henrietta. They can't get him up till morning." His mouth went to a hard line. "He fell almost three hundred feet."

A kind of numbness seemed to paralyze her. "I don't—what can I—" Ramona's brain refused to function.

"He's been conscious. Some of the time. He called for you."

Ramona closed her eyes, suddenly sickeningly dizzy. "Tyler, I can't...I don't..."

"Go put on some clothes. I'll wait."

In the truck, she said, "How did anyone know where he was?"

"He had a friend with him. A soldier from the Gulf War, I think. He's pretty upset. He said Jake just slipped."

"What were they doing up at Henrietta Pass at night?"

"Watching fireworks."

Henrietta. It was a cursed place. Tyler drove to the foot of the cross-country paths and parked next to a rescue vehicle. In the wide parking lot waited a Flight for Life helicopter. Ramona stared at them.

"Three hundred feet?" It was a long, long way to fall.

"Yeah."

High on the mountain waved a plethora of lights—heavy-duty flashlights, and some kind of halogen thing. Ramona steeled herself and got out of the truck.

The path wasn't steep or difficult. It meandered in a graceful, deceptively easy rise in a crisscrossing pattern over the face of the mountain. But Ramona knew it intimately. There were dangerous outcroppings of rotten rock at every turn, and sheer drops that appeared out of nowhere. Jake should have known better than to come up here after dark. What could he have been thinking?

With a needling ache, she knew he wasn't thinking. That was the trouble. She stayed close behind Tyler.

When they reached the meadow, Ramona saw a horde of people. Paramedics and others in forest-service uniforms or wearing the emblazoned red cross of the rescue workers.

Lance was there, and when he saw them, he hurried over and grabbed Ramona's arm. "He's calling for you."

She rushed forward, aware she was numb, that all of this would hit her later. At the edge of the cliff where he'd fallen, several workers had attached a contraption of cables and harnesses to nearby trees. "Hold it," a woman said to Ramona. "Are you the doctor?"

"Yes."

"The friend told us the ground just gave way. Let me fix you up before you go any farther."

Ramona lifted her arms and allowed the harness to be fastened around her waist. "Has anyone been down there?"

"No. We can't reach him."

"So there's no report on the extent of his injuries?"

"We can see him. He's broken an arm, and there's a considerable amount of blood, but he's conscious from time to time. We just can't tell any more until first light."

"I see," Ramona said. The numbness thankfully insulated her from the reality of the moment. Later, there would be plenty of time to fall apart if she had to. Later, she could scream and rage. Later...

A hoarse cry reached her. "Ramona!"

She moved forward instinctively. The woman who'd buckled her into the harness held her back. "Drop down on your belly and crawl forward. We don't want to have to rescue two of you."

Ramona followed directions and inched her way to the edge of the cliff. "Jake, don't talk. I'm here. Save your strength." Someone shoved a flashlight into her hand. "I'm going to turn on a flashlight, Jake, so I can see you. Close your eyes."

She clicked it on. The beam cut through the darkness in a widening arc, making of ordinary rocks and branches an unholy landscape. Jake lay far, far below, his body sprawled at an unnatural angle over a ledge dotted with scrub oak and raspberry bushes. With a cool objectivity that surprised her, Ramona assessed what she could. There was a lot of blood and there was no question that one arm was broken.

But the biggest danger in falls of this magnitude was damage to internal organs, and she couldn't tell anything about those until she could examine him more closely. "Don't worry, Jake," she called. "We're trying to figure out how to get you off that ledge. It isn't a narrow ledge, so you don't have to be afraid of falling any farther."

Ramona moved the flashlight beam slowly up the mountainside. Steep but not sheer, and that gave her hope. Judging by the pattern of snapped branches and fresh scrape marks in the dirt, his fall had been slowed by the shrubs on the way. Even better.

"Ramona!"

"Jake, don't talk. Please. It might hurt you." Her voice echoed oddly, bouncing off the rocks, and the sound gave her a sense of déjà vu.

With a frown, she moved the flashlight in a circle around him, trying to get her bearings. It was difficult in the dark. She was spatially oriented, which meant she needed to have distance landmarks to feel where she was, and in the inky darkness of a mountain night, that was impossible.

The flashlight revealed the gnarled trunk of a piñon, weathered and stunted by wind, and Ramona felt a deep, nauseating jolt of recognition. "Oh, my God," she said. "Jake! Hold on!" She scrambled back from the edge and stood up. "I know how to get to him." With shaky hands, she struggled with the belt of her harness. "I need an EMT to come with me."

"You can't do that. There's no way down!"

Ramona swallowed. "Yes, there is. And I think we can get him out, too."

* * *

Reacting to her certainty, a paramedic grabbed his bag and waited while she shone a flashlight around the meadow. She had not been here since she was seventeen, not even in daylight, and it had changed some. The trees were taller, and there was a grove of aspens, their shiny leaves and white bark catching the light, that she didn't remember.

There—a tumble of boulders shaped like a snail, one big one forming its back, another small one for the head. Without giving herself any time to think, she strode toward it and ducked into the trees just behind, letting the flashlight lead through the inky darkness. Behind her, the EMT followed closely.

Ramona paused and took a breath. It wasn't as hard as she might have imagined it would be, not with Jake waiting—maybe dying, if she couldn't get to him. She deliberately called up memories she had tamped down on hard for many years. Remembered the boys in their red and blue and yellow jackets sitting on this very rock. They had caught her, and one dragged her behind the snail, but in the snow they had slid nearly forty feet before landing in front of a cave on a plateau. He had called his friends and they tumbled and slid down the hill behind them, laughing as if it was just any happy day in the mountains.

Her throat tightened, and deliberately she moved forward, holding out the flashlight to make sure she didn't tumble. The land was dry and covered with scrubby grass in the summer, and it wasn't terribly steep. She looked over her shoulder at the EMT. "You okay?"

"No problem. Wish I'd known this way an hour ago."

She gained the plateau and spied the cave. Lights from the supermarket parking lot at the foot of the mountain cast a faint, cold light over it. It should have horrified her. It should have made her skin crawl.

But she felt nothing but an urgent need to get to Jake. "I came down this way," she said aloud, and followed a flat, wide expanse of stone edging a sharp drop to nothingness one side. The EMT cursed. On the other side of the plateau, she paused to wait for him. "That was the hardest part."

"Good."

The rest of the way was over flat rock. In some places, trees and scrub oak had rooted in pockets of soil, but it was, in general, a simple downward climb.

And finally, finally, there was Jake, lying exactly as he had been when she saw him from above. The plateau spread out to form a wide table, maybe thirty or forty feet wide, then narrowed again and grew steeper, but Ramona thought it was possible they could get him down.

Shivering in relief, she rushed toward him and knelt. "Jake, we're here," she said, touching him gently.

At first, he didn't respond, and Ramona's heart plummeted. She felt for a pulse on his neck, and his eyes opened. "Not dead." His uninjured arm groped for hers and gripped it.

"Good," she said. His pupils were uneven. The damned concussion. She spoke to the EMT in quick, medical language, hoping Jake would miss most of it. Brain swelling was an urgent concern. He'd reopened the cut on his head, but miraculously, there was only a goose egg over one eye and no other cuts she could find.

But his breathing was labored, and when she asked him, he said it hurt. His chest and his side. Ramona looked at the EMT. Broken or bruised ribs—and heaven only knew what else. They had to get him out—and quickly.

Ramona stayed with him, holding his hand and talking quietly, while the EMT made his way back up the hill. She had given him directions to find the place from the bottom, and although the minutes seemed to take hours, the rescuers finally made it, with a hammock stretcher to carry Jake out on.

He could barely speak, but he wouldn't let go of Ramona's hand as they carried him down. Because she was a doctor, they let her fly with him to Denver, and he clutched her hard all the way there. Only when he was taken into surgery did she finally convince him to let her go, and even then, it was a fight. He kept trying to talk and she kept putting her hand over his mouth. "I'll talk to you later," she said, smiling.

"Mr. E," he said fuzzily.

Ramona swallowed with difficulty. "I'll take care of him."

Ramona tried to put on a cheerful face for Jake's family when they drove into Denver hours later, but she understood how grave his injuries were. She tried to phrase it gently, feeling they had to be prepared. In the waiting room, Louise, Lance, Tyler, Tamara and Jake's friend, Robert, sat down and looked at her.

Ramona took Louise's hand. "He fell almost three hundred feet. It's a miracle, and I'm not overstating this, that he lived at all. He must have bounced on the side, and it slowed him down.

"We were lucky he had Robert with him, and that he reacted so quickly. We were lucky to find a way to get him out of there before morning came...." She paused. "We were lucky. He was lucky."

"What's the but, Ramona?" Tyler asked, his face grim. He'd pulled his hair back into a ponytail, but he still looked haggard. His pain was obvious.

She took a breath. "He's injured pretty seriously. He hit his head again, and he had a concussion last week. It's impossible to know the extent of internal injuries, but there were some."

Robert spoke for the first time. His voice was low and

hoarse, and she hated the haunted look in his eyes. "So he might die."

Louise spoke before Ramona had a chance to frame a reply. "He will not," she said fiercely, and stood up. "I reckon I prayed him through worse than this. I'm going to the chapel."

And suddenly, Ramona remembered her prayer earlier—or last night. Whatever. Angels with their strong, swift wings.

With a dizziness born of exhaustion, she, too, stood up. "Excuse me. I'll be back in a little while."

She followed Louise to the chapel and sat down beside her. Louise didn't cease her silent prayer, but she reached out and took Ramona's hand. Fighting hot tears of grief, Ramona bowed her head.

Jake knew he was alive because everything hurt. His head. His neck. His stomach and chest. His legs and backside and even his mouth. He surfaced slowly, aware of the sound of voices somewhere close by, and a faint breath of air moving on his chin.

Slowly, with great effort, he opened his eyes. A white ceiling was all he saw, and it must be night because there was a dim, greenish glow like that cast from a fluorescent tube tinting the white paint. Experimentally, very slowly, he moved his head. It felt as if it weighed a thousand pounds, but he could move it. A very good thing.

Someone was asleep on the other bed in the room. He peered hard at the figure, trying to clear his vision, hoping it was Ramona. It wasn't. He made out the salt-and-pepper curls of his mother's hair, and that was okay, too. He wouldn't bother her just yet.

The memory of the fall came back to him, just a quick, blurred impression of falling and falling, the ground rushing up at him. It made him feel dizzy, and he pushed the memory away. Time enough.

He didn't remember landing. Suddenly, he wasn't sure he could feel his toes and attempted to wiggle them. They moved. With pain, it was true, but they moved. He tried the same with his fingers. The right ones moved fine, but he couldn't seem to locate his left ones. He shifted his head a bit to try to see them. An enormous cast covered his arm from fingers to shoulder. No wonder he couldn't move them just yet.

A fierce, wild feeling rushed through him. He was *alive.*

"Jake?"

He jerked his head to the side, not sure if he was imagining that soft, warm voice or not. The sudden movement sent a zinging pain through not only his head, but all the way down his neck. He grunted.

"Easy." Her hands were on his shoulder, small and warm.

By concentrating very hard, Jake brought Ramona into focus, though there was a nimbus of light surrounding her, as if she were some otherworldly creature. Maybe she was.

He reached for the hand he could feel on his shoulder, found it and closed it tightly in his own. "Hi," he managed. The effort hurt his throat.

"Hi. Do you want some water?"

He nearly shook his head, but remembered how it had hurt to turn it. "No. Throat's too sore."

"I bet." She smiled, and there was a motion at the edge of his vision, then her hand settled very lightly on his cheek. "You had surgery."

"Anything missing?" It hurt to talk, but he had to know.

This time she chuckled. "Nothing you can't live without. They took your spleen. Fixed some torn places inside."

Her hand moved, smoothing his hair gently back from his forehead. It was the best thing he'd ever felt. Ever. He tightened his fingers around hers, wishing he had the wit to lift it and kiss it. But he couldn't. Or didn't. Or something.

"You were so lucky, Jake."

A remembered sensation of falling, falling, falling made him dizzy for a minute. "Yeah," he rasped. "What—" The words stuck in his dry throat, and Ramona turned away then back, putting an ice cube against his mouth.

"This will help."

It was cold and slippery against his tongue and Jake was torn over whether this or her hand were the best sensations ever. "What else?" he said.

"What else did you do to yourself?"

"Yeah."

"Broke three ribs and your arm in two places. Multiple bruises and contusions. Bruised some internal organs, but none seriously." She took a breath. "Your back should have been shattered, the way you landed, but it wasn't."

He had the sense she struggled a little to keep her voice even, and he tried to bring her face more clearly into focus. It was too hard. "Thank you," he sighed, and closed his eyes again.

Ramona stood there for a long time, her hand clasped in Jake's. Looking at him. Touching him. He was battered almost beyond recognition—his face violently discolored from bruises and scrapes. His mouth was swollen and held three stitches—and she didn't think he was going to be happy to learn he'd knocked out two bottom front teeth. His ribs were taped, his arm in a cast, his legs and torso covered with bruises inflicted on the torturous way down. On his back, a wide red bruise from shoulder to hip showed the impact of his landing.

When he really woke up, he was going to hurt. A lot.

She doubted he'd be able to move without help for several days at least.

But he would live. Ramona gently pushed her fingers through the thick, dark weight of his hair, smoothing it away from his wounded and beautiful face. He was warm and breathing and alive. For almost twenty-four straight hours, Ramona had not let herself think, first just to get through the rescue and the surrealistic night. Later, she had not wanted to consider all the things that could go wrong, or recall similar case histories with unfortunate endings. She had practically held her breath, waiting for Jake to awaken and recognize something, someone.

And now he had. It was nothing short of a miracle. In a sudden release of tension, Ramona felt her strength give way. She sank into the chair she had stationed at his side, bent her head to the bed beside him and wept. In gratitude and relief and a recognition that her life was forever changed.

If she had never been raped, if she had never gone cross-country skiing that day, if—as she had wished a million times—that day had never happened, she would never have known the back way down the mountain. She would not have known any way to get Jake off that ledge until morning.

And if they had waited till morning, Jake would have probably died from internal bleeding. He'd been close to succumbing to his injuries by the time they got to the hospital.

She pressed her forehead to his fingers, lax now as he slept, and let the strange, unsettling knowledge of that wash over her again and again, unable to do anything but marvel at it. Too much had happened, and she was exhausted, and she just couldn't think about any of it. Not yet.

A hand fell on her shoulder and smoothed over her back. "Ramona, let me take you home," Tyler said, and she noticed absently that he was using her first name instead of the formal title he'd always insisted upon. "He's going to be okay now. You need some rest."

Shakily, Ramona lifted her head and wiped her face, too tired to even care that she was totally falling apart and revealing everything. He handed her a box of tissues and she accepted it gratefully. "I'm sorry," she said in a breathy voice, still struggling to pull herself together. "I think I'm just overwhelmed."

"He's needed someone to love him like you do. For such a long time."

"I didn't want to."

A shadow crossed his pale gray eyes, and Ramona remembered another hospital room and a long vigil, one that had not ended so well. "I understand."

"I guess you probably do."

He fixed his gaze on Jake's sleeping face. "I still miss her. Every day." Ramona put her hand on Tyler's arm, but said nothing. For another moment, he seemed lost in memory, then he roused himself. "Let's get out of here. I'll buy you a sloppy fast-food breakfast on the way out."

"Is it morning?" Ramona looked out the window. A faint hint of dawn pushed at the horizon. "I guess it is."

She slept a solid, dreamless twelve hours. When she awakened, a soft summer evening had crept into the mountains. Ramona carried a cup of hot, sweet coffee out to the porch and sat on the steps, gazing without thought at the long fingers of buttery light slanting through the feathery branches of pine. Dust motes swirled and danced on the strands of light. Starlings stuttered and sparrows sang from hidden boughs, and through the gilded bars a blue jay flew, calling out his warning.

It made Ramona think of Jake, sitting on her porch that morning in a towel, teasing her.

With a sense of unreality, she realized it had been just over a month since Lance's wedding, since the day Jake had turned everything in her life upside down with his charm and his vulnerable blue eyes and his pain and his kisses.

A kaleidoscopic whirl of images rose in her mind, all of them of Jake. Jake with that devilish grin when he teased her and his sultriness when he taught her to dance. Jake's eyes burning with that fierce blue pain, or dancing with delight. Jake's mouth smiling, frowning, moving toward her, pressing against her lips.

She thought of him holding her so fiercely through the night while he slept, and of his still, pale face as he lay on the ledge in the mountains.

With a small cry, she buried her face in her hands. Next to her, Manuelito groaned softly and pushed his head into her lap. She hugged him, feeling her heart squeeze painfully, as if a fist were crushing it slowly and steadily. Clutching thick handfuls of fur, she tried to breathe deeply, to tamp the fierce sorrow.

She loved Jake, loved him in all his rugged beauty and when he was wounded and low. She loved the dashing slant of his cheekbones and the way he held Mr. E so close and the pleasure he took in sailing and cooking and dancing and music. Loved him for a hundred things, a thousand, some nameable, some not.

But she couldn't be with him. The way he'd called for her when he fell down the mountain, and the way he'd clutched her hand at the hospital told her that he thought he needed her. He might even think he loved her.

And maybe he did. That almost made it worse. She rubbed Manuelito's back idly, watching tiny hairs fly into a bar of sunlight to dance with specks of floating dust. She thought of the way Jake had made love to her, reverently, as if it were a holy act, this joining of their bodies. He had been so serious, so intense.

No, she hadn't imagined the purity, the rightness of that joining.

She sipped her coffee. Even if he loved her, and she loved him back, she could not commit herself to that relationship. Not until he had found a way to make peace with his demons. She could not bear to pick up the pieces like this, over and over again. She couldn't bear to see his face battered, see his body broken.

It would be a life lived on the brink of disaster. And Ramona had spent too many years building a solid, stable peace to let his roaring, unpredictable pain make a shambles of it.

She'd let the lion over the wall surrounding her quiet garden. She'd befriended the dangerous beast and tried to take the thorn from his paw. She'd made a place for him to sleep in the sun and he'd scorned it.

So be it. He belonged in the wild, and she belonged in her garden. As she sat in the calm, peaceful world she had made for herself, her grief-stricken heart shredded into bits, but her resolve was strong. She could take almost anything, but she could not bear to sit back and watch Jake kill himself. She couldn't bear to be on the other end of the line when that last, sober call was made.

No.

Chapter 19

At Ramona's recommendation, they moved Jake to the VA home. He was glad to be there as he began to mend. He wished Harry was there with him, so they could sit side by side in the sun-room in their wheelchairs, but that grief had been blunted a little by the letter Harry had left him.

Jake had carried the letter with him to the mountain. It had been in his pocket when he fell, and there were small tears and smears on the envelope now, but Jake read it every day.

It was a very simple letter, written by a man who had learned not to take simple things for granted. In a thick scrawl that Jake could barely read, Harry had written:

Jake,
Please don't get all choked up about this. I'm going home to Jean. I tried to stick around awhile for you, but I reckon you're in good hands with Ramona, and I'm just tired.

I've always thought of you like a son, and I'm going

to leave you with a father's advice. You're too hard on yourself, and you need to ease up. For me, I wish you'd go to the groups, but I'm not making it a deathbed request. You'll do what you know is right, just like you always have.

Good luck to you, son. Harry.

Jake had read it in the hospital, as soon as he could hold it, and he'd understood that Harry had taken the place of his own father. He wished he'd understood that sooner.

He missed the old vet deeply, but he realized that he could let him go. The truth was, Jake felt extraordinarily blessed. As if there must be a purpose for which he'd been spared, if only he could figure out what it was. For a couple of weeks, he lived in a kind of exalted state. Everything in the world seemed newly made. A morning sky could move him nearly to tears. Raindrops and flowers and apple pie were wonders never to be equaled.

It was just so damned good to be alive.

He didn't go to a meeting and he didn't make an appointment with a counselor. There was time enough for that, if it turned out he really needed it.

The trouble was Ramona. At first, he was so preoccupied with his recovery, he didn't notice that she flitted in and out, never staying long. No one did, except his mother, who patiently mended or put the finishing touches on new clothes for Curtis as she sat with him.

He knew Ramona was busy with her practice. He tried not to mind when she seemed to only give him the same five or ten minutes she gave everyone else. Even though he wasn't her patient, she managed to stop in to talk to him when she made rounds. Even those brief stops lit up his whole day. He looked forward to the evening and Ramona's smile.

But by the end of the second week, he was physically much better. Cranky from being cooped up, as a matter of fact, but Dr. Richards was still worried about some whatsis or another and wanted Jake to stay a little longer. Truthfully, he doubted he had the strength yet to manage a normal life. He felt just better enough to wish for more.

He wanted to go home. He wanted to get on with his life, the life he'd tossed aside so carelessly. He wanted to get outside and smell the mountain air. He wanted to dance and cook and make love.

To Ramona.

But as the days passed, he began to realize she was avoiding him. She kept her visits short and platonic, cheerful and encouraging and completely void of intimacy. And Jake, like all the others, watched for her arrival with a hungry, puppylike eagerness.

He hated himself for feeling like that. It was pathetic the way they all waited, as if for the blessing of some benevolent goddess who deigned to walk among them.

It pricked his pride.

One evening, he hobbled his way outside and stationed himself on a stone bench near the parking lot. He waited while the sun went down and lights began to come on behind the curtains of the rooms. He watched old men turn on their televisions and settle in for a long night of situation comedies, and his irritation grew. One day, he might be one of those old men, but he wasn't now.

Finally, long after the crickets had set up their nightly serenade in the flowers edging the sidewalk, Ramona came out, carrying her leather briefcase in one hand, her keys in another. She didn't see him right away, and that gave him a strange, fierce twist in his gut at first. He could be anyone, any creep, and she'd be vulnerable to him.

But it was crazy to think like that. The truth was, she knew everyone here and she did pay attention to her surroundings. It wasn't exactly a dangerous spot—and, noticing the keys again, he bet she knew how to use them as a weapon.

It was only then that he noticed how drawn she looked, the cheerfulness sliding from her face like a melting mask, revealing a weariness he hated to see. He'd meant to be firm with her, to take a stand and make her see him like a man instead of a weak invalid. Instead, he stood up and called her name.

"Ramona."

She stopped, took a breath and came forward. He saw her attempt to compose her features, but the struggle was evidently too much. "Hi, Jake."

Her eyes were luminous in the night, as if they somehow magically caught the light and reflected it back. He lifted a hand, thinking to reach for her, but let it fall back to his side. He'd rehearsed a dozen things to say in this moment. Strong things. Flirtatious things. Even angry things. But he heard himself say, "I miss you."

Stricken, she stared at him. It seared him straight to his soul, and he stretched out his arm, hooked a hand around her neck and pulled her close. She pressed into him, burying her face in his chest, and he felt a shudder pass through her. Her forehead touched his throat.

Jake closed his eyes, holding tight to the back of her neck, her thick hair tangling around his fingers. Heat and yearning and peace welled up in him, and he couldn't speak. He pressed a kiss to her crown.

Everything would be all right.

But after a moment, she gently pushed away from him. "I can't do this, Jake. I'm sorry." She backed away as if she would just leave it at that.

He limped forward and snagged her arm. "Wait a minute. Tell me what's going on here. I don't get it."

She wouldn't look at him. "I just can't do it."

"Can't do what? Can't love me?"

An expression of sadness crossed her face. "Oh, I can love you." She raised her eyes. "But I can't heal you. I can't be the doctor who always comes running and patches you up. You need something, but I can't provide it." She pulled her arm out of his loosening grip. "I can't," she whispered. "I'm sorry." Quickly, she turned and moved away from him.

Jake stared after her, his body going hollow, like a pumpkin ready for carving. He watched her go, feeling as if he'd been told he'd won the lottery only to find it was a cruel practical joke. A bright pain pressed behind his eyes, and Jake clenched his jaw.

He whirled around and hobbled back into the home. To hell with her, then. To hell with everyone.

That night, his nightmare came back. It was the first time it had appeared since the night at Ramona's house, and Jake had dared to believe it was gone. That his close brush with death had magically cast his demons out.

Sitting bolt upright, his heart racing, Jake was at first bewildered. He couldn't remember where he was. The room and the sounds and the bed felt totally unfamiliar, and he stared into the darkness for long, confused moments before his mind cleared.

Stricken by the realization that he had not, after all, escaped, he fell back on his bed and stared at the ceiling, depression crashing in on him. That night on the mountain, when he'd finally realized it might be possible to live with the memories and somehow move past them, he'd thought that he would be done with this. He'd convinced himself that Ramona had healed him, that her magic touch had made him whole.

He'd felt himself saved.

Staring into the blackness, with the sound of a machine beeping distantly, gradually he arrived at a different conclusion. His body had been so severely traumatized that the need for healing sleep overrode any mental aberrations. Now that he was healing, his mind was going to let the demons back in.

He swore, covering his eyes with his forearm.

He had used Ramona as a shield. In her arms, he didn't need to dream. When he held on to her, he could pretend he was fine, because she was real and whole and solid.

A slow glimmer of understanding finally penetrated his thick skull. This was what she had meant. This was what she couldn't do. She couldn't be his Saint George and slay his dragons for him. He had to do it himself.

And for one moment, he let himself imagine her running toward him, imagine her next to him, warm and soft in his arms, her hair smelling of sunlight.

Ramona. He missed her so much.

It was raining when Jake made his way down to the meeting he knew was being held. A collection of soldiers gathered around the table, everyone from World War II through Vietnam. Jake hesitated, realizing he was the only vet from the Gulf War in the room. Maybe they'd go back to their rooms and tell each other what a wimp he was.

But Dr. Richards was following behind him. "Come on in." He limped to the table and sat down. "This is Jake," he said. "He was a major in the army by the age of thirty. He resigned his commission four years before full retirement. Some of you here might know what that feels like."

"Good to meet you, Jake," a middle-aged man said. "You feel like talking?"

"Maybe not just yet."

"That's fine."

But he did talk. Not the first time, and not the second. At his third meeting, he found himself saying, "The only thing I ever wanted in life was to be a soldier."

And they listened. Nobody pushed him to go further when he felt the tightness in his throat and stopped. Nobody probed his psyche. And when he finally broke down and confessed his "sin" to a room full of old soldiers, he knew he was one of them. That he had not betrayed them, that he'd done the best he could.

Alone in his condo later, Jake held a lapful of cat and let himself remember the feeling of holding that little boy's hand. He let himself think of the look in the big dark eyes—terror of such magnitude it couldn't be expressed except in a dying scream. All he'd ever wanted to do was protect the weak and defenseless—and he couldn't even save the life of one little boy.

Jake closed his eyes and finally let himself mourn that dead child, mourn all the dead children and violated women of the world. He had been so proud to wear his uniform. So proud to be a soldier. He'd wanted to protect and save them all. He'd wanted…

He bowed his head in humility. It would be a long time before he could sort out the finer points. For now, he understood at last that he'd done the best he could.

He was a veteran. That pretty much said it all.

And out there, waiting, was a woman he had discovered he couldn't live without.

Ramona diced plums on her kitchen counter. They were beautiful this year, firm and sweet, with dark purple skins that would turn the jam a vivid, deep red. On the back of the stove, jars rattled faintly in a boiling-water bath. Sugar waited in a snowy mound in a bowl, along with the pectin and lids neatly lined up on a clean dish towel.

Ready. She poured the diced fruit into a heavy cast-iron pot, taking care not to bruise them. Then she added the sugar and stirred it in, grinning to herself over the resulting color—a dazzling shade of ruby that nearly vibrated.

Manuelito, lying on the floor next to the stove, lifted his head suddenly and growled. Ramona glanced at him, then out the window. She absolutely could not stop until this step was done. Naturally there was someone at the gate. She inclined her head. "Go chase them off, baby," she said. The big dog leaped up and streaked toward the screen, knocking it open with his nose.

Outside, she heard his deep, throaty bark, then the curious set of happy yips and whines that meant he was greeting someone he knew and liked. Ramona frowned and glanced out the window again. She couldn't see anyone, but it didn't matter. She trusted Manuelito's judgment, and the jam was too close to finished to stop now.

Deftly, she snatched jars from the water and lined them up, admiring the curls of steam they sent into the air. Humming softly, she took the jam off the burner and began ladling it into the jars. It was as beautiful as she had imagined it would be, and happily she lined the jars up in a row as she wiped sticky residue from the edges with a sterilized cloth, then put the lids on with a twist of her wrist.

She forgot Manuelito had gone out until she turned around to put the pot in the sink and saw the shadow on the floor. Startled, she looked up—and froze. Her heart literally fluttered.

Jake.

She tried not to react. Tried not to stare. But stare she did, standing like a victim of Medusa in the middle of her kitchen with the pot still her in hands.

Jake.

He stood there at the door a little uncomfortably, perhaps unsure of his welcome. In the bright, sunny morning, he looked more handsome than she had remembered, more precious. His hair had been recently trimmed. It hung neatly around his collar and he'd brushed it back from his high, elegant forehead. His jaw was clean shaven, and the bruises were gone, or nearly so. His eyes blazed, violently blue against the darkness of his hair.

Standing beside him, Manuelito had that ridiculously pleased expression dogs sometimes adopted when they found something—ears perked up, tongue lolling out of a cheery dog smile. And just in case she hadn't noticed the prize, he barked sharply.

It broke Ramona's stillness. "I see," she said, and continued on her path to put the pot in the sink. Out of sight, she took a deep breath and steeled herself, then marched to the door and pushed open the screen.

"Hi," he said, and lifted a box of doughnuts. "Brought you a present."

She couldn't help it. She smiled, at once reluctant and wry. "You have to promise not to spill anything if I let you in."

Awkwardly, he lifted his cast and stretched out his fingers. "My hands are steady as rocks."

"No hitting your head, either."

He grinned, and the scar along his beautiful lower lip showed a little, just a thin white line. She'd forgotten how delectable his mouth was. She looked away, then gestured for him to come in.

Manuelito pushed by, licking Ramona's fingers. "Please, Manuelito, you're making a fool of yourself."

He sat, back straight, ears still up, that silly smile plastered all over his muzzle, his tail waving happily over the floor. He barked.

Ramona shook her head. "You really are a dog charmer, Jake Forrest." While he put the doughnuts on the table, Ramona bustled over to the coffeemaker and got out the filters and coffee. "How are you feeling?" she asked brightly.

"Good. How are you feeling?"

The question caught her by surprise, and she looked up at him. "I'm sorry. I do that so automatically." He simply nodded, a soberness coming into his expression. Ramona saw it and reached for a filter. To her dismay, she found her hands were trembling so violently she couldn't pick one out. "Damn," she said.

Smoothly, he moved forward and took the filters from

her hands. She thanked him, then put the one he held out in the basket and reached for the coffee.

Jake stopped her, his big hand capturing both of hers. "Ramona."

She didn't look at him, afraid everything she was feeling, everything she didn't want him to see would be written all over her face. "What?" The word came out on a harsh sigh.

He twined his fingers in her right hand. "When I saw you at Lance's wedding, I thought you would have a kitchen just like this. I thought it would be filled with herbs and plants, and that you would make your own jelly."

His voice rolled like honey over her shoulders, down her spine, seductive and rich and beautiful. His thumb moved over her knuckles, and Ramona focused on his hand, dark and strong, engulfing her own. She couldn't speak.

"Ramona, look at me. Please."

"I can't." Her voice sounded strangled, and that wasn't at all what she meant.

"Please."

"Oh, Jake, can't you just go away?" she whispered helplessly. "I was just starting not to mind every single minute."

He stepped closer, close enough that she was enveloped in that subtle, exotic after-shave he wore. "I miss you," he said, and his mouth fell on her neck, just beside her braid. "I miss you so much."

She shut her eyes, fighting the urge to fling herself into his arms and damn the consequences. She missed him dreadfully. And she'd lied, too. She hadn't got used to being without him. But her heart pounded out a warning that the lion was back, bringing danger and destruction into her calm and peaceful existence.

"I love you, Ramona," he said. "Please look at me."

And at that, she could not resist. She raised her eyes and

met that hypnotic blue gaze. "I know," she said. "I love you, too, but it doesn't change anything."

He put his fingers against her mouth. "Wait. Hear me out."

Mesmerized by the power of those compelling eyes, she nodded.

"I started having nightmares that night after you told me to get lost."

"I didn't—"

"Yes, you did. But it's okay. I started having those nightmares again, and there in the middle of the night, I finally understood what you've been telling me all along. I needed to drain that boil."

For one moment, her heart stopped, then thudded to life again.

He focused on her hand, on the pattern he was making over the knuckles. "So I went to the meetings. I've been talking to a therapist, too." He took a breath. "It isn't easy. I have a long way to go."

Oh, it hurt to look at him! To feel the piercing shards of hope needling through her numbed veins.

"I realized that I was clinging to you, looking to you to make the demons go away. Maybe to protect me from the darkness." He raised his eyes. "And when I found out you had your own darkness, it almost killed me." He grimaced wryly. "Literally."

"Jake, my past isn't a problem for me anymore. It really isn't. I mean, I can't make it go away. But I can live with it. I don't even usually think about it anymore. It was a long, long time ago."

He smiled. "You know, that was exactly the thing I was thinking when I fell. I'm serious." He gestured, still holding her hand. "It just hit me that maybe that's what you have to do. What everyone has to do. Just live with it and go on. I thought seeing that would instantly make me feel better."

Very gently, she lifted his big hand to her lips and kissed it.

"It's not that easy," he admitted. He bent closer and kissed her hand. "But, I swear, Ramona, I'll do whatever it takes. I'll see a shrink every day for the rest of my life if I need to—but please, let me love you while I do it."

Her hope swelled, but she looked at him very seriously. "Jake, I can't be there to pick up the pieces."

"You won't have to." He pressed a kiss to her forehead. "I need you, but not for the wrong reasons now. I need you like any man needs that one woman when he finds her."

Not like any man. He would always do things more intensely, with more passion, than other men. She held his hand close to her cheek, aching at the thought of his loving her like that.

"I just need to be near you, Ramona," he whispered. "I want to hear you laugh and curse and cry. I want to make love to you and give you children, and cook for you and—" He swallowed. "Everything."

She simply let go, and everything in her flowed toward him, into his embrace. "I've missed you so much," she returned quietly. "I wake up alone in the middle of the night and it hurts so much."

His good hand came up to cup the back of her head, and he pressed her close, holding her next to him, and then he was kissing her hair, her forehead, her nose.

"I love you, Jake. I'll be here for you."

"No," he said, cradling her head in his hand. "I'll be here for you. We'll be here for each other. For always, Ramona."

Pure happiness spilled through her, and in her mind's eye, she saw the prowling lion, his wounds bandaged, at last settling in the place she had made for him in the sun. Pressing her head into his chest, listening to his heart beat, she imagined that big, strong lion rolling over on his back and stretching as he let go of a relieved sigh.

Quietly, Jake began to hum, rocking her side to side in a dance, a little smile on his face. Ramona smiled back and stepped onto the tops of his feet, wrapping her arms around his shoulders so they could dance more closely. "What is that song?" she asked. "I feel like I should know it."

"They played it at the wedding reception." He made mock growling noises. "'Listen to the Lion,' by Van Morrison."

Ramona stared at him for a moment, then she laughed and grabbed his beautiful, clean-shaven, healing face in her hands.

"I love you," she said, and kissed him soundly.

And together they danced to the music of healing, to the music of courage, but most of all, to the music of love.

* * * * *

Intimate Moments
is proud to bring
you an unforgettable
miniseries.
BEVERLY BIRD
The Wedding Ring
Wrapped in the warmth of family tradition,
three couples say "I do!"
LOVING MARIAH
(Intimate Moments #790, June 1997)
Adam Wallace searches for his kidnapped
son…which leads him to the Amish heartland
and lovely schoolteacher Mariah Fisher.
MARRYING JAKE
(Intimate Moments #802, August 1997)
Commitment-shy Jake Wallace unravels the
ongoing mystery of stolen babies and helps
Katya Essler learn to believe in love again.
SAVING SUSANNAH
(Intimate Moments #814, October1997)
Kimberly Wallace needs a bone marrow donor
to save her daughter's life. Will the temporary
nanny position to Joe Lapp's children be the
answer to her prayers?
INTIMATE MOMENTS®
Silhouette®

COMING NEXT MONTH

#799 I'M HAVING YOUR BABY?!—Linda Turner

The Lone Star Social Club

Workaholic Joe Taylor was thrilled when his wayward wife returned to him—and pregnant, no less! Then he realized that Annie had no idea how she got that way, at which point joy quickly turned to shock. What a way to find out he was about to become a father—or was he?

#800 NEVER TRUST A LADY—Kathleen Creighton

Small-town single mom Jane Carlysle had been known to complain that nothing exciting ever happened to her. Then Interpol agent Tom Hawkins swept into her life and, amidst a whirlwind of danger, swept her off her feet! But was it just part of his job to seduce the prime suspect?

#801 HER IDEAL MAN—Ruth Wind

The Last Roundup

A one-night *fling* turned into a lifetime *thing* for Anna and Tyler when she wound up pregnant after a night of passion. And now that she was married, this big-city woman was determined to see that Tyler behaved like the perfect Western hubby—but that involved the one emotion he had vowed never to feel again: love.

#802 MARRYING JAKE—Beverly Bird

The Wedding Ring

As a single mother of four, Katya yearned for Jake Wallace's heated touch, for a future spent in his protective embrace. But the jaded cop had come to Amish country with a mission, and falling in love with an innocent woman was not part of the plan.

#803 HEAVEN IN HIS ARMS—Maura Seger

Tad Jenkins was a wealthy, world-famous hell-raiser and heartbreaker, and Lisa Preston wasn't about to let her simple but organized life be uprooted and rocked by his passionate advances. But Tad already had everything mapped out. All Lisa had to do was succumb...and how could she ever resist?

#804 A MARRIAGE TO FIGHT FOR—Raina Lynn

Garrett Hughes' undercover DEA work had torn their marriage apart. But now, after four lonely years, Maggie had Garrett back in her arms. Injured and emotionally empty, he pushed her away, but Maggie was determined. This time she would fight for her marriage—and her husband—with all she had.